PHANTOM OF THE PYRAMIDS

All thoughts of the danger and the thrill of the expedition faded from Ashley's mind as the magnetism of Kasim's will pulled her toward him.

Kasim had completely enfolded her and locked her in an embrace that said more than words ever could.

She felt his energy and his warmth flow into her body as his lips tenderly tasted hers. He caressed her shoulders and back, relaxing away the remains of her resistance to him.

She massaged his neck, ears, and shoulders until Kasim made low growling noises in the back of his throat and his breath burned hotly against her face. She entangled her fingers in his tight curls as his lips flamed against the little hollow of her neck and held him to her. His hands were fiery on her back, his lips pressed greedily against hers, and his tongue scorched hers with the heat of his passion.

Suddenly Ashley remembered the reason she had initially hesitated to give herself to Kasim . . . it was her phantom, the man who haunted the shadows of the pyramids in her dreams, who kept her from embracing Kasim totally.

BOOK YOUR PLACE ON OUR WEBSITE AND MAKE THE ARABESQUE ROMANCE CONNECTION!

We've created a customized website just for our very special Arabesque readers, where you can get the inside scoop on everything that's going on with Arabesque romance novels.

When you come online, you'll have the exciting opportunity to:

- View covers of upcoming books

- Learn about our future publishing schedule (listed by publication month and author)

- Find out when your favorite authors will be visiting a city near you.

- Search for and order backlist books from our line catalog

- Check out author bios and background information

- Send e-mail to your favorite authors

- Join us in weekly chats with authors, readers and other guests

- Get writing guidelines

- AND MUCH MORE!

Visit our website at
http://www.arabesquebooks.com

PARADISE

COURTNI WRIGHT

ARABESQUE

BET BOOKS

BET Publications, LLC
www.msbet.com
www.arabesquebooks.com

ARABESQUE BOOKS are published by

BET Publications, LLC
c/o BET BOOKS
One BET Plaza
1900 W Place NE
Washington, D.C. 20018-1211

First Printing: March, 1999
10 9 8 7 6 5 4 3 2 1

Printed in the United States of America

CHAPTER ONE

Ashley tied a scarf around her short, black, curly hair to keep the dust from covering it as she threw old lesson plans into the trash and took down old, faded posters. Dirt smudges spotted her healthy outdoor complexion and lint clung to the thick black lashes that ringed her coal black eyes. She looked despairingly at the long lists of names on the slightly wrinkled sheets of paper. Her chalk- and marker-streaked medium brown hands shook from the anxiety that filled her. Shaking her head she wondered how she would ever learn all the names.

Every year she thought the same thing and by the end of the second week of September, she knew all of them and their faces, too. Still as her fifth year of teaching started, she was nervous about the prospects of facing a new group of high school students with their usual cynical approach to their lessons and their general distrust of authority figures. She prepared for their arrival carefully, planning to avoid the trite, worn-out summer vacation essay, making new folders to hold ungraded papers, organizing her first lecture, and writing the first night's assignment on the board. Almost as an afterthought, she added her name, Ms. Ashley Stephens, in her bold, confident handwriting. She really did not need to do it; they all knew who she was. They knew more about her than she did about them, but, in short order, she would change all that.

"Welcome back!" Terry shouted, sticking her head in the door on her way to her classroom.

Trying to match her smile, Ashley replied, "Thanks. Did you have a good summer?"

"The best! I got engaged! I'll tell you all about him later. Gotta run. I have so much to do to get my classroom in order. See you at lunch," Terry chirped as she scampered off.

"Best wishes! I'll save you a seat," Ashley shouted, hoping that her voice mirrored her friend's excitement at being back at school.

Returning to her chores, Ashley knew that the jitters that caused her to chew on her bottom lip would pass. They always did. By the end of the last class of the day, tomorrow, she would barely remember that it had been the first day of classes after summer vacation. School would have regained its old familiar feeling, like a pair of old slippers waiting beside the bed. The predictability of the bells would become an almost welcome routine that marked the passage of time and struck off the days before she would begin her adventure in Egypt. The smell, she could not bring herself to call it an aroma, of cafeteria food would have replaced the lingering scent of new paint and freshly polished floors. Life would return to normal within the red brick walls.

But somehow, this school year would be different. Ashley had already filed her lesson plans, put up several new posters proclaiming the wonders of studying ancient history and the excitement of archaeology, and straightened

the thirty-five desks that filled the classroom to capacity.
Everything was ready, except Ashley. She could not make
her mind focus on the task of teaching with Egypt and
the ancient pyramids beckoning. Almost every night, she
dreamed of them and of a mysterious man who was in
some way connected with them. Something about him
commanded her attention as no other man had ever done.
She fairly chomped at the bit to begin the expedition.

Her colleagues had assured her that as soon as she saw
the tanned, smiling faces she would feel the energy and
enthusiasm begin to flow through her veins. They said she
simply suffered from the usual post-vacation syndrome
that affects all teachers when the initial thrill of managing
students and curriculum has faded. But she knew that they
were wrong. Her feelings of malaise and discontent did
not come from having taught the same material often
enough to do it in her sleep, which she often did after
staying up too late reading an engrossing book. Her mind
had been torn between her sabbatical and the dreams of
the adventure she would uncover and the need to focus
on teaching.

And she had met someone. John Edwards had shown
great potential as they strolled along the beach. They had
spent only two weeks together at Virginia Beach as they
shared the companionship of mutual friends, but something had clicked. Ashley had been thrilled to discover
that she and John knew so many of the same people despite
his long absence from the East Coast. It was much too
early for Ashley to think of anything serious, especially
since John lived in California and long distance relationships were not her style, but she had been favorably
impressed by his calm demeanor, his casual easy conversation, and his athletic physique. Already her friend, Toni,
was trying to play matchmaker with the intent of marriage.
Ashley had managed to laugh off her efforts every time.

Somehow, John was not quite right. It certainly was not
that he was unattractive. He was one of the most handsome
men Ashley had ever met. The problem centered around
his predictability. She knew what he would say and how
he would react to things after knowing him for only a short
time. Ashley wanted excitement, fireworks, in a relationship. With John, she had soda.

With the sun streaming through the classroom window,
Ashley tried to push thoughts of Egypt and John to the
back of her mind. She willed herself not to think of either
the antiquities or John as she hung the last of her posters.
She had too much to do to allow John's laughter and his
energy to fill her mind and distract her from her duties.
The posters of sunshine gleaming off the pyramids already
distracted her enough. She needed to prepare her lectures
for the weeks to come and compose her thoughts for the
next day when the children would flood the room with
their stories of summertime adventures and mishaps.
Besides, considering the courses she planned to take
before heading to Egypt, she really did not have time to
think of anyone. Her life was too busy now, with every
minute programmed.

Throwing a dusty handkerchief on her desk, Ashley took
her water bottle and walked down the hall toward the
teachers' lounge. On her way, she passed her colleagues'
rooms where they busied themselves hanging posters, pre-
viewing videos, and arranging lecture notes. They looked
so happy to be back in the comfortable sameness of school
as they waved and smiled when she passed. She wished
she could have been one of them, but thoughts of the
possibilities that lay ahead for a relationship with John and
her great adventure in Egypt detracted from her enthusiasm for teaching.

The teachers' lounge buzzed with excitement as Ashley's
friends and co-workers copied lessons, chatted about their

summer vacations, and discussed plans for the school year. Katherine looked forward with happy anticipation to teaching ninth-grade English for the first time in years. She had spent most of her summer planning how to arrange her classroom and reading the literature she planned to introduce during the first semester. Tim had redesigned a required course and waited anxiously to see if it would be possible to teach a year's English literature in one semester. Paula had visited Francesca and her new baby and filled everyone in on Francesca's tales of the transition from teacher to mom. Helen had rearranged the furniture in the lounge and bought additional pieces to make the work room look more hospitable and less spartan.

Everyone seemed so happy to be back and ready for the school year to begin. Ashley tried to join in with their discussions but found that she could not share their sense of anticipation for a new year. Her thoughts were months away, already in Egypt.

Not wanting to cast gloom on their reunion, she excused herself from the happy group on the sofa and made her way through the crush to the mailboxes across the room. Peering inside, Ashley found a pink callback slip. Surprised, she opened it to find that John had called her at ten o'clock that morning. Unable to suppress the smile that started at the corners of her mouth and quickly spread to encompass her entire face, she dashed out of the room and down the hall to the office in hopes of finding an available phone and much needed privacy.

Reaching the English Department office, Ashley found Connie engaged in conversation on their only telephone. Smiling and waving, she lingered in the empty mauve-colored hall waiting for her to hang up. Pacing, Ashley tried to be patient, but she could feel the little slip of paper with the unfamiliar number hastily scribbled upon it almost burn a hole in her pocket. It pressed warm against her thigh just as his hand had been warm when it held hers. She could still smell his cologne as she leaned against the cold metal door frame. Her heart pounded against her ribs with her desire to hear his voice again.

"Sorry for taking so long," Connie said, leaving the office and bursting into the bubble of memories that surrounded Ashley. "The telephone is all yours."

"Thanks," Ashley muttered, absently easing the door closed. She did not want to appear impolite, but she wanted to be alone when she spoke with John.

Dialing the number on the callback slip with trembling fingers, Ashley counted the rings until his voice would send a thrill down her spine. She swallowed hard to ease the tightness in her throat as she prepared to speak. The usually comfortable room grew too close and too warm. Perspiration had popped out on her top lip and forehead despite the constant hum of the air-conditioning. All sorts of thoughts ran through her mind as she wondered what to say, how to break the awkward silences, and when to end the conversation without appearing anxious to terminate it.

"Hello," a disembodied voice said. "You have reached the office of John Edwards. I am away from my desk in a meeting. If you will leave a message, I will call you back as soon as I return. Thank you."

Ashley's heart felt painfully heavy at the disappointment of having to leave a message on an impersonal voice-mail system when she wanted so much to speak with John personally. Clearing her throat, she was about to speak when another voice interrupted her.

"Hello? Hello? This is John Edwards. May I help you?"

"John, it's Ashley. It's so good to hear your voice. I thought I would have to talk to a machine, which, by the way, is one of my least favorite activities," she said, trying to mask the happiness that threatened to overtake her at actually having a conversation with him.

"Ashley, I hoped it would be you. That's why I picked up. I'm up to my ears in work since the meeting earlier this morning, but I didn't want to take any chances on missing your call. How've you been? I've been thinking about you," John said, sounding genuinely pleased to hear her voice.

She smiled to herself because he had spoken the words that had been on the tip of her tongue. Hoping to keep the conversation going for as long as possible with her question, Ashley replied, "I'm incredibly busy here, too. School starts tomorrow, and I'm trying to get myself together. What are you working on that is keeping you so busy?"

"I've been assigned to a case involving possible anti-trust violations, that's all, but it has been consuming all of my time. By the way, I said I've been thinking about you, and you did not respond. Haven't you thought about me, too, just a little bit? I know we haven't known each other very long, but I thought we had similar thoughts," he commented, sounding a bit hurt and growing distant to protect himself in anticipation of a let down.

"Of course, I've thought about you. We had a wonderful two weeks together. I just didn't know what to say. We're thousands of miles apart, we're busy with our careers, and I'm off to Egypt at the beginning of the second semester. I don't exactly see the chance for a relationship to grow and flourish in the months to come," she replied, falling all over her words. The forceful pounding of her heart made it difficult for her to think.

"We could work at it if we really want our new friendship to become something more. I'll be in New York in two weeks. We could see each other then. We could take in a play, visit some museums, or do some shopping. I've been looking for a woman like you for some time. Now that I've found you, I don't want to miss this opportunity at happiness," John offered.

"As much as I would like to see you, I don't think it would be fair to either of us to start something now. Let's leave things as they are until I return. We have wonderful memories of our time at the beach to last us until next summer," Ashley replied. She sounded calmer than she actually felt, but she knew that the sabbatical came first.

"That's not what I had in mind at all, Ashley. If that's the best you can offer me at this time, I'll have to wait. Promise me you'll think about New York. I'll call you in a few days. I would love to see you again. That might be the last time I'll be on the East Coast before you leave for Egypt," John said in a last effort to convince her that what they felt should not wait until the next summer.

"I'll think about it, John, but I won't make any promises. Now that the school year has started, I don't have much free time. Besides, I have seminars to attend before leaving for Cairo. They promise to be boring, but they are required of all the expedition participants. We'll see what happens," Ashley answered. As much as she wanted to see if John was the right man for her, she knew that other obligations came first. Besides, she still heard the voice of wisdom whispering in her ear that he was not the man for whom she had been searching. Dreams had been haunting her sleep lately, and something in their nature seemed almost prophetic. She had felt so sure about them that she had even consulted a dream book, but without success. She was flattered by John's interest, but she could not bring herself to form a commitment before leaving the States for such a long time. Anything could happen in her absence. He could meet someone else, and so could she.

"That's all I ask. I'll call you tomorrow," John said just before hanging up.

Ashley stared at the telephone for a few minutes before leaving the office. John had said all the right things, but somehow, it was not enough. She wanted more and she would have it. She would not settle for the safe route of love and marriage. She wanted a chance to find herself before she joined her life to that of someone else. With a smile and a light step, she returned to her classroom to continue preparing for the first day of school to begin. The anticipation welled within her as she practically skipped down the stairs. Egypt, the pyramids, and the man in her dreams were only a few months away. Until then, she had work to do and classes to teach.

Over lunch, Ashley listened attentively as Terry bubbled about her fiancé. "He's a professor of history at the university. You'll love him. As soon as we get past the opening school days, I'll invite you over to meet him. We'll have a cookout," she said happily.

"That sounds great," Ashley commented as she munched her salad. She wanted to sound enthusiastic, but she could not quite summon the energy. Her mind was already on seeing John again.

Slipping away from Terry's effervescence, Ashley sought the quiet of Toni's room. Plopping into a chair she said, "I couldn't take any more of Terry's happiness. I know I should have been a better listener and friend, but I just couldn't stand to hear another minute of her raving about her fiancé. I'm so confused about John that I'm having a hard time focusing on anything, let alone listening to Terry. I didn't need to hear that another friend has found the right guy and is planning for a future that's so unclear for me."

"Well, as soon as he calls tomorrow, you'll work it out. You have to decide what's right for you. You tried to make him understand once before that you have to go on your sabbatical. Maybe this time he'll understand,'' Toni replied as she hung the last of her four new posters.

"You still don't agree with me, do you?'' Ashley asked, heading to the door.

"I don't know that I'd make the same decision, but I respect you for sticking to your plans and principles. Besides, it's neither my opinion nor John's that matters. You're the only one who can decide your direction. I don't know for certain what I'd do if I were in your place. I think I'd postpone the sabbatical, but I might not. It's a great opportunity,'' Toni remarked, straightening the books on her desk.

"You're right. Tomorrow will tell. I do have to follow my heart. I know I'm doing the right thing. See you later,'' Ashley replied. She left her friend rearranging the desks for the third time that day.

When John called the next day, Ashley remained true to her decision. She knew in her heart that she would be doing both of them a disservice if she allowed him to think that their relationship could grow into something more than friendship. She needed her time in Egypt to discover herself and what she wanted from life.

"John, I just have to go on this sabbatical. It's the opportunity of a lifetime. If I don't go, I'd regret it,'' Ashley tried to explain.

"I would think you'd want to stay here with me. I understand your argument about the opportunity, but I think our relationship is worth nurturing,'' John countered with little sign of really putting himself in Ashley's place.

"I guess I can't explain exactly how I feel except to say that I have to do this for me. Besides, as much as I like you, I know in my heart that we're destined to be only good friends. I'm sorry, but that's the way it has to be," Ashley replied.

An awkward silence fell between them. Then John slowly said, "I guess I have no choice but to go along with your plans and to wish you well."

"Thanks, John. I'd do the same thing for you if the situation were reversed," Ashley replied. "Everything will work out for the best. You'll see."

As the weeks passed and the presabbatical activity increased, Ashley became even more confident about her decision to break up with John. He accepted her refusal with grace. While he was on the East Coast, he had made a special trip to Washington, D.C., to give her a special going-away present. He bought her the tools of the trade for taking part in an archaeological dig. He had purchased thick-soled shoes as protection from sharp rocks and a pith helmet to shelter her from falling rocks and the unaccustomed sun. He even bought a brush for sweeping away fine sand and had it engraved with her name and the words, "To brush away the sands of the past."

John also gave Ashley a gold pinkie ring with her initials engraved on its flat surface. With a light kiss on her forehead, he slipped it on her finger and whispered, "Be good and be careful. I understand that those deserts can be filled with treacherous sandstorms and thieves."

Before he left town, Ashley gave John a detailed history and atlas of Egypt marked with the location of the dig and the route she would travel from Cairo to the excavation. She wanted him to share the excitement that consumed her.

*   *   *

As the days slipped away, Ashley and Toni gathered all the equipment and supplies she would need for her sabbatical. The separation would not be easy on either of them. They had been close for a long time and had been apart very little since they realized that they were destined to be best friends.

When the cold January day arrived for Ashley to board the flight to Egypt, Toni took her to the airport. Standing among her two carry-on bags, they chatted gaily about Ashley's adventure and Toni's upcoming wedding.

"Flight one seven one to Cairo, Egypt, now boarding at gate three," the voice boomed over the public address system as Ashley and Toni waited for her flight.

"Now, remember, you promised that you would be back home in time for my wedding next summer," Toni reminded her as Ashley fished the ticket out of her pocket and picked up her carry-on luggage.

"You know I would not miss it for anything in the world. Not even the mystery of the pyramids could keep me away. We've been through too much together," Ashley responded, trying to make Toni feel better regarding the trip about which she had dreamed for so long. They had been friends for so long that neither could imagine getting married without the presence of the other.

"What about that dream you told me about? What if you meet HIM?" Toni teased. She hated to see her best friend leave, but she knew that some things just had to be.

Ashley laughed heartily as she walked toward the gate with her arm through Toni's. "Oh, he's handsome and so sexy, but he's not real. You know how dreams are . . . they fade in the light of day."

"Especially this one. It's just your conscience bothering you about leaving John," Toni explained.

"We have talked about this before, Toni, and I simply must go. This is the chance of a lifetime. Look, I've only known John for two weeks. We haven't even slept together and only barely managed to kiss with all the people around us at the beach and when he visited a few weeks ago. He seems like a great guy, but I am not going to base a lifetime decision on so little time. Besides, I just know that there's someone exciting out there for me. I would wait, if he were the one with this opportunity. Stop matchmaking. You have a bad case of 'misery loves company.' Just because you're getting married, you want me to join you. I'm not ready yet. I still have a lot of frogs to kiss. Who knows, I might unearth more than antiquities in the pyramids,'' Ashley replied, a little tease in her voice as she set out on her adventure.

"To each her own, I always say. But, we always do everything together. A double wedding would be perfect,'' Toni said for the thousandth time.

"Well, if I am making a mistake, it's my mistake and I'll be the one to live with the consequences. If I don't go, I'll resent John's hold on my life, and I'll learn to dislike him because of it. I have to do this. Anyway, I'm not sure that I'm ready to settle down yet, and I would want my own, personal special day, thank you very much. I haven't known John long enough to make a commitment to him. There will be plenty of time for Sunday dinners and little league games when I'm a bit older,'' Ashley replied, joining the line of waiting passengers.

The flight announcement burst into their good-natured argument again. Shrugging her shoulders, Toni gave Ashley a last kiss on the cheek and said, "Write to me and don't forget to use your sun block. Even black people can get sunburned in Egypt. This is serious sun you're going into, girlfriend. Keep me posted on your discoveries, especially the male kind."

"You know as well as I do that men are the furthest things from my mind. I have more than enough work to do on this expedition to keep me busy," Ashley retorted, hefting her camera case to her shoulder.

"Maybe so, but men just seem to fall from the sky when we're not looking. The dry season comes when we want someone," Toni laughed dryly, thinking of her own uneventful weekends. Since falling in love with Craig, her life had been a lush, fertile valley of excitement.

Ashley hugged her friend, waved, and walked down the ramp to the waiting plane. She knew Toni was only making small talk, but she could not help but wonder what kind of people, especially men, she would meet on the expedition. The long flight would give her plenty of time to think about her life and her future. So much lay ahead and so much remained behind.

As soon as the plane was airborne Ashley fell fast asleep. She had hardly slept the previous night and, when she did, the old dream returned just as it did now as soon as her eyes fluttered closed. Visions of pyramids, dunes, camels, and relics filled her mind. She dreamed that she and five members of the excavation team became lost in the desert during a nighttime windstorm so thick it blocked out the road in front of them. They pulled their camels off the road and waited until the driving sand subsided. When they could see again, they found themselves in an uncharted valley. Fishing a flashlight from her saddlebags, Ashley searched the flat terrain for signs of people and help.

Suddenly something moved in the distance. It was only a blur of white, almost like a sail moving on a sea of sand. Shining the light toward the movement once again, she saw a man in a long white robe moving along the base of the cluster of pyramids. When he turned toward her, his black eyes shone piercingly in his dark, handsome face. He raised his hands as if to invite her to come to him. His lips moved, but she could not hear him. Shrugging his shoulders, he stepped out of the light and vanished into the darkness. She stared at the spot where he had only seconds before stood smiling at her. All that remained was a haunting memory.

Ashley swung her flashlight frantically, searching for the man. She had to see him again. She had to hear and understand his message. She knew that his words were not a threat. The smile on his face had been kind not sinister, gentle not threatening. He had not been trying to frighten her away. He wanted her to come to him, and, when she did not, he turned away in frustration not anger.

Scanning the area, she observed the massive structures in front of her but could find no trace of him. On the wall of one pyramid someone had written the words in English, "Remember me."

Ashley jerked awake feeling frightened and nervous, yet just as determined as ever to make the trip. She had to find out if this dream man really existed or if he was a pretrip illusion. She looked around to see if she had cried out or spoken in her sleep. The man in the aisle seat beside her slept peacefully with his hands resting on his ample stomach. The two people in the row ahead of her dozed with their seats as far back as they would go. Their slumbering faces showed no sign of having been bothered.

Satisfied that she had disturbed no one, Ashley once again settled into her seat and willed the calmness to ease her mind. Slowly sinking again into sleep, she dreamed of nothing this time as the powerful engines carried her on her adventure to unearth treasures from a previously unknown pyramid that lay slumbering in the shadows of the Great Pyramids.

* * *

Twelve hours later, Ashley found herself and her mound of bags in the middle of an exciting city filled with new and wonderful sights and sounds. She saw women in Moslem attire wrapped from head to toe in black fabric that covered their faces and protected them from the prying eyes of men. She heard the call to worship that filled the air from the loudspeakers mounted on the sides of the mosques. She watched as the faithful flocked to the holy buildings, leaving their shoes and worldly concerns on the steps outside. She smelled the alluring aroma of spices and olives that made her mouth water with the powerful desire to taste the plentiful and exotic delicacies. She was totally captivated by the merchants in the bazaars who beckoned and called to passersby, describing their products as the best on earth and worthy of adorning the bodies and palaces of kings.

Looking around her, Ashley tried to find the driver who would transport her to her hotel. As if on cue, he appeared through the crush of people moving in and out of the airport. Bowing from his waist he introduced himself saying in perfect, lilting English, "Good day, Miss Stephens. I am Khalil Hassan, your driver. If you will allow me, I will escort you to my car. It awaits just over there in the passenger pickup zone."

"Thank you. I am happy to meet you and would appreciate your assistance," she responded with equal formality remembering not to offer her hand. The coordinator of the expedition had informed her that, unlike in the States, women were not on equal footing in Egypt and regardless of their education or position had to remember their place. Contrary to American practices, it was not considered appropriate for a woman to shake hands with a man. Just the idea that she would travel without the protection of a male family member would shock many of the people.

After leading the way to one of the many Mercedes limousines parked along the curb, Khalil proved a skilled guide as he discussed the sights they passed on their drive into the city along a scenic road that paralleled the Nile. As they drove through the bright sun and heavy traffic, he explained that Cairo was a city that never rested or slowed down, making it very similar to New York in temperament, although not in customs. Whizzing between cars and past passengers, he pointed right and left at the monuments to famous Egyptians, massive corporate complexes, and huge bazaars that dotted the streets on both sides. Ashley had never seen such activity in Washington, where the pace was slower. Only in New York's garment district and in Times Square was life this hectic.

After the hair-raising ride from the airport, Ashley was happy to see that her hotel sat slightly off the road and offered a fabulous view of the Nile. The modern face of the building was in opposition to the older structures they had passed along the way, but, somehow, the difference did not seem too jarring. In Cairo, the old and the new appeared to blend without difficulty.

Khalil deposited Ashley and her bags at the registration desk, bowed, and vanished into the crowd before she had a chance to thank him for his kindness and the excellent tour. Turning back to the clerk, she was surprised to see that he already had her key and a telephone message waiting for her. Photocopying her passport and calling a bellhop, he quickly sent Ashley to her room where she could rest until her dinner meeting at eight o'clock that night.

Her room was more than Ashley had expected even from the lavish exterior of the hotel. Everywhere she looked, she saw heavy gold and white fabric. It lined the walls and fell in thick folds onto the gold carpeted floor. Drapes of the same heavy material enclosed the windows in voluminous clouds of opulence. A bedspread of the same white fabric with varying thicknesses of gold threads covered the queen-size bed and eased its heavy corded edges onto the floor.

On the dressing table sat golden brushes and containers of powders and perfumes, each tied with a gold ribbon and sealed with gold tape. Opening one of the bottles, Ashley released a fragrance that she could only describe as overpowering in its thick, sultry spiciness. Lifting the top of the matching powder, she lightly ran her fingers through the delicate velvet texture. Its fragrance was less strong but no less heady.

From her window, she had a perfect view of the Nile's regal path through Cairo. Boats both large and small made their way along its lanes as sightseers, tradesmen, and fishermen made the ancient river their home. She could almost envision the women of the past washing their laundry and bathing their children along its banks. She felt a bond, an overwhelming kinship with the country and its people that she could not explain. It was almost as if the Nile were calling her home.

Suddenly feeling very hot and dirty amid the coolness of the white and gold, Ashley slipped out of her clothes and into the waiting terry cloth robe. She drew a steaming bath scented with the heady fragrance and eased her travel weary body into the depths of the tub. Resting her head against the white satin pillow, she allowed the tension and fatigue to drain from her body into the hot water. Her limbs and eyelids felt very heavy. Closing her eyes, she imagined herself floating along the Nile as a guest of Cleopatra.

Finding herself falling asleep and sliding into the thick bubbles, she shook herself free from the hypnotic spell of the fragrance and the warmth and dried off. Wrapped in the soft robe, she slipped between the sheets and fell into a deep sleep without giving the scheduled meeting a second thought.

Ashley dreamed that all around her people laughed and talked as she reclined on golden pillows at the foot of Cleopatra's throne. She wore a white gossamer gown with gold straps and a belt that matched the gold sandals on her feet. A slave boy catered to her every desire without her uttering a single word. He fanned her moist soft brown shoulders as she lay under the canopy that protected her from the summer sun. Wine and mead flowed freely to quench her thirst. Singers thrilled the mingled throng as they listened to songs of Cleopatra's beauty and glorious army. The grand queen herself listened with rapt attention as her attendants fed her dates and figs.

The fragrance of roasting lamb reached her nostrils as Ashley lolled on her pillows. Just as her attendant lifted a sumptuous slice to her lips, the bell-like tinkling of the telephone burst into Ashley's dreams. At first she did not know where she was, having slept soundly in the comfortable bed. Looking around the room, she suddenly remembered the reason for her trip and why she lay in this opulent bed beneath the draped ceiling. Reaching for the phone, she answered it to find that the receptionist had simply placed a seven thirty wake-up call that she had not requested. The trip coordinator had arranged for everyone in the party to receive one so that no one would sleep through the important information and get acquainted session.

Rising from her bed, Ashley stretched and yawned before slipping into a peach-colored, simple silk dress. She was glad she had packed light clothing because, although it was late January, Cairo was still warm at almost seventy degrees. Picking up a matching sweater and her key, she closed the door behind her and headed for the dining room to meet her fellow archaeologists.

Inside the opulent dining room, the staff cheerfully greeted her at the door, checked off her name, and showed her to her seat. Attaching the name tag to her sweater and easing into her chair, Ashley introduced herself to the others and found that they all came from the States, Europe, and Asia and were filled with the same excitement for the prospects of making a major discovery. They cherished the same goal and desire of unearthing the foundations and contents of the newly discovered pyramid. Each wanted to be the first to discover the entrance, enter the dark recesses, and uncover the long-forgotten treasure that had been buried for centuries under the heavy desert sands.

Breaking into her thoughts by tapping the microphone, a stately older gentleman with glasses resting on the end of his keen nose began his presentation by saying, "Ladies and gentlemen, welcome to Cairo and to the sands of discovery. I am Ben Amad, the leader of our project team. Seated on my left is Kasim Saddam, our co–leader. We are both professors at the University of Cairo. We welcome you to our country and the world's treasures.

"Tomorrow, you will begin work on one of the most important archaeological finds of the century. You will enter the Valley of the Kings from which major treasures have been removed over the decades, yet in which many still remain buried and hidden from our prying eyes. On our expedition, you will experience thirst and frustration the likes of which you have never known. You will find yourselves exhausted and yearning for sleep but too exhilarated to allow it to comfort you. You will want to walk away from the winds that threaten to cover your hours of back-breaking labor. You will look at your partner and wonder what you ever found entertaining, witty, or congenial about him or her as the perspiration soaks your shirt and stings your eyes and turns your companion into a blurred mass. Most certainly, you will wish you were back home in your own bed safe and secure from the biting insects and burning heat of the desert.

"But, when the day comes and you first catch a glimpse of the treasure, you will forget the blisters on you feet, the sweat in your shoes, the hair plastered to your neck, and the spittle caked on your lips. You will know that what you have done has value and worth not only in terms of your satisfaction but for the edification of the world. You will have made a journey into the past that few have been fortunate to experience, and you will return to your regular lives with memories that few are able to share.

"For tonight, I urge you to eat, drink, and make merry. Get to know the other people at your table, for they will be your partners in the months to come. Learn their likes and dislikes and their strengths and weaknesses. You will need to know these things in order to survive where we are going. Study them well, for they are your lifeline.

"Tomorrow morning, we will meet here promptly at six. Our guides will transport us to the site and help us set up our living accommodations before returning to Cairo. Once they leave us, we will be on our own. Your charge tonight is to divide up the living tasks so that we will be ready when we arrive at the dig. Everyone must help with all jobs . . . there is nothing too menial or trivial . . . all are necessary for our survival. Although we will not be far from the city, the constantly shifting sands will make independence a necessity."

Looking around the room at all the eager faces, he raised his water glass and continued with a toast, saying, "So, let us lift a glass to our success and our camaraderie. May Allah grant us an abundance of both."

Everyone clicked glasses and seconded Ben's thoughts

with a resounding "Here! Here!" before eating heartily of the first course of pasta in cheese sauce. This would be their last meal in comfort for quite some time, and they all wanted to sample everything their host had ordered prepared for them.

As Ashley hungrily dug into the Mediterranean and African delicacies, she joined in the conversations of the others at her table. Frank Stewart, the oldest member of her group and of the expedition, was an English widower and retired college professor who spent his time traveling from one archaeological site to another in the hopes of finding something of astounding significance. He told them that he had only just left Syria where he had been close to locating the Holy Grail. When they unearthed a plain copper chalice, everyone in the company had held their breath in anticipation. Unfortunately, it had turned out to be from a time period well after the death of Christ. The cup was a lovely artifact but not the much sought after relic. He had joined the Cairo expedition not only to help with the uncovering of the long-lost pyramid but to forget his disappointment over the failed Grail hunt.

Sallie Barkley was the only other woman in Ashley's group and had joined the expedition as part of her doctoral work at the University of Cairo. She originally came from the States but had not been back in almost ten years. She wore her dark brown hair close cropped. Her trim, athletic figure was tanned a deep brown. Her Egyptian husband was a professor at the university also and had been unable to accompany her. Although she kept up with the major news from home, she was hungry for any tidbits of gossip Ashley could offer her. Ashley was glad to see her not only because Sallie was female and an American but because her vivacious personality would keep her from becoming homesick and lonely on the long days in the sun and sand.

Sun Chin originally came from China and studied for his doctorate in ancient history at Oxford University in England. He, too, was on a fellowship that brought him to the deserts of Egypt in search of buried treasures from days long forgotten. Like Ashley, he was a historian rather than an archaeologist and looked forward to the excitement of uncovering history rather than simply reading about it.

One member of their group was strangely remote and reserved. Until he spoke, Ashley had assumed that he was an African-American. But the sound of his voice quickly told her that he was Egyptian just like Ben Amad. His short, tight brown curls, deep brown skin, and smoldering black eyes accentuated his tall, lean good looks. His voice, sometimes accented by years in an English boarding school, rumbled from deep within his broad chest. His broad hands never lay quietly in his lap as he gesticulated freely to emphasize his discussion points. He looked in top physical condition. She did not think that he was a sedentary academic on holiday or sabbatical. The name tag he wore revealed that he was Kasim Saddam, the man Ben Amad had introduced earlier.

Feeling Ashley's gaze on his face, Kasim Saddam stopped his conversation with Frank Stewart and returned her stare. The corners of his lips turned up in a slight smile of appreciation as he took in her eyes, cheekbones, mouth, and bosom. After having drunk his fill of her and without stopping to introduce himself, he returned to his conversation, leaving the print of his eyes on her face. She had to shake herself free from the hold the few moments of exchanged glances had placed on her psyche.

Shifting uneasily in her chair, Ashley turned her body away from Kasim to join the conversation between Sallie and Sun. She was not particularly interested in their discussion of photography, but she could not bear the idea that

Kasim would see the blush that had consumed her cheeks and the frustration that his penetrating eyes had caused in her soul. She was amazed at her reaction to this total stranger, knowing that she had not responded so suddenly to any other man at first sight. Slightly ashamed of her lack of control, Ashley scolded herself for so quickly being attracted to Kasim's exotic dark looks.

As if sensing her discomfort, Kasim chuckled softly to himself. He was accustomed to the reaction of European and American women upon first meeting him. More than one key and invitation to a private dinner had been discretely pressed into the palm of his hand or slipped into his jacket pocket by women on expeditions, at seminars, or in hotel lobbies. He usually deposited the keys with the concierge and tore up the notes. He was not interested in picking up women as trophies while on the quest for antiquities, but something about this woman made her different. Rather than coming on to him, she had been genuinely distressed by the meeting of their eyes, and he found that intriguing. He wanted to know more about the bewitching member of his group with the soft voice and deep dimples in her cheeks.

As Ashley engaged her table mates in conversation to avoid Kasim's eyes and her thoughts, she discovered that she quickly formed a friendship with Sallie, who seemed to understand that she suffered from a touch of homesickness. Listening attentively, Sallie asked with a chuckle, "What brings you to Egypt other than the usual desire to sift through the sands of antiquity for long forgotten treasures? Tell me about yourself."

"There's nothing to tell really. I'm a history teacher, and I'm here on sabbatical. I decided to spend this semester and part of the summer pursuing a dream of a lifetime. I can't remember a time when I did not want to be part of an archaeological dig. When the sabbatical opportunity arose, I hopped on it. I needed something to revitalize my teaching and my imagination. I thought the expedition would do both," Ashley answered, relieved to have a diversion from Kasim's penetrating eyes.

"I used to live in the States, you know. I miss not having the beach summers myself," Sallie replied. "Cairo is a far cry from a beach town. Tell me about your summer place."

"Well, it's not actually mine. It belongs to my best friend, Toni. We've spent summers together since we first met in college. When Toni's parents retired and moved to Arizona, they gave her the house on the beach where she had spent her summers as a child. Naturally, she invited me to spend my vacations there, too. I'll miss the waves, sand, and sun this summer, but I couldn't let a chance like this slip through my fingers," Ashley answered, feeling very homesick for her best friend.

"Sure sounds as if you two are great friends," Sallie commented.

"We sure are. I'm going to be her maid of honor at her wedding this summer. We've been best friends for a long time. During our college days, we traveled together during breaks and summer vacations if we could scrape together enough money for the airfare. We visited Spain, Italy, Turkey, France, and England on a shoestring, eating in the little bistros, sleeping in youth hostels, and traveling by bus and train as much as we could. Since graduate school, we've been inseparable. We teach in the same high school and share an apartment a few blocks away. We're the perfect duo, except that Toni has a sandy complexion, gray eyes, and freckled skin. And she'd never think of going on an expedition into the dust of the past. Now, it's your turn. Tell me something about yourself," Ashley said, as she sipped her wine.

"You already know the gory academic stuff from the bio sheet. I guess the only thing not mentioned there is that

I'm a photographer in my few spare moments. I plan to record this trip on film, so you'll see a lot of me from behind my trusty lens," Sallie said, filling in the blanks about herself.

"What do you know about our guides?" Ashley asked, feeling confident in her new friendship with Sallie.

"They're both highly respected in their fields. Ben has been in the business longer, but Kasim has gained international acclaim from some stunning discoveries. He's part African-American, you know. His father studied for his bachelor's degree in the States where he met Kasim's mother. They returned to Egypt via England as newlyweds. He credits them with interesting him in archaeology. I read an article in which he wrote that, unlike other kids who played on the beach during the summer, he spent his vacations digging in the sands of the Egyptian dessert," Sallie confided willingly.

"He's very attractive," Ashley commented, sending a furtive glance at Kasim.

"And very private. I've never read anything in his biography or any news clippings about a wife or girlfriend. He's dedicated to his work and nothing else," Sallie concluded with a shrug.

As the evening grew late, Ashley became too tired and sleepy to notice the sideways glances that Kasim continued to cast in her direction. Occasionally, she could sense the warmth of his gaze as it swept over her body or studied her face, but she was too jet-lagged to react. Ordinarily, she would have found his attention flattering, but after the hectic pace she had kept for the last two days, she could only file it away in the recesses of her mind for further consideration. Besides, she had not come on this expedition to attract the attention of an undeniably handsome man. She had come for the purpose of expanding her horizons, unearthing antiquities, and joining in scholarly discourse about history. Kasim and his penetrating eyes were an unexpected bonus.

As the effects of the strong dinner wine served only to the visiting archaeologists weighed heavily on her eyes and the excited conversation dulled, Ashley excused herself from the table and retired to her room. She was too tired to notice that Kasim's gaze followed her through the door and as far down the hall as he could see through the wall of windows that separated the dining room from the lobby. She also did not see the appreciative little smile that lifted the corners of his lips as he watched the sway of her hips and the carriage of her proud but exhausted shoulders.

Reaching her room, she eased the key card into the lock and successfully opened the door on the first try. Switching on the light, she found that the covers had been turned back and a chocolate candy placed on the pillow. Throwing her clothes carelessly into the waiting chair, Ashley slipped into the welcoming bed without bothering to wash off the tiny bit of blush that added a hint of color to her naturally rosy complexion. Pulling the sheet under her chin, she fell asleep instantly with visions of the next day's trip into the desert spinning through her dreams.

Kasim did not rest as easily as memories of the bewitching American woman filled his mind. He knew that as the group's leader and a seasoned archaeologist, he needed his full strength after a good night's sleep to help him guide and direct the energies of the inexperienced archaeologists. They would need his advice on the methods for conserving one's energy while working in the hot sun, for locating the dig, and for maintaining a sense of direction in the large expanse of sand. Still, he could not force the image of Ashley from his thoughts. She stood before him in shirt, jeans, and boots or in a clinging evening gown or in a revealing silk gossamer nightgown. She came to his mind without encouragement and would not give him peace. Finally, he understood his father's attraction to his mother.

Chuckling at his own folly, Kasim checked his watch to find that it was already two in the morning. They were to meet at six in the dining room for a quick breakfast and last-minute reminders before boarding the vehicles that would transport them to the site. As the illuminated hands of his watch again reminded him of the lateness of the hour, he forced himself to fall asleep. The success of his group depended on his leadership, skill, and clear head. For the next few hours, he forced thoughts of Ashley deep into the recesses of his mind.

Dressed in jeans or heavy twills, thick-soled shoes, white shirts with long sleeves, and pith helmets, the subdued members of the expedition assembled as instructed as the early rays of the sun shone on the Nile. Ashley was among the first to enter the dining room and take her place at the table. She had slept well and had risen before the wake-up call feeling refreshed and ready for the day's adventure. Helping herself to servings of oatmeal, fruit, yogurt, juice, coffee, and bran muffin, she looked anxiously around the room for Kasim. When she did not find him, she smiled happily at Sallie who could hardly contain her excitement long enough to sit through breakfast. Her desire to begin their adventure was so infectious that Ashley quickly found herself just as anxious to board the bus and travel into the desert.

As Ben called the group together, Ashley again looked around the room for Kasim. There was something very familiar about him. She wondered where she had seen him before as a vague memory tried to surface through her excitement to begin the expedition. Not finding him, she turned her concentration to what Ben was saying to them as he prepared the amateur and experienced archaeologists for their trek into the desert. Leaning her face on her hands, she listened as he said, "With luck and hard work we will find the hidden treasures we have come here to uncover. Let us remember that what we do here is not for our individual glory but for the good of the whole world as we prepare to share the rewards of our toil. Now, let us board the bus and return to the time of the pharaohs."

Picking up their bags, Ashley and Sallie joined the others as they walked out of the hotel to the waiting bus. She had hardly stepped aboard when she felt his presence. Looking toward the back, she saw Kasim standing among the tents, food supplies, and excavation tools frowning over the checklist as he gave it one last scrutiny. Even with a scowl on his face, he still struck a handsome pose. He looked up from his clipboard as they boarded. When he saw her, his face broke into a smile and he nodded in recognition. Ashley quickly returned it as she settled into the seat beside Sallie.

Despite the early hour, the streets were already packed with people rushing to work in smoking cars, on bikes, and on foot. Sallie kept up a steady stream of nervous chatter as the bus driver slowly eased into the press of traffic and began the drive out of town to Giza. Already the sun shone hot through the windows as Ashley absent-mindedly listened to her companion's discussion of the assorted artifacts she had uncovered on previous expeditions. She wished Sallie would be silent for a while so that she could relish the excitement of her first true adventure without the intrusive voice in her ear.

Sallie's voice droned on in the warm bus as she clicked shots of people and buildings. Ashley found herself dozing behind her sunglasses and dreaming about the expedition into the burial land of the great pharaohs of Egypt. The exotic aromas of olives, spices, rice, meat, and grain floated in through the open windows and filled her nostrils. In her mind, Ashley could see herself sailing down the Nile on a barge made of heavy wood encrusted with sparkling gold that shone brighter than the sun and precious jewels that glittered more dazzlingly than the evening star. Her flowing gossamer gold silk robes fluttered in the warm air. Her attendants had carefully braided her hair with gold and silver threads. Gold serpentine bracelets encircled her bare wrists and arms, dangling gold earrings hung from her ears, and gold cloth slippers enfolded her oiled feet. By her side lounged a huge mastiff in its emerald and gold collar, and beside it, on a pillow, slept a black cat with a coat so smooth it looked like the softest velvet money could buy.

Resting on a down-filled pillow on one elbow, she delicately nibbled on figs and dates as her servants fanned and shaded her against the heat of the sun. On a matching chaise, reclined her lover, a bronzed, muscled specimen of the male Egyptian form, whose barely clad body glistened with fragrant oils. He appeared indifferent to the attention of her coyly smiling handmaidens as he paid homage only to her, peeling grapes for her and massaging her shoulders and feet with his strong, powerful hands. He tenderly planted kisses on her cheeks and fingers while gazing up lovingly at the controlled, disinterested expression that concealed the desire the closeness of him caused to burn in her body. As they made their slow progress down the sleepy river, he kept his eyes fixed on Ashley, anticipating her every desire.

He eased into a reclining position beside her, and she could feel his hard maleness pressed against her thigh as his hands lovingly caressed her shoulders and back. Her hands responded by gently massaging the muscles in his arms and chest. Under the protection of the gossamer fabric that surrounded her throne, their lips clung together as sea birds soared overhead uttering cries that blocked out their passion sounds as the need for each other mounted.

No one saw into their secluded hideaway as they pulled up the fabric that barely covered their oiled bodies and made love with the water gently lapping at the side of the barge. They were totally alone as her lover slipped over her body and entered the deep recesses of pleasure between her shapely thighs. Only the birds witnessed the rise and fall of their motions as their primal urges drove them to explore each other with total abandon. Nothing interrupted the increasing frenzy of their movement as she matched her thrusts to his. And when they lay exhausted as the last tremors of passion left their bodies, no one heard the words of love that slipped easily from between their kiss-swollen lips.

Just as she was about to raise her eyes to his face, a voice burst into the haze of her dream, shattering the serenity and destroying the moment. Allowing her mind to return to the present, Ashley woke to discover Kasim leaning across the stretching Sallie. Smiling, he repeated before moving to the next row, "It is time to gather your things. We will be in Giza in a few moments."

Embarrassed that she had been caught in such a provocative dream by the owner of the knowing smirk, Ashley quickly thanked Kasim and began gathering the camera and duffel bags she had carried on board the bus. The driver had stowed her other two bags in the bus's luggage compartment along with those of the other expedition members. All of them would soon lie in piles and clusters on the pavement.

Almost immediately, Sallie began to speculate on their success enthusiastically saying, "I bet we will unearth something fabulous that will set the world on fire. I just know we will. I can feel it in my bones." Ashley was amused at the energy her companion displayed despite the frequency with which she participated in archaeological digs. Sallie had a gift for making all activities fun and novel.

As the caravan of buses pulled to a stop, Ashley gazed out the window at her first sight of the famous pyramids. Rising from the sand into the bright sun, the massive stone structures stood as proud testimony to the architectural skill of the early Egyptians. She marveled at the complexity of the designs and the wealth that had once been preserved in each one. She felt small and insignificant in the shadow of such greatness.

Stepping from the bus into the sunshine, Ashley shaded her eyes from the glare as she scanned the flat, dry expanse of desert that lay before her. Although only a few miles outside of the bustling metropolis of Giza with its flowering gardens, she could feel the vastness and danger of the ancient sand. She promised herself that she would not stray from the group. She would resist the temptation of taking an unaccompanied camel ride into the desert where she might possibly meet villages of people hostile to outsiders or become lost amid the never-ending whiteness.

As Kasim emerged with his arms full of boxes and camera supplies, Ashley was once again struck by his exotic appearance, which was enhanced now by the flowing cream-colored robe that fluttered around his ankles. Over his white trousers and shirt, he had donned the extra layer of protection from the sun after all the passengers had left the bus. He now appeared before them looking more Egyptian and handsome than ever. The light color of the fabric further enhanced the striking darkness of his skin, his chiseled features, and his piercing black eyes. On his feet he wore the traditional leather sandals instead of shoes.

Looking at him, Ashley once again had to remind herself that she had come on this trip to work not to fall in love with a stranger who could never really be part of her world. With a crooked smile, she told herself that she must not confuse the excitement of the expedition with feelings for this man.

Whistling softly to himself, Kasim assumed his place at the head of their little group and awaited Ben's instructions. He had gone ahead of them to make sure the staff had prepared their accommodations to his satisfaction. Although informal and bordering on primitive, everything still had to be properly arranged inside the structure, which stood within easy walking distance of the recently discovered underground tomb. The last work team had just vacated the site yesterday, and he hoped that they had left the compound clean for the new inhabitants.

Seeing Ben's signal, Kasim hoisted the boxes to his shoulders and summoned the group to follow him down the planks that served as a temporary path to the temple. As they walked, Ashley studied the looming strength of the Great Pyramid. The symmetry and the lasting quality of its structure impressed more completely than she had anticipated. Knowing that each one of the more than three million stone blocks weighed two and one half tons, she marveled that people could have built such a massive structure with their bare hands without the help of machinery. She stopped briefly for a few photographs before rushing to catch up with the others. Ben had promised them some free time that morning before the tourists arrived for touring the other pyramids. Later that evening after the sunset, Kasim had already planned for them to attend the sound and light show so popular with visitors to Egypt. They could play tourist to their hearts' content then, but now they had work to do.

CHAPTER TWO

When they finally reached the building that would serve as their quarters for the duration of the expedition, Ashley discovered that her shirt had become drenched with sweat and her makeup had all but washed off from the walk in the hot sun. To her surprise, Kasim appeared cool without even a drop of perspiration on his forehead. She promised herself that on their first day off, she would venture into Giza and purchase several of the flowing robes. Although she had dressed in cool cottons, western clothing was no match for the heat of Egypt even in January.

Stepping inside the structure, Ashley was relieved to find that it was cool and dark after the harsh glare of the sun. The interior was arranged dormitory style with each sleeping area containing a cot, protective netting, a little bedside table with a small reading lamp, a privacy curtain, and shelves and a chest at the foot of the bed for clothing and extra linen. The communal bathroom and laundry room were situated at one end of the long narrow room. Near the door was the conference room where they would eat their meals, debrief after a day's work, examine artifacts, and relax while watching the television or listening to the radio.

Although there was little privacy except for the curtains that separated the common sleeping area into cubicles, Ashley found that she did not object to the shared accommodations. There was something strangely comforting about living so closely with the people on whom she would have to depend for the next few months. Searching down the row of bunks, she discovered that Kasim's space lay at the other end of the room near the bathroom. She was relieved that he was so far away, but she doubted that anything would develop between them anyway in these close quarters and with the long, tiring hours they would keep. Still she liked the idea that he would not be sleeping too close to her.

Turning her attention to her bags, Ashley quickly unpacked and neatly folded her things on the provided shelves. When she reached the bottom of the suitcase, she found the excavation brush John had given her. As she fingered the inscription, her mind turned to the weeks they had spent together on the beach. She could still feel the warmth of his hand on hers and smell the fragrance of his cologne. Tossing the brush into the drawer, Ashley smiled at the memories and prepared to make new ones on this expedition.

The next thought came uninvited to her mind. The sight of Kasim's dark muscular body and his deep accented voice again rocked her senses. Ashley shook herself for being so easily distracted from the purpose of her sabbatical. Reminding herself that she was on expedition for scholarly purposes and not personal ones, she again turned her attention to settling into her new quarters.

Sharply brushing Kasim from her mind, Ashley promised herself that she would never again allow herself to become

entrapped by him. The months would quickly pass and
too soon she would return home. Ashley did not want to
take a broken heart back to the States along with her
journal and album of photographs.

Yet, Kasim was hard to resist. Ashley knew that some of
his display of attention was financially motivated. After all,
the guest archaeologists needed to be kept happy so that
they would enthusiastically spread the word among their
friends and associates and inspire others to follow in their
footsteps. Without their positive evaluation of the program,
the excavation would be slowed by the absence of funds
and willing hands.

Still, Ashley knew that some of his warmth toward her
was genuine, making him very difficult to dismiss. She was
drawn to him as if for a reason she could not explain. At
the same time, she knew that it was not he who was familiar
but someone very much like him. Shaking her head at her
behavior, Ashley decided that Egypt and its handsome
people had cast an even greater spell on her than she had
originally thought. She would have to be careful lest she
find herself in love with the wrong man. Joining the others
outside as they prepared to walk the short distance to the
underground pyramid, Ashley continued to berate herself.
She had been in Egypt only a matter of hours and surely
should be able to keep her mind on her work and off
Kasim.

Stepping into the glare of the bright sun, Ashley shaded
her eyes as she joined the others. She matched her stride
with Sallie's, and they trudged along the makeshift walk
that led to the dig. Her untrained eyes saw nothing in the
horizon except a great expanse of sand. But as they drew
closer, she saw the outline of the kind of pyramid used for
the burial of the pharaohs' wives and children as it rose
from the camouflaging sand. The crew that had recently
vacated the site had spent months uncovering it. Their

funding had expired before they could enter and see the treasures that had been buried for centuries. The pyramid was just barely visible in the shimmering sun until they stood almost in front of it. Then, suddenly, it loomed before them in all of its majesty. Although massive, its size was dwarfed by the Great Pyramid. Ashley wondered how much of it lay below the surface of the sandy desert.

As they stopped within arm's reach of the perimeter, Ashley stumbled on a small brush that had been left behind by the last group of archaeologists. She felt herself tumbling headfirst into the bruising stone but could do nothing to stop her forward motion. As she extended her hands to protect her face from coming in contact with the massive stone blocks, she felt strong arms encircle her waist and yank her to safety. Resting against his chest, she knew immediately that Kasim had saved her from a potentially nasty spill.

"People should be more careful where they leave their tools," Kasim muttered into her ear as her pulse raced in her neck and her heart pounded in her chest. He held her close in an effort to steady her. His face nestled in her hair. She could feel his warm breath on her neck. Cool shivers and rivulets of nervous perspiration ran down her spine.

Shaken by her near disaster and her reaction to Kasim's closeness, Ashley replied through her tightly constricted throat, "I'll have to be more observant in the future. I was so busy looking at the structure of the pyramid that I didn't even notice the brush. It was foolish and quite amateurish of me to walk without scanning the area. But I'm fine now. Thank you. You can turn me lose now, thank you."

"Reluctantly, I will do as you request," Kasim replied.

As Sallie's gaze bore into her flushed cheeks, Ashley muttered, "Thank you for your kindness."

Bowing slightly at the waist, Kasim backed away and

smiled before picking up his hastily abandoned load. Without a backward glance, he continued the last few feet to the staging tent from which the delicate work of the excavation would proceed. Ashley watched his shoulders bulging under the weight of the supplies and shuddered, not from her near tumble but from the memory of the smell of his warm body and the strength of his arms. She would have to be more careful in the future. She did not like the thrill his nearness caused to course along the length of her slight frame.

"What was that all about?" Sallie asked, studying Ashley's flaming cheeks.

"Nothing. Kasim just saved me from a bad spill. I tripped, that's all. Let's join the others," Ashley replied, trying to distract Sallie's inquisitive mind.

"Do you think he'd look at me like that if I stumbled?" Sallie inquired with thinly veiled sarcasm in her voice.

"You're reading too much into a purely innocent happening. Let's go," Ashley retorted, giving her new friend a slight push in the direction of the pyramid.

Pushing thoughts of Kasim from her mind, she joined the others and listened to Ben's instructions for the division of labor and the assignment of work areas. The previous groups had unearthed the buried pyramid and the hidden entrance. Her task was to uncover, preserve, and record the treasures deep within the massive structure. Like all the other members of her group, Ashley excitedly awaited the start of the work. But she also had a personal reason for being anxious to begin—the hard physical labor would keep her mind off Kasim.

She and Sallie had been paired up for the remainder of the excavation work, and now they stood by impatiently while Ben led the first two teams as they carefully eased the huge stone block from the entrance. It was tedious work that required a great deal of patience. First, they had

to remove the ages of sand that sealed the slab to the body
of the pyramid. Then, they had to wedge a large clawlike
structure between the tiny crack and the doorway and
gently but firmly pull the stone away from the opening.
Helping with the preliminary efforts as much as they could,
Ashley and Sallie waited for their opportunity to be really
useful.

By late afternoon a sense of anticipation filled the hot,
dry air as the wench pulled the embedded stone away from
the opening and to the side of the pyramid. All of them
cheered as the black gaping mouth of the interior presented itself. Ben shone his massive flashlight into the
recesses, illuminating first nothing and then the painted
walls of the tomb. He shone the light on stairs and passages
that lead downward and deeper into the burial chambers.
Finally, he positioned a massive fan inside the entrance to
blow out some of the stale gases and help with air circula-
tion. Deciding to explore the walkway to the right of the
opening where the path was wider, Ben called for them
to follow him.

As they slowly entered, Ashley breathed the dusty stale
air of her first excavation. Her heart pounded against her
chest in anticipation of uncovering the treasures so long
forgotten. Sand swirled around the floor at her feet, and
the eerie sound of ages of silence filled her ears. Clutching
her flashlight, she followed Ben along the entrance passage, which they hoped would lead to the treasure and
burial chambers. They stopped along the way to shine their
lights on the drawings that covered the walls in vivid colors
as if they had been created only yesterday instead of thousands of years ago. From the nature of the art, they thought
that this might have been the grave of a queen whose
interests included agriculture and sailing. Each picture
contained drawings of sailors and farmers going about
their daily routines. She marveled at the detail as Ben

explained the meaning of the hieroglyphics that accompanied them.

Following the path as it wound ever upward toward what they hoped would be the burial chamber, Ashley and Sallie stayed in close contact with the others in their group. They were not afraid of becoming lost or disoriented since behind them they could see the sun streaming in through the opening, but they had felt a strange stillness descend upon them as soon as they entered the pyramid. It was like the quietude that accompanies entering a church or the waiting moments before the orchestra plays the first notes of a symphony. When they spoke, they spoke in whispers. Every fiber of their beings waited for something to happen. They both sensed that whatever it was, it would be big.

Suddenly Ben stopped his forward progress and signaled for all of them to be silent and still. Listening, but at first hearing nothing, they strained to catch the sound of a distant rumble. It seemed to come from outside the pyramid and only filtered through the thick walls where it was muffled by the silence of the ages. But as they waited, it grew louder and closer and began to sound like the noise made by a rushing herd of cattle.

Turning toward them with panic written on his face Ben shouted, "Run! Head for the opening. Get out of here!"

Quickly making their way in the direction of the light as the sound came closer and the stone under their feet began to shake, Ashley and Sallie ran with the others in their group. No one dared to stop and look back. They knew that an unseen something wanted them out of the tomb and was hurrying toward them.

As the group leader, Ben was the last to exit the pyramid amid a shower of sand and small rocks. As soon as he entered the sunlight, a massive boulder filled the opening, sealing the entrance from inside. The ground shook with its force as it came to rest inside the narrowing passageway, undoing months of hard labor.

"Is everyone all right?" Kasim asked, joining them at the entrance. He had heard and felt the rumble from the work tent where he had been cataloging their supplies. When the ground began to shake beneath his feet, he had dropped what he was doing and had run to the pyramid, reaching it as a cloud of dust billowed from the blocked entrance.

Obviously shaken but not discouraged, Ben brushed the grit from his clothing and said, "We're fine. We heard the rumble in time to get out without any casualties. I guess we have more work cut out for us than I originally thought. There is no way we can move that boulder from the outside. We will have to look for another way in. Most of these pyramids had more than one entrance so that the workers would have an escape should something go wrong. Let us get cleaned up and have some supper. We will start early tomorrow morning before the sun gets too hot. With luck, we will find another route inside very quickly."

"What do you think caused that boulder to come rolling down from nowhere?" Ashley asked, brushing the dirt from her hair with hands that trembled with fear and excitement.

"You probably tripped an ancient booby trap set to protect the treasures buried inside the tomb from robbers. Now that we know that the ancient Egyptians went to this much trouble, we will have to be more careful. This was a close call. It is a good thing that no one was hurt. There must be considerable wealth buried inside the pyramid for the builders to have rigged it against thieves. No one spends time building sophisticated burglar alarms unless they have something to protect," Kasim replied as Ben absent-mindedly surveyed the structure for signs of another entrance.

"How exciting!" Sallie added. "To think we were nearly buried alive in an ancient Fort Knox!"

Members of the assembled group rolled their eyes at her outrageous enthusiasm as Ben said, "There might also be nothing in this pyramid. It just might be a decoy to lure us from a richly appointed one we still have not found. If I am not mistaken, I believe that the inscription on the wall beside the opening predicted that we would encounter many obstacles to our success. We will not know for certain until we find the treasury and the burial chambers. In the meanwhile, let us return to base, get cleaned up, and have some supper. I am really quite hungry."

Clutching Sallie's hand and almost dragging her away from the freshly sealed tomb, Ashley followed the others down the path. As they were about to enter the lodge, she stopped Ben by asking, "What exactly did the hieroglyphics say? You only read bits and pieces. I had the feeling that you didn't share everything with us."

Shading his eyes with his dirty hands, Ben replied slowly as if the memory caused him great pain. He said, "You are right. I did not tell you everything because I did not want to upset everyone. Often the ancient Egyptians wrote messages to frighten off intruders, which today often scare fledgling archaeologists. I usually only point out the obvious messages or the pleasant inscriptions. Usually I am correct in doing so, but this time I was not. The hieroglyphics warned that anyone entering the tomb should beware the rolling rock that would crush him to bits or trap him in the narrow passage from which there is no exit. There is more, but I will share it with you later when we are not standing in this devilishly hot sun."

Not waiting for Ashley's reply, Ben entered their quarters and walked immediately to the conference room and closed the door behind him. This was not the first time an inscription on a tomb wall had come true; everyone knew that the Tut expedition had been plagued with curses. It was, however, his first brush with death and the possibility of losing the people in his charge. He needed some time to be alone. He also had to plan their alternate entry route. The detailed drawings he had made of the exterior would come in handy for that task.

"Is he all right?" Ashley asked Kasim, who stood silently at her side.

"He will be fine. It is just unsettling to know that our entire team could have been killed. That does not happen to us every day. In fact, this is our first close call," Kasim replied, leading Ashley through the sunlit doorway and into the coolness of the enclosure.

Easing her into a nearby chair and fetching two tall glasses of ice tea from the counter, Kasim settled into the seat across from her. He stretched his long legs out into the aisle between them under the folds of his robe. Drumming his fingers on the table, he seemed quite lost in thought and almost unaware of her presence. Ashley wondered if she should quickly drink the refreshing tonic and leave him in peace. As if reading her mind, Kasim said resting his hand on hers, "It feels good to have someone to sit with and not have to say anything. I do not feel the need for small talk since we just shared the same experience. It is very nice."

Ashley sat perfectly still as the heat from his body flowed through hers. She wanted to pull away, liberate her hand from his, pick up the glass, and sip nonchalantly from it, but she found she could not move. It was almost as if Kasim controlled her will. The weight on his long thin tapered fingers and broad palm totally covered her hand and pinned it to the table, holding it prisoner. The pressure reminded her of the boulder's frightening weight. She needed to turn away from his piercing gaze, but the intensity of his stare would not allow her to budge. She knew that she should not allow him to take control of her this way, but she was powerless. All of the will power and reserve had left her body.

Feeling the color flush her cheeks as the heat from his hand and the temperature of the room mixed, Ashley experienced a giddy sensation that made her stomach sick, her ears ring, her throat constrict, and her heart hammer irregularly. The room slowly began to spin until it swirled around her. She could not force her eyes to focus on anything as the pictures on the walls, the tables and chairs, and the other members of the expedition spun past in the mad, blinding chaos that enveloped her. For an instant, she saw Kasim's lips moving and heard a voice coming toward her from a distance. Then darkness descended and all was forgotten.

When she awoke, Ashley lay on her cot in the darkness. The low hum of the ceiling fan and the voices around her slowly penetrated her mind as she struggled to open her eyes. A cool cloth rested on her forehead and a woman spoke softly in a familiar voice saying, "Don't try to sit up. The heat and the excitement caused you to faint, but you're all right now. Just lie still until I return with a cup of broth."

Unable to speak, Ashley did as the voice commanded. She was too tired and confused to rebel against the gently spoken orders. Allowing the pillows to cradle her head and dreams to claim her mind, she drifted off into a fitful sleep in which she found herself alone in the dark, lonely desert. Stumbling amid the miles of sand, she walked with outstretched hands toward a flickering light in the distance. Instead of coming closer, with every step the glow seemed to move farther away, leading her deeper and farther into the silent night. Suddenly a man appeared directly in front of her. He stood draped all in black and blocked her path with his broad shoulders. In his hands, he carried a torch that illuminated the area around them but could not shed light on his covered face.

As Ashley reached up to touch him, he whispered, "Remember me." Then he turned and vanished in the darkness, taking the only source of light with him.

Easing her eyes open, she stared at the figure outlined in the glow from the harsh ceiling florescent lights. At first, she thought it was the man returning for her. Slowly, as the last of the sleep fogginess left her brain, she recognized Sallie.

"Have I been out long?" Ashley asked, accepting the spoonful of nourishment her friend offered.

"Only about two hours. The doctor said that we should let you sleep. He thought you fainted from the heat and excitement. How do you feel now?" Sallie asked, ladling yet another spoonful into her charge's mouth.

"Embarrassed. I've never fainted before. That's such an old-fashioned thing to do. Let me get up. I'm being such a bother," Ashley said struggling against Sallie's restraining hand.

"You're no trouble at all. Now lie back before you faint again."

"No, I'm fine. Don't worry. I don't know what happened. One minute I was sitting with Kasim and the next I was lying here with a cloth on my forehead."

"We had enough excitement today to make anyone ill. Even Ben is still in his room trying to collect his thoughts. Oh, by the way, Kasim is really worried about you. From the expression on his face, I'd say you made quite an impression on him, and I don't mean just the fainting part."

"You're imagining things. He doesn't even know me. I'm sure Kasim is simply being nice to a novice archaeologist. It's part of his job," Ashley replied, finishing off the last of the healing broth.

"The way he looked at you when he laid you on this cot was anything but casual and detached. I think he's falling for you," Sallie said with a knowing wink.

"Don't be silly. I certainly don't need a man adding to the excitement in my life at the moment. Enough has happened to me already without anything else complicating it further," Ashley objected, hoping that her voice sounded confident and secure in her response.

"Really? You could have fooled me. I've seen the way you study his face when you don't think he's looking. I saw you two holding hands at the table, too. I'd say that you already have your hands full whether you want the added attention or not," Sallie continued in an annoying know-it-all tone of voice as she scrutinized Ashley's tired face from the top of her glasses.

"Well, you're wrong. He simply placed his hand on mine for emphasis. We were not holding hands as you called it. Besides, there's something strangely familiar about Kasim. I vaguely remember a dream I had a few nights ago. In it there was a man who looked a lot like him only different. They have the same build, the same sturdy shoulders under the flowing robe, the same dark eyes and coloring. They even have the same face, except for a scar in the right eyebrow, but the man in the dream had a certain arrogance that Kasim doesn't. He's really very nice. That's one of the reasons why I don't need to complicate matters any more than they already are by starting something with him."

"Want it or not, you've got it. Your friend back home had better get himself on the next flight to Cairo if he knows what's good for him. Looks to me as if his days are numbered," Sallie replied over her shoulder as she walked toward the snack room with the coffee cup in her hand.

Sitting on her bunk with Sallie's words still echoing in

her mind, Ashley admitted to herself that there was indeed
some truth in what her new friend said. She had tried to
ignore the feelings that blossomed in her toward Kasim,
but she had not been able to shake the appeal of his
trim body and the excitement of his conversation. Telling
herself that her feelings had mingled with the exotic fragrances and sights of Egypt, she had tried to overlook
them, but his hand on hers had forced them to the front
of her mind.

Resting her chin on her hand, Ashley thought about
home. Suddenly very homesick and confused about her
feelings for Kasim and the man in her dreams. Surprisingly,
she missed her classroom—certainly not the mountain of
papers she graded every week—but the children and their
stories. John had offered her stability, and school provided
routine. Kasim and Egypt meant excitement and intrigue.
She was not certain she was up to the challenge of an
adventure. The one thing Ashley did know was that she
could not build a relationship with Kasim. Their worlds
were too far apart. They had lived such different lives that
a future with him was out of the question. Ashley refused
to allow an expedition fling to develop between them.

Allowing her mind to drift, Ashley could hardly believe
that only a few short months ago she had returned to the
classroom after her refreshing summer. Now sitting on her
hard bunk in the middle of the desert and fingering the
soft bristles of the brush John had given her, Ashley
thought about home and safety. She hoped the excitement
of the dig and unearthing the treasures would compensate
for her confusion. Something deep within her said that
being true to herself was the most important lesson that
she would learn from this sabbatical.

But then there were the dreams. Those confusing
dreams about the man who warmed her from the depths
of sleep. At first Ashley had convinced herself that Toni

was right and the dreams were simply her excitement about the trip playing tricks on her. But when they continued and increased in length, she began to wonder if they meant something more.

Now, to complicate matters, she found Kasim attractive in a strangely familiar way. Ashley was not sure of the connection between Kasim and the man in her dream, and the effect that either would have on her thoughts about John, but she had to find out before she could be content.

When the others slipped into their cubicles and turned out their lights, Ashley eased into her nightshirt and slid between the covers. Immediately, fatigue overpowered her limbs and sleep snuffed out her thoughts about the man from her dreams and Kasim.

Yet Ashley did not sleep soundly despite her weariness. Dreams of the runaway boulder crashing down on her and pinning her inside the pyramid haunted her and caused her to toss and turn fitfully. She could feel the dust and closeness of the tomb closing around her. She could hear the silence of the ages fill her ears. She clawed and pushed at the massive rock, but it would not move from the mouth of the pyramid. Feeling eyes burning into the back of her skull, she turned to stare into the darkness.

Listening, Ashley heard no one. Just as she was about to scream for help, a familiar male voice reached her ears. Moving slowly toward the sound, she made her way in the darkness with only the light from her flashlight to guide her. The voice grew closer and closer until she could almost recognize it. Her heart pounded wildly, and perspiration dotted her shirt. Shining the light upward, she could almost make out a face at the opening above her head.

"Ashley, wake up! You're talking in your sleep and making an incredible racket. Anyway, it's time to get up. We have to meet in the briefing room in ten minutes for breakfast and the day's instructions. That must be some dream. Your nightshirt is stuck to your body. Are you okay?'' Sallie's voice penetrated the darkness and kept her from seeing the person who had come to save her.

"I'm fine. Sorry. I hope I didn't wake you and everyone else. I'd better get a move on. I'll just grab a quick shower and meet you at breakfast. Save me a seat next to you,'' Ashley said, swinging her long, shapely legs over the side of her cot. She quickly spread out the sheet and light blanket before grabbing her robe and darting from her cubicle.

"No, you didn't disturb me, but I sure would like to have a dream like that. It must have been quite invigorating,'' Sallie replied as she stood in the doorway watching Ashley's frenzied actions.

"It's nothing really. I keep having this vision of being lost or trapped and being rescued. It's all too confusing. I haven't been able to make sense of it yet. When I do, I'll share it with you. I'd better hurry or I'll miss breakfast,'' Ashley said as she rushed to the shower.

When she joined the others at breakfast, Ashley looked surprisingly refreshed and rested. Everyone inquired about her health as they assembled around the table for a hearty meal that would likely be their only one until they returned to camp later that afternoon. If they became hungry, they could snack on the candy, fruit, and bread they carried in their backpacks. Taking the offered seat beside Sallie, she listened attentively as Ben described the new route through the ancient air and worker escape tunnels that would now become their entry into the pyramid. He felt confident that no further booby traps awaited them.

Looking around the room at all the attentive faces, Ashley discovered that Kasim was not among them. He had explained that he would often be absent from their communal meals while tending to their supply needs, refueling the machinery, and arranging for transportation. She was somewhat glad of his absence this morning. She did not want to face him after the fainting spell. She did not trust herself with him, knowing that it was not the heat or the fright from the rolling boulder but his nearness that had made her lightheaded.

Walking beside Sallie, Ashley gave her supplies one last mental check. She had her essential water canteen hooked to her belt, her pack securely strapped to her back, a rope around her waist and over her shoulder, and the brush in her breast pocket. She smiled at the irony of carrying John's gift next to her heart as if its closeness would keep him on her mind.

Looking up at the bright, cloudless sky, Ashley could tell that the day would again be hot and sunny. The interior of the pyramid, once they reached it, would be a welcome haven from the heat. She hoped that Ben's plan of entering through the ancient workers' exit would be the right approach. She certainly did not need a repeat of yesterday's close call.

To her surprise, Ashley found a newly erected ramp leading to the workers' entrance eight stories above the ground. As they gathered around Ben, she listened as he explained that Kasim and his crew had assembled it late last night and during the early hours of the morning from prefabricated sections constructed for just that purpose. By climbing it and lowering themselves down the steep incline inside with the help of their ropes, they could reach the flat walkways inside. From there, they would be able to explore the rest of the pyramid and, if they were lucky, find the treasury and burial rooms.

The waiting tomb called to them. Again it invited them to explore its treasure, yet warned of its dangers. Ashley wondered which one of its personalities they would meet this time and exactly which was more dangerous in her life . . . the pyramid, Kasim, or the man in her dreams.

CHAPTER THREE

Ashley's heart skipped a beat at the thought of Kasim. Mentally, she scolded herself for acting so childishly. True, he was handsome with an exotic appeal, but no more so than many of the clean-shaven American men whose ruggedness usually appealed to her. And yes, his body was muscular from the exertion of the expeditions, but so were those of her male friends who spent long hours in a gym. She could not quite put her finger on the pulse of the matter or fully uncover what it was that drew her to Kasim. Could it be his likeness to the man in her dreams? The phantom who nightly came closer and closer until she could almost hear what he said before he turned and vanished into the darkness. Whatever it was, she would have to work through her attraction later since Ben had finished speaking and was once again leading them toward the pyramid.

As they approached, Ashley looked up to the steep ramp to the top where Kasim stood waving to them. His dark skin shone with health as the sun beamed down on him,

reflecting off the white of his cotton robe. Around his waist
and shoulders was a rope identical to the one worn by the
others in her group. The sun glinted off the buckle that
would fasten them one after the other to the tether rope
above his head. Using it for support, they would slowly
make their descent into the cool, silent, stillness of the
tomb.

After fastening his clasp to the rope and helping Frank
do the same on the second line, Kasim stepped into the
opening and began his backward descent. As soon as they
reached the level floor below, he called to Sallie to follow
his example. Stepping up to the tether and checking the
knot at her waist, Sallie clicked onto the rope and slowly
followed him into the tomb. As each person vanished into
the darkness, the next took up the position at the opening
and waited for the call from below.

When Ashley's turn finally came, she waved down to
Sallie and Frank before stepping backward into the pyramid's opening. Immediately she was struck by the sensation
of falling as she struggled to maintain her footing on the
steeply inclined marble. Leaning forward for balance and
looking straight ahead at the shrinking opening, she carefully placed one foot behind the other in a backward walk
that reminded her of a slow-motion step from the moon
walk dance.

Keeping her gloved hands on the rope as it fed through
her fingers, Ashley examined the walls that passed close
to her body. As the perspiration collected on her top lip,
she marveled at the construction skill that held the massive
structure together without the help of mortar. Moving at
this incredibly slow pace, she was able to study the hieroglyphics that covered even these simple passages. Considering the time spent on this humble passage, she could only
guess at the majesty of the burial room, which should

contain the best art to help the dead pass into the under-world with ease.

As her arms and legs began to ache with the effort of maintaining her balance and the slow backward descent, Ashley grew bored with studying the wall paintings. She wanted desperately to reach level ground where she could relax her body and assume a more natural posture. Looking toward the opening, she realized that for all the effort of descending into the pyramid, there would soon be an equal task of ascending from it. Now she understood why Ben had insisted that they eat a large breakfast and pack bread and cheese along with their usual supply of water. It would be too time consuming for everyone to leave the structure for lunch and only to return an hour later.

With a slight shudder at the memory of the boulder, Ashley realized that the tomb would be her work station for eight hours every day for many weeks to come and that one small hole at the top of this steep walkway would be the only exit. She hoped that, Ben's men, led by his assistant Mohammed, would soon dislodge the rock from the main entrance or at least discover another exit.

Finally reaching the level walkway that they hoped would lead to the main chambers, Ashley unbuckled her rope and recoiled it around her shoulders. Stretching and bending, she tried to unknot the muscles held so long in the rigorous pose of descent. Pulling off her thick leather gloves, she checked her fingers for signs of blisters that might need treatment as they waited for Ben to descend.

As she waited, Ashley was once again struck by the grandeur of the art that lined the walls. Like many lovers of Egyptian history, she had thought that the ancient people had decorated only the main chambers and was thrilled to find so much display of their talents in what she had expected to be barren areas. The vivid colors untouched by sunlight dazzled her mind as she carefully sketched the most intriguing sections showing a family bathing by the Nile while their pet dog frolicked in the water at their feet. Although one-dimensional in form, she could almost feel their excitement at being together and hear their happy laughter.

Preoccupied with her thoughts and sketches, Ashley did not at first notice that she was not alone in her concentration on the drawings. Looking over her shoulder, she found that Kasim had joined her as she stood at a little distance from the others who chatted excitedly about their expectations now that they were finally within reach of their goal.

"You are quite an artist," he said, peering at her sketchpad in the half darkness.

"Thanks. I do what I can, but in this low light I'm not too sure how successful my efforts will be at capturing the essence of the art," she replied as she tried to keep her hands and voice calm despite his nearness. She was still a little embarrassed about the fainting episode.

"It looks very professional to me. Sorry that there is not more light but exposure to excess illumination either natural or artificial would damage the pigment before we could have the time to study it. That, unfortunately, is one of the hazards of this kind of work. There is never enough light or time to do the job as we would like. We, too, do the best we can," he commented with a sad smile. Ashley could see from this small exchange just how much the work of uncovering the past civilizations of his country meant to him.

Ashley studied his face as Kasim continued to tell her about the precautions archaeologists took to preserve the dignity and splendor of artifacts. His expression was very similar to that of the man in her dreams, but it was missing the arrogance and the self-confidence that her mystery man exuded. He said that their efforts were especially strict concerning works of art as he categorized these wall paintings.

Kasim's love for his work shone in his face as he pointed out the different symbols that to an Egyptologist spoke of the importance of this tomb. He reveled in the glory of the discoveries yet to come, not in terms of his own success, but for the information the world would learn from them. He made his contributions to discovery unselfishly and without desire for financial gain or fame.

Ashley wondered if the man in her dreams would have been that selfless when surrounded with such vast wealth. He might actually be more. After all, Kasim worked for the university's museum where the artifacts would be locked away on display. Maybe her dream man would sell them and use the proceeds for the poor.

Returning her full attention to Kasim's words Ashley responded, "Oh, I wasn't complaining. It would be great to have more light, but I understand why we can't. I'm just thrilled to be a part of this historic discovery. My sketches are for my personal journal and for my students when and if I return to teaching, not for publication. Do you think we'll really find treasures in this pyramid? The others would be terribly disappointed if we didn't. I guess I would be, too. Everyone always dreams of uncovering the grandest treasure ever found in a pyramid. I doubt that we're any different."

"That boulder booby trap was a good indication that something of value was buried here thousands of years ago. We will have to wait until we find the burial and treasury chambers to know for certain, but I have a strong gut sensation that we are on to something big here," Kasim replied as they walked back to rejoin the others.

"Do you think we might uncover a tomb as valuable as Tut's?" Ashley asked, gazing in awe at the paintings that surrounded them.

"I cannot promise anything that spectacular, especially in what we originally believed to be the final resting place of a lesser individual. However, I think we have stumbled upon a very important discovery in history. It is possible that we have mislabeled this tomb. It might actually be much more important than we thought," Kasim confided as he directed her toward their leader.

"That certainly would explain the booby trap at the door. This is very exciting. Much more so than I had thought when I first applied for this sabbatical expedition," Ashley remarked enthusiastically.

"One thing I have learned during my years in this business is that you can never be too sure of the contents of a tomb from the outside. We have discovered some pretty spectacular items from lesser pyramids and nothing from grand ones. We will have to wait and see," Kasim whispered as they waited for Ben to speak.

After the group had assembled, Ben began to brief the members on what to expect and how to act under the different circumstances. Speaking clearly and with a tone of authority he said, "We are to stay together. No one is to venture off alone for any reason. We have already encountered one anti-theft deterrent; we do not need to set off another. The inscription warned of many incidents yet to come. Everyone has to stay at top alert. There is to be no day dreaming. What one person does not see must be observed by another. We do not know what might be of utmost importance to our work, so we will treat everything, every drawing, rock, tool, or artifact as if it is the only one and the sole purpose for our expedition.

"According to the traditional layout of pyramids, we are somewhere between the treasure and burial rooms, about equal distance I would say. For the sake of expediency, we will divide into two groups of fifteen. The first group will go with Kasim to find the burial room, and the other will go with me to locate the treasury. Once we find them, we will have the arduous and rewarding task of cataloging, photographing, and packing every artifact we uncover. Listen while I call your names," Ben instructed as he began the roll call.

Ashley paid close attention to the roster of those assigned to each task. Her heart pounded against her ribs as Ben came within the last eight names, four of which would be assigned to Kasim's group. She felt herself being torn between wanting to be with him on this momentous expedition and needing to keep her distance from him for personal reasons. Sallie told her that he had repeatedly popped into her cubicle while she rested before his other duties pulled him away from the lodge. Ashley knew that he had been genuinely attracted to her and concerned. She also knew that she could not faint every time she had a moment alone with him. The excuse of heat prostration and near disaster would grow thin very quickly.

"Sallie, Frank, Sun, and Ashley will join Kasim's group," Ben concluded as he returned the note pad to his pocket and picked up his pack. Hoisting it onto his back, he waved to his group to fall in behind him on the descent along the path that he hoped would lead to the treasure room.

Kasim's group! Ben had made it official. He had assigned her to Kasim's group for the remainder of the expedition. There was no avoiding him now. They would work and eat together every day until they either finished the task at hand or her time on the project came to a close. Either way, Ashley knew that she would spend every waking hour with him until she returned home in August.

Falling in line beside Sallie, Ashley could feel the excitement grow at the prospects of spending her time with Kasim. Maybe Kasim was "Mr. Right," or maybe he was the man in her recurring dream. One thing Ashley knew for certain, she had never fainted at any other man's presence, but she had grown weak with Kasim. True, she had never experienced the fear of a runaway boulder or the heat of the Egyptian desert while with John, but even without these things, Kasim's strength made her feel light-headed and giddy. He was so exotic, so mysterious, and so handsome. Kasim's keen features, tight dark brown hair, piercing almost black eyes, and wiry frame draped in flowing robes certainly made him attractive. Even the sound of his voice that rumbled from deep in his chest with its gentle lilting accent was difficult to resist. He showed a deference toward women that came from being raised in the Egyptian culture of his father and had inherited none of the hurried manner of Americans from his mother.

However, the differences between them scared Ashley and made her hold her emotions in reserve. She knew that she would not have reacted this way to an American who so obviously found her attractive. Yet, with Kasim, she found that she had no choice but to take a wait-and-see attitude. Besides, the expedition would last for six months, giving her plenty of time to get to know him.

Clucking her tongue in displeasure at her own foolish thoughts, Ashley reminded herself that this emotion she felt for Kasim was caused by the excitement of the expedition and the hot Egyptian days mingled with the aroma of spices and sweat . . . it was not real and it would not last. He was her passion, nothing more. He was as unreal as the man in her dreams, who did not exist in the real world outside of the fog of sleep, although she wondered if maybe one day he would appear in the flesh.

Most of her friends had already passed through the stage of being drawn to the "wrong" man, a man who could never really make them happy. She had never experienced that wild abandon of reason. She had always chosen reliable, dependable, stable, marriageable men as her companions. Kasim was the first man to whom she had ever been attracted who did not fit that description. Yet, there was something settled about him, too, only it was tinged with the exotic. He was very organized and highly responsible in making the arrangements for the group. He certainly had not missed any details. She hoped that her new adventurous sense of exploration would not lead her astray and into a fruitless relationship.

"Ashley," Sallie whispered giving her sleeve a jerk, "you're not keeping up. You know what Ben said about daydreaming. Catch up before Kasim sees you lagging behind. And be careful. We don't want any mishaps today."

"I'm with you. There's no need to panic. I'm the last person who wants to meet a boulder again in these dark passages," she replied, stepping carefully in the glow of her flashlight.

The path was narrow and treacherous as they climbed the incline to the chamber above them. Kasim positioned special smokeless flares along the way to mark the route for those coming behind him and so that they would be able to find their way out at the end of the day. Still, their glow barely brightened the darkness. Her leg muscles rebelled against the unfamiliar uphill exertion, and her eyes stung from the acrid smell of the flares and the dust. With each labored step, her backpack grew heavier.

They stopped briefly along the way to read a hieroglyphic message with Kasim's help. As he translated it, Ashley could feel her skin grow cold and the hair on her arms rise. In a voice laced with dramatic effect, Kasim read, "Beware the silence of this tomb. Break it not. Enter not into the chambers of the dead. Trespass not into the sacred halls. Speak not a word to disturb those who slumber here. Death unto you who enter uninvited into this place." Turning to their somber faces, he chuckled and beckoned them to continue on their upward climb. Ashley was not too sure

that the message was laughable. She remembered all too
well the crashing boulder.

After what felt like an eternity, they came to a halt in
front of a wall. The path they had been following ceased
to exist and there was nowhere else to go. No branches
off the main walk lured them in perpendicular directions.
No hints of long-ignored parallel pathways beckoned. They
had simply reached a dead end.

Easing his pack from his shoulders, Kasim felt along the
blocks that made up the wall. To the untrained eye, it
looked as if they had followed a path that ended before it
began, another booby trap of sorts for the curious and
uninvited. But to Kasim, the unevenness of the placement
of the blocks and the slight irregularity in their shape told
him that he had discovered a closed-up entrance rather
than reaching a fruitless end.

Feeling with fingers that could see in the darkness, he
traced the outline of the original opening. Taking a crow-
bar from his pack, he chiseled out the clay facade that the
workers had used to camouflage the opening and make it
appear constructed of the same large heavy blocks as the
surrounding walls. Slowly and carefully he brushed away
debris to reveal the outline of an entrance. As Ashley and
the others stared in disbelief, Kasim gripped one of the
central blocks and methodically rocked and pulled until
it began reluctantly to slide out of the position it had held
for thousands of years. Its mournful rumble filled the path
with each fraction of an inch it relinquished to him. The
sound of grating stone on stone and stone on sand was
almost unbearable as it echoed off the walls and reverber-
ated in the silent passages.

Calling to the men to help him, Kasim lifted the heavy
block from its resting place and lowered it to the ground.
Then, peering into the dust-filled opening, he shone his
flashlight into the space behind the wall. The silence sur-

rounded them as they held their breaths, afraid to speak for fear of breaking the spell of suspense that bound them together.

Finally unable to remain silent any longer Sallie asked, "Kasim, do you see anything?" The sound of her voice startled the others around her.

His answer was so long in coming that they wondered what could possibly have mesmerized him into silence. Looking at the others, Frank posed the question on all of their minds saying, "Do you think he's all right?" Remembering the warning on the wall, they exchanged looks of concern.

As if hearing their voices from a distance, Kasim turned from the hole in the wall and looked at them. His face in the glow from the flashlight shone an eerie ghostly iridescent gray, his eyes sparkled with a strange fire, and his hands shook with emotion. As he struggled to control his excitement his voice further added to their tension and worry.

Swallowing hard Kasim spoke in a hushed tone saying, "We have found the burial chamber of what I think was a great and wealthy king. Our purpose was to investigate what we thought was the pyramid of a queen, but, from the wealth concealed behind this wall, I can only surmise that no woman was buried here but a man of great stature. Of course, as archaeologists we must reserve our final verdict until all of the artifacts have been catalogued and appraised, but on first inspection this appears to be a tomb of no small value to history.

"It is our task to open this sealed doorway and proceed with the utmost respect and caution. We must remember that the spirit of a great personage was put to rest here. We must respect the dead and the history of Egypt's greatest years. To that end, we will work carefully and diligently

to open this wall for our safe passage and to secure it
against vandals and thieves after we leave in the evening.

"Now, let us begin. As we remove the blocks, let us
carefully place them along the walls of the passageway until
we can move them inside the chamber. Remember that
the walls themselves are treasures that must be preserved.
Do not touch the drawings with your bare hands or allow
anything that might deface them to come in contact with
the work. We must number and identify in the log everything we remove before it can be crated for transport to
the university in Cairo.

"Let us start by sketching the wall before we remove any
more boulders. Number each as it is removed and match
that number with the sketch. All of our records must be
precise. Although our effort will temporarily be redundant,
until we can bring in a laptop, everyone will record all
discoveries for backup purposes. When we have the compu-
ter with us tomorrow, we will backup the hard drive to
three disks and on paper. The records we keep will be as
important to furthering the understanding of the tradi-
tions of the ancient Egyptians as are the treasures we will
remove."

Stepping aside so that they could make their sketches,
Kasim drank heavily from his canteen. Ashley surmised
from the tension that emanated from his body that he
wished he were not Muslim and had brought more than
water with him. She wondered if he ever resented growing
up under the dictates of his father's culture rather than
the more liberal views of his mother's American ways. Ashley had never seen anyone become so charged with energy
and purpose as he was from this monumental discovery.
She wondered if it were the value of the treasures, the
notoriety for the discovery, or the sense of history that
gave him the most pleasure.

As she sketched, Ashley cast furtive glances at Kasim.

Pacing the length of the passageway where they stood in concentrated effort, he looked like a caged panther waiting for someone to open the gate and set him free. The muscles in his jaws worked constantly. He clenched and opened his hands repeatedly. He glanced at his watch countless times. He needed this tedious initial work to be completed so that he might get on with the real work that lay ahead.

Finally, their drawings completed, Kasim and the men of the group began the slow, careful dismantling of the wall. One by one they removed and tagged each of the blocks until fifty of them lined the passageway to a height of three feet. Breaking often to record the progress in their sketchbooks and to flex their tired muscles, the team worked until all but two of their flares had burned to ashes. No one had noticed the passage of time as the treasure and history slowly came within view.

Stepping inside and swinging his flashlight in a large arc that slowly illuminated the entire chamber, Kasim was the first to enter. He beckoned to the others to join him, and they eased into the room as if entering a church or temple, which in fact they were. As they walked, the light glinted off gold and silver vases, chests of jewelry, statues encrusted in precious gems, and, in the middle of the room, a massive gold throne with its plush, gold-embroidered seat still intact.

In awe of the civilization that had once flourished in this desert, Ashley drew an audible breath of the stale tomb air. Her lungs ached from the unaccustomed closeness and the dust. Her eyes burned from the fine particles that rose from the floor with their every step. Her skin burned from the touch of the grit that fluttered from the high burial room ceiling and clung to her clothing like white powdered sugar. It had already dulled the shine of the pinkie ring John had given her on his brief visit to Washington.

Yet, Ashley felt an exhilaration she had never before experienced. She could hardly contain her excitement at the enormity of the discovery in terms of historical significance and hard, cold cash. A quick glance at Kasim's face told her that he had done some quick mental calculations also and was quite impressed with the scope of their discovery. They had expected to discover the tomb of a wealthy man's wife. They had not anticipated the discovery of the man's tomb itself. It was obvious from the size of the chair and the sarcophagus that neither a woman nor an ordinary man had been buried here. Everything was far too massive and elaborate. Sallie stepped into the opening and began the process of shooting the rolls of film that would help to document the enormity of the findings. She could hardly work fast enough to capture everything she wanted to see and record.

As they gaped at the enormity of the find, Ashley did not notice at first the increasing swirl of the dirt around her ankles. Gazing up at the paintings that lined the walls and the chests of treasures on platforms around the room, they were all too engrossed in their thoughts of interviews, books, and photography sessions to notice. Even if they had realized that an ever increasing flow of air stirred the ancient dust, they probably would not have thought anything of it. They might even have welcomed the increased ventilation. When they did finally perceive the change in the tomb, it was already too late.

Moving carefully among the overflowing chests and mounds of artifacts, they approached the sarcophagus as a group. Knowing that they could not budge the massive lid, they contented themselves with walking around it as they made sketches from all sides. Deep in thought, they did not hear the soft sound from deep within the darkness of the chamber until it changed from a barely audible whisper to a distinct but distant grumble.

"Kasim, do you hear it, too?" Ashley asked pausing in her drawing to strain her ears in the silence broken now and then by the sound of their pencils scratching lightly on the drawing paper each member carried and the distant sullen voice.

"I have been listening to it for some time. At first, it was only a faint sound that I thought was more from the air pressure affecting my ears than from anything real within the tomb itself. Now, I am not so sure," Kasim responded looking a bit concerned. Considering their close call yesterday, it was understandable that he would not want to take any chances now.

"Whatever it is, it hasn't come any closer in the last fifteen minutes. Do you think we should leave?" she inquired, unable to quell the slight tremble of her hands.

By way of an answer, Kasim folded his pad and turned to the others saying, "It is getting late, everyone. Let us return to base. We will get an early start tomorrow."

"Come on, Kasim. There's so much to see and sketch. I'm nowhere near ready to leave. Just give us a few more minutes," Sallie begged, reluctant to put away the tools of the trade when so much lay around her waiting to be recorded and examined. She still wanted to shoot some more film, too.

"No, it is late and time to leave. I do not want anyone becoming tired and careless," he answered. Then turning to the others he added, "Time is up, everyone. We will return in the morning."

Just as the others looked up in preparation for a combined effort against his authority, the distant sound grew louder and more insistent. Loud enough, in fact, so that those who had not heard it earlier suddenly looked startled at its presence.

"What's that?" Sun demanded with real concern on his handsome face.

"I do not know, but for now, I think we should leave. We will return tomorrow," Kasim said, giving the no longer recalcitrant archaeologists a collective shove toward the opening.

No sooner had they reached the only exit from the treasure room than a great howling wind filled the chamber, disturbing the dust of the centuries and causing little twisters of activity on the floor. Fascinated, they watched as the little funnels grew and united to form larger ones that merged into more massive ones until a cloud of dust as tall and as wide as a man buzzed angrily around the room. With every rotation, its anger appeared to grow and the roar increased in volume. Dust and bits of rock started to fall from the ceiling and heavy necklaces fell from their pedestals. An occasional spark of lighting flashed within the interior of the funnel as it whirled around the room bumping into the overloaded chests and massive vases. In amazement they watched as its fury took possession of the room but stayed clear of the sarcophagus almost as if the relic buried inside controlled its will.

Suddenly, the angry little storm rushed toward them. It stopped short of the opening as if its powers were not strong enough for it to travel any farther. As the grit and sand slapped their faces, Ashley could feel the cloud's anger pelting her. She shuddered from its force and malevolence without really knowing the reason for her reactions, yet she could not turn away. She stood riveted to the spot unable to pull her attention from the circle of wind.

As if sensing her turmoil, Kasim took Ashley by the hand and led her out of the burial room. Retracing their steps, they joined the others waiting at the workman's exit. Already Sallie had made the ascent to the opening above them, using the ropes as her guides.

Snapping the ring of the tether securely around Ashley's waist, Kasim gave her a gentle shove to propel her up the steep, narrow escape route. She felt strangely secure knowing that he was climbing the walk behind her. Nothing would be able to harm her as long as Kasim was there to protect her.

Automatically, as if programmed, she placed one hand over the other on the rope and pulled herself toward the last rays of sun shining through the opening in the pyramid's wall. Reaching the top, she disappeared into the light as Sun and finally Kasim exited the tomb with the voice of the wind echoing in their ears. Brushing the dust from their clothes, they took deep breaths and sighed with relief at being safely outside again.

"Wow!" Ashley exclaimed to Sallie, brushing the dust from her hair after safely reaching the sandy desert floor. "What else is going to happen to us? First a boulder locks us out of the pyramid and now a tornado practically blows us out. What's next?" Sallie looked up at the silent tomb and laughed as she straightened her shirt. She had a wild expression in her eyes. Ashley could see that her new friend was really enjoying herself.

"I don't know, but this is certainly the most eventful dig I've ever been on. The others pale by comparison. Not only have we unearthed a fabulous treasure, but we've awakened an ancient booby trap. This is so wonderful. I've almost filled three diaries already and we've only just begun!" Sallie gushed.

"I wonder what Ben will have to say about all this. Last time he tried to pass it off as a chance happening. Somehow a tornado in a tomb does not sound like a fluke. It feels like a warning to me," Ashley commented as they walked with the others toward their headquarters. Maybe when they all sat down together over soothing cups of coffee, they would get to the bottom of these perhaps related events.

* * *

As the group assembled in the conference room, Ashley searched the dirt streaked faces for Kasim, who she found standing in the back of the room. His white robe was covered in the reddish dust of the pyramid floor and his hair was flecked with grit; yet, his eyes shone with excitement.

The buzz slowly settled as the members of the excavation took their seats. Standing at the head of the table, Ben cleared his throat and began his discussion of the plans for the next foray into the pyramid. Looking into each excited face he said lightheartedly, "This has been one of the most eventful expeditions I have ever led. Never in my twenty-five years as an archaeologist have I encountered run-away boulders and indoor tornadoes. With any luck, we have seen the last manifestation of the tomb's protective devices or curses, if you will.

"Kasim and I believe that what we have witnessed, however mystical it may appear, has a basis in natural phenomenon. Undoubtedly, the ancient builders of the pyramid left behind the strategically placed boulder with the intention of having it roll toward the opened tomb door, scaring off the intruders, and resealing the opening against further invasion. Our investigation uncovered an ingenious pulley system arranged to trigger the release of the massive stone when anyone removed the door. Ingenious people, those early Egyptians!

"The tornado is a little more difficult to explain if we look upon it as a natural display of wind activity such as that which sweeps across the plains of the United States. If, however, we consider it as a disturbance in the air currents inside the pyramid after we opened the main entrance, we can see that our tornado was nothing more than the wind that blows balls of cat fur around the bare living room floor. Larger, of course, but no more destructive or threatening.

"At any rate, we will return to the pyramid tomorrow to begin cataloging its riches. Both teams uncovered tremendous wealth in both the treasury and the throne rooms. We will not be deterred from our goal of preserving these wonderfully preserved monuments to the spirit of the Egyptian people for all humanity to enjoy.

"So, for now, I suggest that we all enjoy dinner and get some much needed rest. We return to the tomb at seven o'clock sharp. Any questions?"

Seeing that everyone was content with his explanation of the day's events, Ben summoned the cooking staff to begin serving the evening meal. Ashley would have preferred to bathe and change before eating dinner, but the food looked and smelled so inviting that she could not bring herself to leave the table no matter how thick the dust that covered her curly hair. Digging in ravenously, she ate every bite of the thick lamb stew, crusted dark bread, and crisp salad. She even ate heartily of the thick chocolate pudding served for desert, although she hardly ever ate sweets.

When she finally entered the showers, she was both sated and relaxed. The soothing water washed away all traces of the grit and further refreshed her body. Moving slowly, she toweled off and slathered lotion on her lithe body. She marveled at the suntan lines forming on her neck and arms despite the long sleeves she wore to protect her from the burning rays. Her face had begun to wear the telltale sign of her sunglasses even though she was only outside for a few minutes every day. She decided that the pyramid's white blocks must have intensified the sun's penetrating rays.

Feeling refreshed and exhilarated after her shower, Ashley decided to go for a walk in the cool desert air before

turning in for the night. Pulling a sweater over her jeans
and T-shirt, she quietly eased out of the complex and
strolled toward the Great Pyramid. The sound and light
show for which droves of tourists gathered every night had
been over for almost an hour. The sky no longer flickered
with the lights that danced across the face of the pyramid
to the beat of the music that filled the quiet slumber of
the ages.

Walking along the paved road that led the tour buses
to the staging area, Ashley fell into deep thoughts about her
stay in Egypt. It had taken the members of the expedition
almost a week to find the opening to the cave, only to have
it closed by the boulder. She had experienced two major
mishaps in the pyramid and had almost lost her life in one
of them. She had touched unbelievable treasures, spent
countless hours meticulously recording them, and been
chased by an unearthly funnel cloud and survived to tell
about it. Any sane person would have been having second
thoughts about continuing with this expedition after days
spent covered in the dust of antiquity and nights tormented
by dreams. However, to Ashley's surprise, the idea of leaving had not really entered her mind. She wanted to see the
adventure through to the end regardless of the dangers.
Besides, Ashley did not believe in ancient curses. She
agreed with Ben and Kasim that the rock and tornado
were easily explained away as a booby trap and a natural
although bizarre occurrence.

Ashley knew that she should write to her friends at home
to share the events of her days in the pyramid, but she
could not bring herself to sit down and take pen in hand.
She had much to tell Toni, but she found that every adventure contained a reference to Kasim. Ashley was not ready
to share her thoughts about him since she had not sorted
them out herself. She did not know how to separate the
thrill of the expedition from her feelings for him. She

needed time for reflection on her emotions and did not want Toni's phone calls, her letters, or, in worst case, her unexpected arrival to interfere. Yet, Ashley knew that she owed her a letter. Toni would soon read in the paper about their near misses, and she would worry unless she communicated with her personally. She promised herself that as soon as she returned to the compound from her walk, she would write.

After all, it was not Toni's fault that the sight of the sun on the sand made her heart feel light and that the stars shone more clearly over the pyramids at night than at home in the States. She was not responsible for the mystery and majesty of the artifacts that glistened more brightly with each stroke of her brush and recalled the legacy of a time long ago when slaves toiled in the hot sun to erect the massive temples, tombs, and obelisks. Toni had nothing to do with the charge of electricity that coursed through her every time she unearthed a new treasure. She had not planted them for her to discover; that had been done by ancient ones who had not even imagined that one day she would invade the privacy of the tomb.

Neither was Toni responsible for the gentle lapping of the Nile as it caressed the shore outside the walls of her hotel in Cairo. She had not painted the sunset on the desert sand. She had not created the images that danced on the pyramid walls and in her dreams. She did not even know about the man who almost nightly beckoned to her to come away with him.

Ashley was so deep in thought that she did not hear someone stealthily approaching her in the silent night. Suddenly, a hand covered her mouth as an arm encircled her waist from behind. She struggled against the unseen assailant as he pulled her toward the parking lot which sat empty except for one van. Trying to think of some way to strike out against him, she tore at his face with her flailing hands and tried to sink her nails into his flesh. Cursing angrily under his breath, he shoved her against the van, leaned his weight against her, and threw open the door. Ashley tried to scream but the force of the blow to her face momentarily stunned her and caused her ears to ring. He clamped his hand tightly across her mouth, bruising and crushing her lips. She could taste her own salty blood as it welled in her mouth. Her cheek throbbed angrily. Panting heavily into her ear from the exertion of their struggle, the man tried to lift and push her into the cargo space as perspiration dripped into his eyes, blinding him.

Seizing the moment of hesitation, Ashley kicked back with her foot and planted the heel of her heavy boot on the man's toes and instep. As she ground it into the tender flesh of his sandal-attired foot, he shrieked in pain and loosened his grip on her arms. Twisting around to face him, she kneed him in the groin as she stripped the ski mask from his face. Quickly she jabbed the two fingers of her right hand into his exposed eyes. Screaming in pain, the man reeled away from her and ran away from the glaring lights that illuminated the Great Pyramid into the darkness. In the distance, she heard the sound of screeching wheels as a second vehicle sped away.

Shaking uncontrollably on legs that wobbled under her, Ashley sank to the sandy pavement and collapsed into helpless tears. She had never been so frightened in her life. Not even the runaway boulder or the whirling winds of the tornado had been as terrifying as the hands of the man in black as they held her prisoner.

"Ashley! Ashley! Where are you?!" shouted voices from the compound as flashlights darted through the darkness searching for her.

"I'm over here . . . behind the van," she sobbed unable to stop the tears as the sound of familiar voices broke through her torment.

Rushing to her side, Kasim, Ben, Sallie, and the others found her leaning against the vehicle. Her blouse had ripped with the struggle and tears streaked her face. Sand and the man's blood had dried on her hands. Blood dripped from the corner of her lip where he had smacked her to silence her.

"Did he hurt you?" Sallie asked cradling her gently to stop the tremors that shook her body.

"Only my lip. I'm mostly just frightened. I've never been attacked before. I guess I've been lucky, growing up in a big city the way I did. Who do you think he was?" Ashley asked as they led her into the building.

"He was probably someone after the treasure. Not long ago, there was a kidnapping attempt of an archaeologist at the Luxor temples. When the police caught the men, they confessed that they had planned to hold the archaeologist prisoner until someone met their demands for gold and treasure in exchange for his life. Fortunately, their plans were interrupted by security guards assigned to protect the temple. It looks as if we will have to be more careful now that we know we are being watched. I will call the university and request more guards. A call to the police seems to be in order, too. I will leave you with Sallie and Kasim if you think you are all right," Ben answered looking closely at Ashley's bruised face.

"I really don't think you need to call the police. There isn't anything I can tell them. I was too frightened to see his face, although I poked at his eyes and scratched at him. The man had appeared a rather ordinary type without any distinguishing features. He could have been one of any number of Egyptian men who linger around here all day, one of the workers, a tourist." Ashley said, dabbing at the cut on her lip. She only wanted to be left alone. The thought of discussing the attack with the police was just too much for her to handle so soon.

"I cannot agree," Ben stated firmly. "This intruder struck against you and put all of us in danger. My first priority is for the safety of the archaeologists in my charge and my second is for the protection of the artifacts. I must notify the police. I will make my report to the university and ask for more security as well."

"I'm fine, really. A cup of tea would fix me up, if you wouldn't mind, Sallie," Ashley replied sending Ben off to make his call. She did not want to detain him from contacting the university. She felt sure that the man would return since he did not get what he wanted on his first try. Something in the set of his lips and the cold light of his eyes spoke of his determination.

Leaving them alone in Ashley's cubicle, Sallie rushed off to fetch the restorative cup of tea. She chuckled to herself when she looked back and saw Kasim dabbing Ashley's cut lip with a cotton ball saturated in peroxide. It was clear to her that they wanted to be alone but were unsure of what to do with their privacy. Sallie made a mental note to complete her errand slowly. She wanted to give them plenty of time to sort out their feelings.

"I hope I am not hurting you too badly," Kasim said, lightly touching the cotton to the puffy lip.

"Only a little," Ashley replied. In truth, his nearness kept her from feeling the sting of the medication at all. Her heart fluttered wildly each time his soft, warm breath touched her cheek. The smell of his skin was intoxicating as he examined her split lip.

"Your lip is looking much better. There is a little swelling but not much. Now that I have cleaned off the blood, I can see that it is really not that bad. You will not need any stitches," Kasim commented, leaning a little closer and examining his handiwork.

"Thanks, Kasim," Ashley muttered, trying to maintain some degree of composure when all the while what she really wanted to do was throw herself into the comfort of his warm embrace.

Looking deeply into her eyes, Kasim gently took her trembling fingers in his and kissed each one. Softly he said, "I would kiss your lips only I am afraid I would hurt you. I cannot begin to tell you how angry it made me when I heard about your attack. I wanted to strangle that man, not simply because he had violated our camp, but because he had put you in danger. You are very important to me, you know. If I ever get my hands on him, I will make him pay for what he has done to you."

"Promise me that you won't do anything foolish, Kasim. I'm not hurt really, and he didn't steal anything. He's not worth risking your life over," Ashley replied with anguish in her voice.

Pulling Ashley against his chest, he said, "I will not make a promise I know I cannot keep. But I will promise that he will never harm you again as long as I am around."

Ashley saw written in his face a depth of concern and emotion she had never seen in any of her former male friends. The intensity of Kasim's feelings both excited and frightened her. She did not know if she was ready for the kind of relationship that could easily grow in the heat of the desert sun, if she would allow it. Part of her longed for the tenderness Kasim's eyes said he could offer her, yet deep inside her lived a secret voice that wanted to be free from the constraints of a deep relationship. She did not know which voice to heed. She wanted something exhilarating, something unique, and something different. She still looked for the sparkle and the bubble of champagne.

Allowing the intensity of Kasim's gaze to entrap her and to control her will, Ashley no longer felt the soreness of her split lip. The fear that had so totally possessed her after the attack slipped away. All thoughts of the danger and the thrill of the expedition faded from her mind as the magnetism of his will pulled her toward him. Everything and everyone except the smell and the feel of Kasim vanished.

Ashley did not know when it happened, but suddenly she was kissing him. Kasim completely enfolded her and locked her in an embrace that said more than mere words ever could. She felt his energy and his warmth flow into her body as his lips tenderly tasted hers. He caressed her shoulders and back, easing the last of the soreness from them and relaxing away the remains of her resistance to him.

She massaged his neck, ears, and shoulders until Kasim made low growling noises in the back of his throat and his breath burned hotly against her face. She entangled her fingers in his tight curls as his lips flamed against the little hollow of her neck and held him to her. His hands were fiery on her back, his lips pressed greedily against hers, and his tongue scorched hers with the heat of his passion. The pounding of their hearts blocked out the sound of everything around them.

Suddenly Ashley remembered the reason she had initially hesitated. Her feelings toward the man in her dreams had stopped her from being able to give herself to Kasim. It was her phantom, the man who haunted the shadows of the pyramids in her dreams, who kept her from embracing Kasim totally. She knew from Kasim's closeness that he was not the man who tormented her nights, although she had hoped desperately that he was. Until she found him, Ashley would have to continue to search.

Pushing him away, Ashley muttered softly, "Kasim, please, we must stop. I'm not ready for complications in my life just now. I need time to find myself. I left behind a man who wanted more of a relationship than I could give, and I don't need to start anything here under the

spellbinding Egyptian sun. I'm so sorry, but I just can't.
I'm awfully attracted to you, but I simply can't."

"Ashley, this is more than mere physical attraction. I
cannot explain it, but I feel drawn to you. Maybe it is your
bravery in the face of disaster that pulls me to you. I do
not know what it is that makes me feel this way. I only
know that I must be with you," Kasim argued as he kissed
the frown lines between her eyes.

"Kasim, I'm incredibly impressed by your knowledge
and intoxicated by the splendor of this magnificent country, but I can't get involved with you. I don't know if it's
you or the pyramids that intrigue me. Until I do, I can't
risk making a mistake. Besides, there are other concerns,"
Ashley tried to explain.

They did not hear the squeal of Sallie's boots on the
tile floor as she returned with Ashley's tea until she stood
at the opening of Ashley's cubicle. Clearing her throat
and uttering a polite "Oh, excuse me," she entered with
downcast eyes and placed the tray on the chest at the foot
of the bed. Without waiting for a reply, she backed out,
smiling as she went on her way to the common room where
the others were discussing the events of the day.

Shaking her head at her understanding of Sallie's smile,
Ashley said reluctantly, "That's another reason why we
can't start something in this fishbowl. I don't want to be
the topic of gossip. I suppose we should join the others.
We'll be missed if we stay here any longer."

Trying to smile into her sadness-clouded face, Kasim
replied, "I am sorry, too, Ashley. I have been looking for
the right woman for a long time and had hoped that I had
found her in you. Your bravery tonight and in the pyramid
says that you were different from the others I have met.
Maybe later when the expedition is over you will have a
change of heart. Anyway, you are right. This is definitely

not the place for us to have any privacy or to get to know each other."

"Thank you for understanding, Kasim. Shall we join the others?" Ashley asked, leading the way to the opening of her cubicle.

As the voices and music from down the hall wafted to her cubicle, they walked down the hall to where the others had gathered. Ben had scheduled a meeting to discuss their new security. As Ashley took her place beside Sallie in the last row of seats, she felt a heaviness fill her heart. She hoped that she had not been mistaken in her decision to postpone building a relationship with Kasim. He had so many of the traits for which she had always searched in a man, but so did her phantom. Inwardly scolding herself, Ashley acknowledged that she had met two wonderful men and put them both aside for a dream that never lasted in the light of day.

After dinner, Ashley took Sallie aside for a talk. She needed someone to help her sort out her feelings. Sitting on her bed, Ashley cried, "I don't know what's come over me. I came on this expedition for the pleasure of discovery not to fall for one of its leaders. I left a perfectly delightful man at home. Now, I find that I can barely remember the face of the man about whom I thought I might have strong feelings. I'm hopelessly drawn to another man. I don't know what to do."

"I've noticed the attraction between you and Kasim. The desert plays all kinds of tricks on people's minds the first time they see it. It's so vast and lonely. I'm sure it's a combination of the moonlight and the sand and that dream you've been having. I wouldn't be too worried about it," Sallie advised as she studied Ashley's tormented face.

"It's all so unfair. I shouldn't be having these feelings about Kasim. I've never been so helpless to control myself. I hope you're right about the desert's magic." Ashley smiled bravely.

"I know I am. It happened to me," Sallie confided with a smile.

"Really? What happened? How did it work out?" Ashley asked.

"I left home thinking that I loved a colleague only to find myself drawn to a member of the expedition. It was my first time completely alone without friends for support. He was nice to me and always ready to lend a helping hand. His knowledge was tremendous. I felt just as guilty for caring about him as you do about Kasim. In time, after some of the novelty of the dig wore thin, I started looking at him a bit differently. He didn't seem superhuman with dust all over him, but he was still a great guy. I returned home for a short visit to see the man I thought I loved. He had changed, or at least I had. He didn't seem as stimulating. He wasn't as witty."

With a sigh, Ashley interjected, "I'm afraid that the same thing will happen to me when I return to the States after being here. How did you handle it?"

"When I returned to the dig, I married the archaeologist," Sallie replied with a chuckle. "We've been blissfully happy ever since."

"Oh, my! That's not exactly what I wanted to hear. You see, I'm not sure that Kasim is the man I really want. It would be so much simpler if he were. But that man in my dream continues to exist as a real person for me. I know he's out there somewhere," Ashley lamented.

"I wouldn't worry too much if I were you. Whatever should happen in your life, will happen. It's in the hands of fate," Sallie commented, motioning toward the conference room. They were late for a meeting.

CHAPTER FOUR

Sipping strong Egyptian coffee and tea, the assembled team listened attentively as Ben explained the increased precautions for personal safety that he had initiated. The group seemed surprisingly relaxed as it faced the new reality of always traveling the grounds in pairs, locking the compound doors, and posting double guards around the tomb's entrances. They accepted their new restrictions as part of life in a world full of constant turmoil. Since most of them lived in big, urban cities, they did not find the regulations too confining. They all knew that it was imperative that they become more vigilant inside the tomb during the day as well as on the grounds at night.

Ben spoke slowly and seriously as he said, "As you know, a member of our team was attacked in the parking lot. We must increase our vigilance and be ever mindful that there are people in this world who would take for their own use the precious treasures we unearth for the good of all humankind. I have notified the university, and it has sent us more police protection. Until the person or persons responsible for this deed are apprehended or until we complete our expedition, we will proceed with greater caution. Let us not be disappointed or disheartened by the uncivil acts of our fellow man. Let us continue to do what is right for all of humanity.''

After Ben's talk, Sun distributed the mail that had been completely forgotten in the aftermath of Ashley's attack. To her surprise, Ashley received a letter from Toni. As the group disbanded, she sought the limited privacy of her cubicle to read what she knew would be a gossip-filled letter.

Sitting at the foot of the bed, Ashley turned the envelope over several times before deciding to open it. She was afraid that her lack of correspondence had aroused her friend's suspicions. She should have written, but so much had happened that she did not even know where to begin.

After reading the first few words, Ashley relaxed. Her fears had been for nothing. Toni had not written to scold her; she only spoke words of wedding plans, teaching chores, snowy weather, and the latest love affairs among their friends.

Laughing, Ashley turned one page after the other as Toni's words flowed freely from them. Several of their buddies had recently become engaged and were planning to be married during the summer. Toni lamented that they were obviously trying to outdo her plans with their own, but she would not let them. Her own wedding would be more glorious than any event that they could construct in their attempts at imitation.

Toni rambled about the affair that had sprung up between two married colleagues. According to her, someone had discovered the lovers in a passionate embrace in the faculty room after hours. They had assumed that everyone had gone home for the evening and were quite chagrined at being the topic of discussion over the coffee pot the next morning. Toni closed the long letter by reminding Ashley that she had promised to return in time for her wedding. According to Toni's parting words, if she did not, the boulder and tornado would not be the worst of the natural causes to befall her.

Ashley stopped reading to wipe away the tears that streamed down her face. She had not laughed so hard since arriving at the expedition. Anyone seeing her would have thought that Toni's letter had contained bad news rather than the hilariously funny gossip. Shaking her head and chuckling, Ashley folded the letter and returned it to the heavily marked envelope. When she was not so tired, she would write to Toni to assure her that she would be home in time to walk down the aisle at her wedding.

Laying her tired body on her cot, Ashley thought about all the things she would tell Toni when she finally had enough energy to pick up the pen. The first topic would, of course, be Kasim and the second would be her phantom man. She was so terribly confused about both of the men in her life. These conflicting emotions were so new to her. She always lived such a well-ordered life. When she was a student, she had always turned in all of her assignments on time, she had always written clear, accurate notes, and she had always annotated her books carefully. Now that she was a teacher, her students counted on her control to guide them through their studies and to provide a shoulder to lean on during the ups and downs of their social lives. But now her own life was in total chaos.

No matter how confused she felt about finding Kasim so appealing, she could not deny that she was inexplicably drawn to him, although she had only just met him. His handsome exotic looks, his lively sense of humor, and his knowledge of history pulled her to him. He was kind, caring, and a total gentleman. And then, there was the man who haunted her dreams . . . the man who seemed so much like Kasim, yet so different . . . the man who always stayed slightly out of reach. He was the phantom and the promise of life just beyond her fingertips.

As the quiet of the evening lengthened, Ashley fell into a sound sleep on top of her covers. She dreamed that she was running across the desert away from masked men carrying long knives. The thick sand grabbed at her ankles and tried to suck her into its warmth. Her legs became tired from the effort as she struggled to keep ahead of them. Reaching a distant village, she ran into the crowds, trying to hide herself from her pursuers.

Lifting the flap from the doorway of a nearby tent, she stepped inside and out of the blazing sun as the men approached with their weapons drawn. Inside sat three women who looked at her menacingly and rising advanced toward her with outstretched hands. They made tearing motions at her clothing and face. Shrinking from them, she backed out of the tent directly into the arms of the men. She sensed that the tallest of them was the man who had attacked her at the van. His right eye was red and watering. He had covered the left with a black patch to keep out the light. Before she could open her mouth to scream, they bound her and carried her away.

In the distance, she could just barely make out the figure of another man rushing toward them. He shoved through the crush of people who lined the streets, watching the spectacle of a man carrying a woman in Western clothing over his shoulder like a bag of flour. She felt that if he could only reach her, she would be safe. She looked at him and wordlessly begged for his help.

His face was vaguely familiar but his piercing eyes flashed with an arrogance and determination that she had never seen in those of anyone she knew. His hands reached for her as if promising more. His mouth called to her. When she did not move or answer, he slowly dropped his arms and walked away, leaving her feeling alone and lost. The people filled in the space where he had been standing wiping out her memory of him.

Ashley struggled to free herself of the bonds that held her captive. Finally loosening the ropes, she pounded on the head and shoulders of her captor until she broke free. She ran into the crowd in search of the man with the piercing eyes, who had awakened something deep within her. The people only watched in awe-struck silence as she passed. Drawing near to him, she touched him on the shoulder. When he turned around, she looked into the face of the man she had seen at the base of the pyramid. Only this time, a scar had appeared over his eyebrow and a beard had obscured his other features. His eyes with their piecing gaze seared into her soul reading all of her hidden thoughts and desires.

He sensed without words that they shared the same needs. He took her into his arms, and Ashley allowed him to propel her toward a cabin that had suddenly appeared in the desert behind the pyramids. Leaning against his strong shoulder, she smiled as he gave her a gentle shove and closed the door behind them.

Unbuttoning the tiny pearl buttons on Ashley's gray silk blouse, he helped her ease it off her shoulders. The sight of her slender body, the soft mounds of her breasts, and her small waist made him shudder with desire. His hands ached to explore her body and to press his mouth against her luscious lips. He pulled her skirt up to reveal her shapely thighs and buttocks, and his groin grew tight as he looked at her trim runner's calves.

Seeing her full breasts, he hungrily ran his burning fingers over the velvety soft flesh. A groan caught in his throat as her nipples grew hard and erect at his caress. Looking deeply into Ashley's half closed eyes, he saw that he had aroused a similar passion in her. His fingers locked in her short curls as he pulled her head back to look into her half closed eyes. Gently he guided her mouth to his as his fingers continued to create flames of passion that coursed to the hidden region between her thighs.

Ashley's hurrying fingers quickly untied the strings of his robe and helped him discard it on the floor. Finding his belt buckle, she released it and unzipped his trousers, gently brushing her hands against the bulge of his manhood as it strained against the white of his cotton briefs. She helped him ease out of them. They joined the pile of discarded clothing on the floor.

Lying back on the pillows, Ashley moaned as his hot tongue entrapped first the right nipple and then the left as he traced a path down her flat stomach to the waistband of her bikini panties. She lifted her hips as he tugged them over her thighs and flung them aside. His lips rained kisses on the silky skin of her upper thighs as they parted in invitation.

Caressing his broad shoulders and well-muscled back, Ashley whispered gentle urgings as her body burned from the passion his probing fingers incited. She gripped his tight buttocks and encouraged him to release her from the flames that burned deep within her.

Breathing only her name, he entered the flaming recesses of Ashley's body. Together they moved with the same desire, the same longing, and the same need to join their bodies, souls, and passions. Lifting her hips to meet his thrusts, he plowed into her as she writhed in response to the waves of desire that overtook her body and carried it toward the heights of longing and to a place almost beyond human tolerance. She shuddered as their flesh meshed and their essence mingled.

Then, slowly they rode the tide of passion as it released them. They returned to the tangled sheets in a twisted labyrinth of legs and arms. Barely moving, he reached down and pulled the covers over their intertwined bodies.

Just as she reached for his hand, Ashley awakened to the darkness of her cubicle. She lay drenched in cold sweat. Her pulse raced, her heart pounded, and her mouth felt dry. Slowly, Ashley regained control and realized that she was safe inside the compound with no one chasing her. But, sadly, no handsome bearded man waited for her.

Wiping the sleep from her eyes, Ashley slipped out of her clothes and into her nightshirt. The bed felt comforting as she crawled under the sheet and light blanket. Her head ached from the realism of the dream. The pain in her bruised lip had returned. Lying down in the dark silence of the night, she listened to the sounds of her fellow archaeologists. Their peaceful snoring helped to comfort her. Turning onto her side, she fell asleep. This time she dreamed of nothing as Toni's letter lay forgotten on the hard floor. Her dream lover did not return.

Kasim's sleep was equally as plagued by thoughts. He worried about the safety of the members of the expedition now that violence has thrust itself upon them. Mostly, he wondered about the distance Ashley insisted on keeping between them and contents of her letter. She had seemed so distant after receiving it that he made a mental note to ask Sallie about it in the morning. He hoped that on top of the attack she had not heard anything distressing from home.

Sinking into his pillow, Kasim also listened to the silence punctuated by snoring and deep breathing. This was the time when he did his best thinking after all of the responsibilities of the day had been satisfied and all was quiet. He often lay on his bunk planning the next day's activities or his free weekend trips into town. Since meeting Ashley, he had spent the majority of his leisure thinking about her.

Ashley had captured his attention in a way that no other woman had ever managed to reach him through his carefully constructed world of academia. The tilt of her head, the sway of her hips, and the sound of her laughter had immediately made him notice her sensuality, but usually that initial attraction did not last long. He had met many beautiful women on these expeditions, yet he had never found any whose appeal was so great that he did not forget her as the intensity and excitement of his work increased. Ashley was different somehow. She was beautiful, graceful, and elegant, but, above all, she was intelligent, curious, and brave. No one would have thought ill of her if she had decided to call it quits. After being frightened from the tomb by a boulder and attacked in the darkness by an unknown assailant, she had every reason to be frightened. However, these events had only made Ashley more determined to uncover the contents of the pyramid and the reason for the episodes. Kasim liked bravery and spunk in a woman. He found the combination of personality traits alluring and incredibly difficult to resist.

Yet, he had seen a different side of her when Ashley had picked up the letter postmarked in the States. She had looked almost frightened, as if the sender had looked into their moment of shared affection and stood accusing her of doing something terrible. She had immediately fled the common room for her cubicle and had not returned for the rest of the evening. Kasim was very curious about the letter's contents, yet he was reluctant to inquire for fear the information would cause a change in their relationship. He did not want to face the possibility that Ashley would turn from him. Already he was looking forward to being alone with her away from the other members of the expedition where he could get to know her better.

A man met the perfect woman only once in his life, and Ashley was his ideal. He planned to keep her in Egypt with him for the rest of their lives, if she would have him. Now, he had found out that she could not allow him into her life. She had spoken of another man she had left behind; someone who had also tried to win her heart. Although she said that the relationship had ended, Kasim wondered if Ashley would risk letting him into her life. She acted as if some memory stood between them.

Tucking the light sheet under his chin, Kasim forced himself to put thoughts of Ashley out of his mind. He needed to be alert tomorrow and every day so that he could protect and lead his group. He did not need his mind cluttered by thoughts of soft skin pressed against his, sweet tasting kisses tantalizing his soul, and gentle hands roaming his body. Yet, he could not keep his mind away from the thought of making a life with a woman he had known for only two months but planned to marry.

Kasim did not know that his competition was the phantom who visited Ashley every night in her dreams. He had no way of knowing that when Ashley lay her head on her pillow, she dreamed about the man at the base of the pyramid. She replayed the same scene with only minor changes as she tried to reach him and the safety he offered. It was not that he was part Egyptian that caused Ashley to hold him at arm's length. He could overcome that obstacle, but not the one he could not identify.

As Kasim slumbered peacefully, Ashley was for the second time that night tormented by the knowledge that the almost faceless man would be the source of her happiness if she could only reach him. Try as hard as she could, she was never able to touch him or to hear him or to see more of his face than simply his startlingly black eyes. Ashley thought tonight she might have been saved the effort after the experience she had suffered earlier in the evening.

This time, the dream took on a different focus. Instead of standing in front of the pyramids, Ashley was standing in her parents' gardenia-bedecked church. Music played softly in the background. People wore their Sunday finery as they sat in readiness for a wedding.

Slowly the fogginess of the vision began to clear, and Ashley became aware that she was not sitting among them. She was not waiting for the bride to enter. Rather, she was the bride. Looking down, Ashley saw herself dressed in a silk gown she had recently admired in a fashion magazine. On her head sat a gossamer veil that swept to the floor in a cloud of silk. She held a bouquet of red roses that seemed to drip from her fingers onto the white runner on the carpet.

Gazing around her in slow motion, Ashley became aware that she stood at the altar on her wedding day with her father at her side. He smiled and patted her hand, making a shower of petals fall to the floor at their feet. She tried to smile at him, but a strange silence kept her lips from moving. She could only stare at him and wonder why he looked so happy when she felt as if something heavy lay between and around them.

Even the priest looked as if he were totally unaware of the presence that loomed there. Her mother and other relatives, too, seemed oblivious to it. Only Sallie and her friend Toni who served as her matron and maid of honor appeared to feel it. They wore frowns that matched hers on their beautifully made up faces. They disapproved of something just as she did. They shared her emotions and her feeling of loneliness as they waited for something to happen.

Slowly the organ music stopped and a figure moved to the center of the church. Ashley had not seen him until he appeared there from nowhere in particular. He simply stood among the dropped rose petals and lifted his arms to her. Studying him, she saw that he was the same man who stood beside the pyramid. The sun from the window behind him shone in her eyes. She could not see his face. Now she understood that he was the one who had written the words "Remember me" on the pyramid wall as she heard his voice float toward her as he repeated the words once again.

Ashley felt as if she could not breathe. The fragile fabric of her gown was too tight, too confining. She tried to pull it off, but it would not leave her body. She opened her mouth to call out to him for help, but he lowered his hands and turned away. As he walked from the church, she called out to him, but her words evaporated in the warm air before they could reach him. He never heard her say that she would always remember him.

As her father patted her hand and smiled down at her, Ashley shuddered and cried. The music started again and the priest began to read from the book he held open in his hands. When he asked if anyone had an objection to the marriage, Ashley tried to answer, but her lips would not form the words. Instead, she watched as the gold pinkie ring suddenly clamped tightly around the fourth finger of her left hand. She tried unsuccessfully to remove it, but it would not budge. She looked toward her father for help, but he smiled sadly and faded into a soft mist.

Sitting straight up in bed, Ashley struggled to turn on the little light. Her bare fingers trembled as she fumbled in the darkness. Perspiration streamed down her face, flowed from her armpits, and ran between her breasts. She gasped for breath as she pulled at the neckline of the wet T-shirt that clung to her body in an effort to suffocate her. Finally finding the lamp's pull chain, she chased away the fears that surrounded her as light flooded her cubicle.

Pulling her wet shirt from her body and wiping herself dry with it, Ashley slipped another over her head as she quietly paced her space. She had never been so frightened. Not even the monsters hiding in her closet when she was a girl had scared her as badly as the dream of the wedding. Her nerves were so raw that she occasionally jerked to a halt at the sight of her silhouette on the drapes that separated her space from Sallie's. She stripped the soaked sheets from her bed, wishing it were as easy to remove the images from her mind, and remade the bed.

Easing into the cool, dry sheets, Ashley calmed her breathing and allowed the silence of the night to lull her into a fragmented sense of peace. She listened to the gentle snores of her colleagues and took comfort in their closeness. She could always call to Sallie who would come running to her as quickly if she needed her. Resting her head on the pillow, she felt the tension flow from her body as the promise of sleep returned. She forced her thoughts to stop swirling and questioning. In the light of day, she would think about the meaning of the dream, the man, and her friends' frowns.

Ashley turned out the light and allowed her eyes to flutter shut as her mind turned blank. She breathed in the silence of the night and allowed its peace to enfold her. She hoped that her dream and feelings of regret about Kasim and the mystery man would not interrupt the tranquillity again.

Ashley did not know that deep in the desert her attacker was busily making plans. Her valiant struggles had thwarted his efforts, but he would not allow anything to stand in his way a second time. It was a matter of honor that he would succeed. His team depended on him, and he would not fail again. He knew that the managers of the expedition would increase security against another attempt at kidnapping, but he would not let them stand in the way of his success this time. Not even the woman's screams would keep him from this goal.

CHAPTER FIVE

Ashley's morning did not begin any better than the prior day had ended. Security was so tight around the pyramids and especially their compound that she needed to wear an identification badge whenever she left the building. She forgot it when she went out for a jog and had to call Sallie from the guardhouse to vouch for her when she tried to reenter for her shower. The armed guard was certainly successful in frightening her. Ashley wondered if thieves and robbers would be as intimidated.

As they assembled for breakfast and their usual briefing, Kasim searched Ashley's face for signs that his boldness had not permanently affected their budding relationship. Something in the way Ashley initially avoided his eyes and appeared uneasy in his presence told him that another man occupied a significant place in her heart, too. He hoped that the mystery and magic of the desert would give him the upper hand and help him to win her love. When Ashley finally looked in his direction, his heart fluttered with relief as her eyes spoke of her feelings for him.

*   *   *

Ben's talk and Ashley's morning outing had made clear
to her the realities of living under increased security protection. However, nothing could have prepared her for the
way she would feel on the walk to the pyramid. Passing
the armed guards that lined the path to the pyramid, Ashley
felt a cold chill run down her spine. The sight of the
automatic weapons they carried as they patrolled the
perimeter caused her to shudder just as she had when she
first saw the soldiers in the airports in Italy on one of her
summer trips with Toni.

Walking along beside Sallie, Ashley thought of her phantom and realized that her feelings for both men imprisoned her as much as did the presence of the guards.
However, until she could solve the puzzle of the pyramid
and the identity of the man who plagued her dreams, she
could not think of a future with Kasim. The right man
might be only an arm's length away. Ashley could not take
the chance that he was waiting for her around an unturned
corner.

The work in the pyramid did not take her mind off the
situation either. She found that, although the treasure
shone brightly and proved to be an even more historic
find than they had originally believed, Kasim's sad face
and voice interfered with her enjoyment of the discovery.
Each jewel she photographed and catalogued, each vase
she crated, and each sketch she made reminded her that
at the end of the day when she lay down to rest, her
phantom lover would keep her company. Instead of looking forward to an evening in Cairo with Kasim, Ashley
would have to explain to him that until she satisfied her
curiosity about the phantom of her dreams, she could not
become involved with anyone.

All day Ashley stayed as far away from Kasim as she could.

She avoided his penetrating gaze, which usually filled her with a tingling expectation but now only served as a reminder of the conversation they had shared earlier. She had decided that until she could come to terms with her own infatuation with a man who existed only in her dreams, she would not allow herself to be pulled any further into a relationship with Kasim. Regardless of how important to her he had become or how much Ashley longed to feel his arms around her again, she would hold herself away from him until she was free of her obsession with the phantom. Only then would she feel comfortable sharing herself with Kasim.

Forcing herself to push the men in her life into the recesses of her mind, Ashley began to take enjoyment from the treasures that filled the room and sparkled through the ages of dust stirred up by the angry wind that had ripped through the pyramid. Each item proved more glorious than the last as she carefully photographed, tagged, and bagged the contents of the gold chest at which she knelt. Gently placing each necklace on the white cloth she had spread on the sandy pyramid floor, she brushed off the traces of dust and grit before making a photographic record of the find. Ashley packed each one with a photograph and ledger notation as to where it was found. When the curators at the University of Cairo unpacked them, each artifact would be accompanied by detailed information of its original condition when uncovered and the articles that had surrounded it.

Turning the hammered gold and emerald inlaid eagle-shaped necklace over in her white-gloved palm, Ashley marveled at the exquisite detailing in the etching and the splendor of the stones that managed to shine despite being covered for hundreds of years in the fine sand that sifted down from the pyramid's ceiling. Each perfectly matched gem captured the glow from the bright work lights they had set up inside the tomb and reflected it back as if it had been cut only yesterday. None of the splendor had been diminished.

As if reading her mind, Sallie leaned over and whispered, "Wouldn't you love to have pieces this exquisite in your jewelry box? Can you imagine the time and labor that went into fashioning this thin chain? And to think, they didn't even have the modern machinery we have now."

"The problem is that on a teacher's salary, I don't have anything to wear with this stuff. I'd have to buy a whole new wardrobe," Ashley replied with a giggle and smiled at the awe and wonder in her friend's voice. The majesty of the treasures was certainly overpowering and, fortunately, distracting. Diving back into her work, she submerged herself in the delights of the treasure chest, forgetting the men in her life. They had to take a back seat to the once-in-a-lifetime opportunity of uncovering fabulous antiquities.

As they sat on the sandy floor, Ashley became aware of an itchy sensation on the exposed skin between her thick socks and the cuff of her hiking shorts. Seeing that little red spots covered her legs, she noticed that Sallie was scratching absently too. Calling over to her she said, "What do you think is causing this itching? Could there be spiders in here?"

Sallie half turned to her and said, "I haven't seen any, but my legs are starting to burn from whatever it is. Look at Frank and Sun; they're scratching, too. There must be something in the sand." Suddenly, she jumped to her feet and began patting at the almost invisible intruders that attacked her body. Her eyes were wide with the terror of being covered by insects. It was almost like a scene from an old Hitchcock movie.

Just as Sallie finished speaking, Ashley saw them. Thousands of tiny red spiders crawled around the base of the chests, the throne, the vases, and them. They came from

every corner of the room as if they were an army staging
an attack. Soon they were all surrounded by the pesky,
stinging creatures. Ashley brushed furiously at them as they
climbed up her legs toward her shoulders and arms, but
every time she swept away one wave of assailants, another
battalion appeared to take its place. Her skin itched
unbearably and was covered with tiny moving spots.

Taking Sallie by the arm, Ashley pulled her toward the
opening. They watched as the spiders crawled away from
them to continue their torment of the others in the throne
room. One by one, Frank, Sun, Kasim, and the others
joined them in the hallway. From where they stood, they
could see the slow reddening of the sand as the army of
spiders massed over every square inch of floor and began to
spread over the boxes, chests, chairs, and carefully bagged
treasures.

As Ashley and Sallie were joined in the doorway, they
noticed that not one of the spiders came into the area just
beyond the opening, where they had sought shelter. They
carefully checked each other for signs of any clinging
insects. Looking at each other, Ashley voiced the question
that was on everyone's mind, "Kasim, do you think that
those spiders are protectors of the tomb in the same way
that the tornado and the boulder were?"

Scratching the backs of his hands and surveying the faces
of his team members, Kasim replied, "I have never seen
anything like those spiders anywhere in Egypt. They must
be some type of ancient insect that lived in the sandy floor
of this pyramid, perhaps unnoticed by the builders. I do
not know if they were intended as an ancient anti-theft
device, but they are certainly effective as one. I hope everyone is all right."

While they spoke, the spiders had covered everything in
a carpet of red, Ashley and the others turned to Kasim
for direction. Looking from one to the other he smiled

crookedly and said, "I guess our work for today has ended. I will send a cleanup team in to exterminate, but until the chemicals have subsided, there is not much more we can do. We'll return tomorrow. Let us call it quits. It has been a long and productive day anyway. We are about due for a rest and something to eat. Maybe we can even have a proper tea time for a change."

Stepping out into the late afternoon sun, Ashley realized just how true Kasim's words had been. She had sat inside the tomb for hours without feeling the passage of time. She had bagged, tagged, and identified hundreds of artifacts with such concentration that she had forgotten to eat the fruit she had hastily packed for lunch. Chuckling, she wondered if the ants had covered her banana and figs, too.

As she walked with Sallie past the sentries, and toward the compound, Ashley reflected on the tomb's efforts to keep its treasures intact and private. From the moment they arrived, something had tried to keep them out and to keep the artifacts in. She wondered if maybe they should simply close the tomb and forget that they had seen the treasures. Smiling at her own naïveté, she acknowledged that if they did not unearth the treasures, another expedition would. Once the word of their success spread, nothing inside the pyramid would be safe from seekers of fortune. At least their group worked for a university rather than for individual gain. Still, she marveled at the desert's ability to protect its own.

As she entered the building, Ashley had the strangest feeling that something had changed, almost as if someone new had joined the group. Shrugging her shoulders, she slipped into her cubicle planning for a quick shower and a change of clothes before joining the others for dinner. Pulling back the curtains that served as the doorway, she uttered a brief exclamation before stopping dead in her tracks. Someone had placed a newly unearthed treasure in the center of her bed.

Stepping cautiously forward, Ashley bent toward the glistening bracelet and almost touched it. Suddenly standing upright, she backed away and into the corridor. She did not want to take the chance that her fingerprints would replace those of the thief.

"Sallie, come quickly!" Ashley called as she stood staring at the artifact.

"What's the problem? Is there a snake on your bed?" Sallie inquired as she joined Ashley at the opening of her cubicle.

"No, it's even worse. Look!" Ashley demanded as she pointed toward her bed.

Following Ashley's gesturing hand, Sallie gasped and asked, "Where did that come from? I thought you crated that for transport yesterday."

"I did. I don't know how it got here, but I don't think this is at all funny. Stay here while I get Kasim and Ben," Ashley replied as she hurried away.

Ben and Kasim quickly arrived. The sudden appearance of the intricately carved, jewel-encrusted gold bracelet flabbergasted them, too. Only the day before Ashley had discovered it among the treasures in the tomb. Immediately Ben ordered everyone into the conference room and summoned the police. Kasim stayed behind to guard the artifact during fingerprinting and join them with it later.

"Ladies and gentlemen," Ben began as he quieted the muttering archaeologists gathered around the table, "we have experienced another breech of security. As I am sure you have heard, Ashley found a bracelet from the tomb on her bed when she returned this afternoon. Until Kasim joins us, we will not know if the bracelet is the original or a copy. At this point, I am not sure that it matters. Of utmost concern is the fact that someone, despite the guards on the door and the perimeter of the compound, has breached our security measures. He has had sufficient time and opportunity to study the artifacts and either steal or copy at least this one. Without fear of discovery, he then placed the item in Ashley's cubicle. This is yet another indication that we must be on our guard."

Frank asked, "Aren't all the artifacts locked in the vault prior to being loaded onto the vans? How could this happen?"

Nodding his head, Ben replied, "They are indeed stored in the safe and then transported by secure trucks operated by museum officials. In the past, they have arrived at their destination without any difficulty. This is the first time in my career that anything like this has ever happened. I am completely at a loss to explain this occurrence."

"Why is this person targeting Ashley?" Sallie demanded. "First, she was attacked, and now someone has left a priceless treasure or its copy on her bed."

Raising his hands for silence, Ben commented helplessly, "Unless the person identifies himself, I can only assume that he is mocking our efforts to stop him from infiltrating the security of our dig. In my opinion, he is trying to tell us that nothing we do to try to keep him away will stop him."

"But exactly what does he want?" Ashley asked over the other voices.

Turning to her, Ben replied, "Unfortunately, we cannot begin to speculate on his motives. We have not received any written communication from the intruder. We can only wait. However, this latest entry into our compound says that he is never far away."

The excited voices quieted again as Kasim entered the room with the bracelet in his gloved hands. Its brilliance shone brightly as he carefully placed it on the table. Slipping into the seat at Ben's right, Kasim explained, "The police have completed their search of Ashley's quarters and have fingerprinted the bracelet. Unfortunately, they did not uncover any clues as to the identity of the intruder."

Frank asked, "Is that bracelet an original or a copy?"

"It is definitely one of our artifacts. How the intruder managed to remove it from the vault, we do not know," Kasim replied with a shrug of futility.

Voicing everyone's concern, Sallie said, "This is dreadful. We are totally at a loss to defend ourselves or protect the treasures. It's almost as if someone is watching our every move."

Kasim replied, "Unfortunately, that seems to be the case. The police think that someone who works on the expedition committed the attack on Ashley and the breech of security. However, until we have definitive clues to the person's identity, there is nothing the police can do for us. We must be very careful."

With that they adjourned to their rooms for rest and tea. Sallie linked her arm through Ashley's as they strolled down the hall toward their cubicles. "Let's take our tea together. The men might feel helpless to do anything, but we have to make plans to protect you," Sallie said, carrying her tea tray into Ashley's cubicle.

"I agree, but what can we do? He's able to enter without being stopped by security, which to my mind means that everyone knows him. I didn't recognize the man who attacked me because I was too terrified to get a good look even after I pulled off his ski mask. I just can't believe how bold he is. Just think of the arrogance of the man," Ashley commented as she drank deeply of the sweet elixir.

Nodding Sallie replied, "That's what makes him so dangerous . . . and so exciting. I can hardly wait to tell my husband about this. He said that all expeditions were alike. He really missed a good one.''

With a shrug Ashley rebutted, "If I weren't the target, I'd agree with you, but right now, I'm scared."

"Oh, I know, dear, but I don't think you really need to be. At least this time he didn't do anything physical. You weren't hurt by the little gift he left on your bed," Sallie rejoined, drinking down the last of her tea.

"But what about next time? I don't like knowing that he's so close," Ashley replied as they placed their trays on the cart in the hall. The kitchen help bowed and rolled the cart down the aisle to the next cubicle.

Sallie patted Ashley on the arm and said with her familiar gush, "You'll feel better after a nap. I'll see you at dinner. I'm going to write that letter to my husband now. He'll be so sorry that he missed this trip."

To Ashley's surprise, she fell asleep as soon as she stretched out on her bed. The tension and the heat of the day had sapped her energy and left her more tired than she had thought. The gentle hum of the overhead fan made it impossible for her to resist the comfort of her fluffy pillow.

Later that evening, as Ashley walked down the hall to the dining room, Kasim's voice reached her ears. He had already started the evening's discussion on the subject of cataloging and preserving antiquities from the ravages of twentieth-century polluted air when she entered and took her seat beside Sallie. Seeing her, he paused ever so slightly in midsentence before continuing. He tried to read her face but could find nothing written there that would tell him of the depth of her fears.

As Kasim's discussion eased to a close, Ashley signaled that she would like some time alone with him. Immediately, he joined her for a stroll around the compound. They passed alert armed guards as they ventured into the Egyptian night. With a sad chuckle Kasim commented, "With all this security, you would think that the intruder would have difficulty penetrating our compound, but he does not appear to experience any difficulty. We can just barely find the opportunity to be alone, but he manages to enter without being questioned."

Looking toward the illuminated pyramids, Ashley replied, "That's what has me so terribly frightened. He appears to know what we're doing, but we haven't a clue to his identity."

"Sadly, I cannot provide you with protection past this moment, but for now, let us put the thought of this intruder far from our minds. There is much that we need to discuss and much that has remained unspoken between us," Kasim responded, gently taking Ashley's hand in his.

"Kasim, your nearness only confuses me further." Ashley sighed as the warmth of his body penetrated hers.

"If you will only allow yourself to care for me, I will take away your worries forever. Tell me what it is that you need, and I will give it to you," Kasim said, lightly kissing the back of Ashley's hand. The touch of his lips sent thrills coursing through her body.

"Kasim, I cannot make you understand what I don't myself. When I left the States for this expedition, I expected to find an intellectual experience beyond compare. I did not anticipate that the desert and you would be so compelling. I am not ready for a relationship with you." Ashley tried to explain but stumbled over her own words.

"Do you have a lover at home? I thought you gave me signals that you were available. If I misread them, I am very sorry," Kasim said, gazing into her eyes.

"No, there's no one waiting for me to return. I was seeing someone, but I broke up with him before coming here. He did not understand the importance of the sabbatical and this trip to me. It's something else entirely."

"Tell me. I feel I have a right to know. I thought I felt a mutual attraction between us. Was I mistaken?" Kasim asked as he reluctantly released Ashley's hand and stepped back a pace.

"No, you didn't misread me. I am attracted to you. It's just that I . . . I . . . I can't explain it. I have this feeling that someone is waiting for me. I can almost feel him watching me. I almost expect to see him step from behind the pyramids at any minute. He's just that close." Ashley struggled to make Kasim understand.

"So, what do I do in the meantime? Should I sit around twiddling my thumbs while the woman I care about dreams of another man?" Kasim demanded with more than a little sarcasm in his voice.

"I said that this would be difficult for you to understand. You'll just have to give me time to sort through my feelings. It might just be the majesty of the desert, but I have to find out for myself," Ashley replied, determined to stick to her own direction.

Seeing the pain written on Ashley's face, Kasim sighed and offered, "Maybe I should ask the university if I could work as the inside man on this project. That way I would be in Cairo and unable to add to your confusion."

"You're right. That would be a great solution. But you'd miss the initial thrill of discovery, I'd really hate for you to do that. Do you think your department would agree?" Ashley asked feeling hopeful that she would have some time alone at last.

"I have unearthed many artifacts in this desert and, fortunately, will have the opportunity for many more, but this is the only chance I have with you. I would do anything to convince you that I am the man for you. I do not want to take any chance that by staying here I will win or lose by default. I will make the call right now. I will let you know as soon as I can," Kasim responded. He slowly escorted her back to her cubicle with the heavy tread of an old man under the weight of his distress at having to leave the dig and Ashley.

Ashley sank into her pillow as the privacy flap of her cubicle closed. She had never felt so lonely or in so much despair. If she had known that she could feel this much pain or see so much agony written on another person's face, she never would have allowed herself to think about Kasim at all. Berating herself, she thought that she had not planned to fall in love with him, but it had simply happened. She had not counted on the dreams or the excitement of the dig either. This sabbatical was definitely turning out to be more than she had anticipated.

Burying her face in her pillow, Ashley cried quick hot tears. What a mess she had made in her search for a sparkling, exciting life rather than being content with simple happiness and the comfort of good companionship. Yet, even as she pounded the pillow in frustration, she knew somewhere in the depths of her heart that she would do it again if she had the chance. She had to have more than the ordinary life . . . and love.

After a quick group dinner at which Kasim was absent, Ashley and Sallie decided to join a few of the others on a camel ride into the desert. She wanted to see the surroundings with the glow of sunset making the sand shine blood red. She had heard so much about the splendor of the desert that she could hardly wait. Besides, riding a camel was in itself a unique and exciting prospect. She needed to share her feelings with Sallie, too. She knew that her friend would be able to provide some advice for dealing with her conflicting emotions.

As remorseful as she felt over the mess she had made,
Ashley could not remain sad when she saw the fun the
others were having with the camels. Their levity immediately made her spirits soar as she watched them struggle
to make the willful animals comply with their wishes.
Laughing with delight, she clung to the saddle's pommel
as the great smelly beast rose on its thin, fragile-looking
legs. Flies swarmed around its body and her head as she
waited for the others to mount up. Gripping tightly, Ashley
looked at the Great Pyramid standing stately and serene
in the warm afternoon as its surface began to take on the
rosy hue of the sunset.

Every year as she had taught her history classes, she had
dreamed of visiting the splendor of Egypt, but she had
never quite believed that she would ever see more of it
than what was shown in the pages of her books. Looking
over the desert, Ashley could hardly believe that she was
actually here. The months had passed so quickly, almost
in a blur of activity. She had experienced so much in such a
short time, met wonderful people, discovered unbelievable
treasures, and fallen in love with a delightful man. She
asked herself what more she could ask of a lifetime.

Without giving her more opportunity to reflect, the
group of four started following their leader away from
the compound and the familiar sights toward unexplored
territory. The desert with its mystery lay ahead of them.
Their guide had told them that they should all stay
together; no one should wander off alone. Tribes of
unfriendly people lived in the desert on the outskirts of
established towns. They hated the noise and bustle of civilization and the intrusion of strangers into what they considered their own personal desert. Often they reacted with
hostility to lost tourists who happened upon their compound. Looking at each other, Ashley and Sallie acknowledged that they would definitely follow his instructions.

The last thing they wanted was to be attacked by people with the same fury as they had experienced from the spiders earlier that day.

The desert did not disappoint them as they ambled along. Its glowing expanse of white sand reflected the red of the sun, spreading its endless grandeur as far as they could see. Ashley quickly understood how the uninitiated could become lost in the sameness of the flat, sandy surface as she gazed out into its splendor. She had seen the deserts of North America and the wonder of the Grand Canyon, but the Nile Valley and the Western Desert of the Sahara held their own majestic, ageless charm and cast an undeniable spell over all who beheld them. Looking up at the sky, she saw that the stars twinkled more brightly here than at home. She knew that the absence of city lights made them appear closer, but she still felt as if she could reach out and touch them in a way she could not in Washington, D.C.

Riding along on the rolling gait of the camel, Ashley and Sallie barely spoke as the sights passed before their eyes. All the emotional conflict she had wanted to share flew out of her mind as she watched the magnificence of Egypt open its arms to her. The changing personality of the valley as it blended with the arid desert land struck them silent with the realization that this had been the cradle of civilization since man first began to walk the earth. Ashley wondered how she would ever be able to share with her students the sights, smells, and sounds she experienced. Sadly, she doubted that she would ever find just the right words. Egypt was a feeling as much as it was a place. To really know it, they would have to visit it themselves.

The time passed as they trotted along at such an easy pace that she barely noticed the sunset changing from pink to red to claret to darkness. As the night air grew cool,

Ashley wondered when their guide would turn around
and begin their return trip. Sallie seemed to have been
snatched from her desert-induced tranquillity at the same
moment because she looked around as if awakening from
a deep sleep. Their guide, too, seemed to have been lulled
by the silence into a sleep-walking state and appeared oblivious to their discomfort. Noticing the darkness and without
saying a word, he turned his camel in a wide circle and
began to retrace their steps.

The breeze started to blow as they made their journey
back to the compound, making Ashley quite happy that
they had not taken the camel trip alone. Already the wind
had started to sweep the sand clean of any traces of their
presence. Looking behind them, she could not see any of
their prints. Frightened, she realized that nothing lay
ahead of them except darkness. They had traveled so far
from the compound that she could not see even the bright
lights on the Great Pyramid.

Suddenly they were joined by riders on camels who
appeared out of nowhere. At first Ashley could not make
out the masks that hid the lower portions of their faces
and the weapons they held in their hands. By the time she
realized that these men were not simple travelers, they had
totally surrounded her group. Without saying anything to
the others, their guide saluted the masked men and
spurred his camel into a gallop. As she watched his vanishing back, Ashley understood that he had deliberately
led them into the silent desert away from the sounds and
sights of civilization. He and the masked men had worked
together to engineer a kidnapping on the dark expanse
of sand.

With a quiver in her voice, Sallie whispered, "What are
they doing? Do you think we're being kidnapped?"

Before Ashley could answer, one of the men shouted in a
brusque commanding voice, "Quiet! No talking, anyone!"

He waved his long menacing weapon in the air for emphasis. He was a rather crude type—definitely not the leader. Immediately, they fell silent as they rode beside their captors. They did not look around as they followed the fierce looking leader.

At first it looked as if they would retrace their tracks until the masked men forced them to turn left into the uncharted darkness. Although Ashley could barely see the rider in front of her, the man at the head of the line did not appear to experience any difficulty in directing them away from the pyramids. As they slowed to a stop, she peered through the darkness as the silhouette of small, nondescript cottages came into view. With no physical landmarks to tell her their location, she could have been anywhere in the desert. The sound of animated voices whispering floated through the open windows as they approached the larger of the dwellings.

Reining their camels, the men forced Ashley to dismount and follow them inside the dimly lighted structure. They pushed at her lightly with their riding crops and muttered something in a language she could not understand. Carefully picking her way through the semidarkness, she stepped into the cabin. With Sallie at her side, she blinked as her eyes adjusted to the glow of the candles. The men, covered in ski masks or bandannas, turbans, and flowing robes, glared at them in the eerie light. She could feel their hostility and their lust as they stared at the American women who dared to dress in the attire of men and ignore the ancient custom of covering their bodies and faces from view. Their lack of respect was almost palpable as they licked their lips and glared brazenly at her breasts under the white shirt and her thighs in the close-fitting jeans. For the first time in her life, Ashley felt uncomfortable with her liberated American upbringing.

"Please sit down on these chairs where we can keep an

eye on you. It would be most inconvenient if you suddenly vanished," the man who was obviously the leader directed from behind his bandanna as he pointed with his rifle. The tone of his voice and the expression of determination in his eyes told Ashley that he meant business. Yet, something told her that he would not harm her. She did not feel that he wanted her, but only planned to use her for a larger purpose.

He shoved them toward two straight-backed, hard wooden chairs one of the leering men quickly produced. Watching as Ashley and Sallie hastily obeyed his orders, the men laughed at their discomfort and fear. The sound of their voices sent chills of terror through Ashley's body as she perched on the hard seat waiting for them to make the next move. With a wave of his hand, the leader silenced them. His finger rested frighteningly close to the rifle's trigger. Pulling their arms painfully behind the chairs' backs, the man in the red mask and dirty gray bandanna bound their wrists and taped their mouths while the leader watched.

"We will not hurt you as long as you do what we say. It is not you that we want but the pyramid's treasure. As soon as we get it, we will turn you loose. As a matter of fact, one of you will leave here tonight with a message for Ben and Kasim. Do not worry. The one who stays behind will be perfectly safe. We have no interest in you as anything other than ransom for a far greater reward," he said as his controlled, refined voice met their ears in a harsh whisper. He spoke in heavily accented English not unlike that spoken by Kasim and Ben.

As Ashley looked from the leader to his men, they muttered agreement and nodded assent. Yet, something in their manner told her that whatever control he had over them held them together thinly. She doubted that she would be safe for long, especially not from the man with

the healing scratch showing on his cheek above the handkerchief that covered the lower part of his face. With a
shudder, she recognized him as the man who had attacked
her in the compound's parking lot. His eyes told her that
he wanted revenge for his foiled efforts . . . and more.

She wondered what cause held together this ragtag
assembly of men. Their leader appeared quite refined. His
posture was regal, and his speech clipped in the British
manner. He had obviously been educated in England.
Although he carried a rifle, he held it in the relaxed manner of those who are accustomed to duck hunting with
the barrel pointing downward. His nails were clean, unlike
those of his men. What she could see of his hair was neatly
combed. His eyes sparkled brightly and showed a clarity
not reflected in the expressions on the dulled faces of his
comrades. His slim yet muscular physique could have been
comfortable on horseback as well as on the tennis court.
He was certainly an enigma. Ashley wondered what she
would have discovered if she had been able to assemble
the pieces of the puzzle.

Ashley looked around the small cabin for any signs of
the style of life he had enjoyed there. Aside from the two
chairs in which she and Sallie sat, one more sat to the right
of the fireplace. There were four open and unmade cots
along the walls and three extra ones stacked in front of
the dirty, unused fireplace. On the mantel lay a collection
of mismatched plates and cups, most of which were
chipped and faded. She counted five plates and seven cups,
but she had no way of knowing if that were representative
of the number of men in the group. The only cooking
utensils were a cast iron skillet and a large greasy spoon.
To the left of the door were coat pegs, but nothing hung
on them. She did not see any indication of a closet in the
tiny one-room cabin. She also did not see a bathroom or

a kitchen. Whoever lived here was accustomed to the bare
necessities of life.

Looking toward the windows for signs of life outside the
cabin, Ashley noticed that they had been soaped over to
keep people from being able to look inside. No blinds,
curtains, or shades hung at them. She assumed that no
women lived here. She wondered if this group of men
actually inhabited the cabin or if they simply borrowed it
as a hiding place for her.

The only thing she saw that indicated any connection
with the modern, outside world was the telephone that sat
on the small table in the middle of the room. It looked
new as if it had been installed for this occasion.

Unlike Ashley who surveyed her surroundings with a
mixture of curiosity and defiance, Sallie sat whimpering
in her chair. Her eyes were wide with childlike fear. Tears
flowed steadily down her dirt-streaked cheeks. Soft sobs
escaped from her parched lips.

The men moved to the other side of the small room
away from Ashley's and Sallie's straining ears. The minutes
moved slowly as they deliberated on the details of their
next action. When they returned, a sort of glee accompanied them as their leader described the next step in their
plan. Pulling over the empty chair, the leader put his
scuffed but obviously expensively booted foot solidly on
the seat of the chair next to Ashley. She noticed that it
was the kind of boot usually worn by archaeologists because
of the thickness of the sole and the soft flexibility of the
leather. Ben and Kasim owned boots of the same design.

Leaning toward her so that she could smell the mixture
of peppermint and strong coffee on his breath, he said
confidently with a slight teasing sound in his voice, ''We
will take the blond woman back to the excavation site.
You will stay here with us until Ben and Kasim meet our
demands. We have noticed that Kasim seems to have a

weak spot in his heart for you. You might prove to be a
valuable bargaining tool for us, and, if you do not, you
would make a good worker on one of the remote oases."

Pointing toward Sallie he added by way of instruction
to his men, "Untie the blond; she leaves immediately. Slip
this blindfold on her so that she cannot tell anyone our
location. You two drop her off near the compound. Do
not stay around to see if she makes the walk safely. Get
back here as soon as you can."

Ashley reeled at his words, almost as if he had struck
her across the face. She would have to stay with these
masked men indefinitely unless Kasim and Ben agreed to
their terms to trade treasures that did not belong to them
for her safe return. She wondered if the Egyptian government would play along with them, or if they would leave
her to fend for herself. Somehow she knew that no good
would come to her if she were left alone with the man
with the angry, piercing eyes and the scratched cheek. She
would have to throw herself on the mercy of the leader if
she were to survive.

Watching Sallie being pushed and half carried out of
the cabin, Ashley felt her heart grow heavy with fear. She
was alone with this band of ruthless masked men. The only
thing that stood between her and harm was the leader,
who gave the impression that he cared as little for her as
did his men. Listening to him whistle a tuneless song while
he filed a rough spot from his well-manicured nails with
the long, slender blade of a stiletto, she could easily imagine the skill with which he could filet meat or an enemy.
Yet, something in the way he watched his men when they
were near her suggested that he might be an ally after all.

As if reading her mind, he spoke softly yet firmly, "As
long as I am in charge of this little band, you will be safe.
But I hope your friends do not try my patience. The longer
we remain here, the greater our risk of discovery. Leaving

here and moving farther into the desert would be risky for you. The terrain is most inhospitable, should I say. Let us hope they act quickly before the heat and anxiety stretch our hospitality. My men are not ruthless killers. They are in this for the money not for revenge on the government or to make a social comment. They want their share of the treasure in order to better their lives. They will not harm you as long as things progress smoothly, but I would not like to see them become frightened about being apprehended."

Ashley shuddered at the menacing tone he applied to the word hospitality. She doubted if she would ever hear it spoken again without remembering the hissing sound his breath made as it rushed through the handkerchief that covered all but his deep brown eyes that held her imprisoned as securely as the ropes bound her hands. Although she knew that she was only a pawn in this unpleasant game, Ashley could sense that something more lay beneath the surface. At the same time, she had no choice but to trust him. Her life depended on his good graces and Ben's expeditious response to his demands.

"Here, drink this. It will soothe your nerves and help you sleep," the man instructed, thrusting a cup under Ashley's nose.

"What is it?" Ashley asked, turning her face away.

"Do as I say. Do not question me," he barked.

The slightly bitter lemon drink felt cool as it slid down her throat. Soon Ashley found it difficult to stay awake, although she was determined to listen to everything that transpired in the little cabin.

As the hours ticked away Ashley's arms ached and her throat grew dry. The leader seemed to have all but forgotten her presence as he read a magazine and worked the crossword puzzle. However, the men impatiently waited for the return of their comrades and contact with Ben and

Kasim. She wanted a glass of water desperately but was afraid to ask for it even though the leader had long since removed the tape from her mouth. She tried to appear as small and inconspicuous as possible in the hopes of keeping the men from noticing her. She did not want to feel the rude stares trace over her body. The liquid she had consumed had caused her to feel as if she were standing outside herself watching the events unfold around her. She was not frightened, only curious and very tired.

Her head pounded painfully at the memory of their initial treatment of her. She could still feel their insulting, insolent gaze wandering over her breasts and thighs. She knew even before they spoke to her that her white linen blouse and stylishly snug jeans set her off from their expectations of women and made her a candidate for ridicule.

Yet Ashley had not anticipated the degree of disrespect they would pay to a woman in Western apparel. As they had looked her over from head to foot, she had felt almost violated, raped . . . certainly striped naked and paraded before them. She had actually regretted having a lush, feminine figure rather than being built like the boyish models who graced the pages of the fashion magazines. Their slight figures would not have drawn the same attention, but her full breasts pressing against the white cloth of her blouse and her shapely thighs and buttocks straining within the confines of the heavy denim caused them to visually strip her naked. Their hungry leers had filled her with fear for her safety. Their grumbling conversation did little to soothe her spirits.

Suddenly, as if everyone were straining to hear something from a great distance, the room grew quiet. The men stopped their good-natured quarreling and the leader looked up expectantly. They all listened as the faint sound grew stronger. They held their breaths as the thunder of hooves slowed and finally stopped outside the cabin. Their hands sought their weapons as the door swung open and the two men sent to return Sallie to the compound entered.

Breathing deeply from the quick ride in the warm night, one of the men said as she settled heavily onto one of the cots, "We delivered the woman as you instructed. There was no one outside the compound or at the windows. Even the guards did not stand duty in the guardhouse. Not that it mattered; most of them were our men anyway. They are deep in the desert by now. No one saw us. The last I saw of the blond, she was running across the parking lot shouting at full volume for Ben. By now, he has probably alerted the police. We should hear something very soon."

"Good work. It is getting late. Let us get a little rest until it is time for me to make contact with him," the leader replied, clapping both of the men on their shoulders. He was obviously pleased with the progress of the operation.

He limped over to one of the cots for a quick nap before placing the telephone call that he hoped would make significant changes in his group's financial status. Almost immediately, he was up again and on the phone with someone whose voice Ashley could not hear. From his conversation, Ashley could tell that he did not mean that they should belong to the government or the university.

Ashley overheard him say, "Do not forget, my friend, that I detest the snobbery of institutions of higher learning, although I am a self-made expert in art history. I detest the way those book-educated people look down their noses on working people. They have mistreated us and ignored our poverty and suffering long enough. I cannot stand to see the suffering on the faces of our children any longer. I plan to put the money to good use helping the poor in the little forgotten villages. The university is already wealthy enough and its collections are immense. It always makes me feel good to give something to others especially when the art I steal and resell buys so much on the black market."

Looking at Ashley to see if she were asleep, he continued in hushed tones, "I can buy cases of supplies, books, food, and medicine with just one artifact and still have plenty to pay my men and give myself a healthy sum."

Feigning sleep, Ashley could tell from the smile on his face that he enjoyed stealing from the rich and giving to the poor. He seemed to feel that the wealthy contemptuously held themselves above everyone else, and that it was his duty to try to even the score.

Ashley listened carefully as the man continued, saying, "I have already contacted several prominent art dealers who will pay top dollar for the artifacts without asking any questions as to the manner in which I have acquired them. The only thing they demand is authenticity of the product. They know me and have dealt with me on several occasions. They know me to be a man with superior taste and an eye for bona fide objects of art. I have already supplied them with jewels and art carefully selected from the mansions of famous people who kept silent about their missing objects, having themselves originally acquired them under dubious conditions.

"Do not worry, in a few hours, the treasures of this pyramid will belong to me if I have not underestimated Ben's concern for the welfare of others over the need to protect the antiquities. He has always been driven by compassion more than fame. Until then, I will contact you again, I need some rest. Goodbye."

As silence overtook the room, Ashley found that she could not fight off the effects of the drink any longer. A feeling of serenity deepened as she drifted into a deep sleep.

Glancing at Ashley, who sat slumped in the chair a few feet from him, the leader smiled. His one and only regret in this endeavor was that he would not have the opportunity to get to know her more fully. He had watched her from a distance ever since she had arrived at the dig and had been inexplicably drawn to her. Many times he had almost taken the chance of ingratiating himself into the company of archaeologists. No one would have recognized him as an outsider. They might even have confused him for someone else they knew. He was extremely knowledgeable about their actions and their leaders. He would have had the chance to be near her.

His reaction to her surprised him. He was not usually attracted to American women, but this one was different. She was no more beautiful than any other woman he had ever seen, but something in her demeanor attracted him as no other had. He admired her bravery in this time of crisis. He would have like to have loved her . . . made her a part of his life . . . introduced her to the finer things that his share of the treasure money could buy. As it was, he would have to content himself with watching her sleep and thinking about what might have been.

As the silence of the night deepened, the leader dropped his chin onto his chest for a brief nap. Even in his sleep, Ashley dominated his thoughts. He had known many women but none had appealed to him as much as Ashley. She was not only intellectually stimulating with her interest in antiquities, but she possessed a sensual beauty of which she seemed totally unaware and an astounding ability to withstand hardship without cracking. Even under pressure, she remained calm. No sobs of despair wracked her body. No sighs of self-pity disturbed her sleep. She was composed and self-assured even in the face of danger. She had never flinched at the sight of their weapons or rough treatment unlike the blond she had called Sallie, who whimpered constantly. Even if he had not already decided to keep Ashley with him until ransomed, he would not have detained the other one. Her sniffling would have driven him insane. He might have been tempted to return her without the exchange of goods, and that was something he could ill afford to do. Too many hungry people depended on him.

As sleep overtook him, he thought that maybe he could still win Ashley's heart if he had the time and the opportunity. He did not think that Ben would comply with his demands in the next few hours. Considering her interest in Kasim, he thought that his chances were pretty good that she might be receptive to him. He had often been told that the similarity between them was unmistakable.

CHAPTER SIX

Ashley did not know that Ben was already in conference with the Cairo police trying to work out a plan for her rescue. Scribbling madly on the white board used for plotting their expedition routes, he drew maps of the area based on Sallie's description of the sounds she had heard and the sights she had seen as she and Ashley rode with the others through the desert. Unfortunately, the leader had blindfolded her for the return trip, but she thought some of the sounds were familiar. Based on her sense of time, they tried to pinpoint the exact location of the encampment in relation to the pyramids.

Using the most current map, they worked feverishly combining her memories with the known villages in the area. Unfortunately, Sallie had been so frightened for her own life and Ashley's that she had not paid very close attention as she rode through the stillness of the night. She thought she had traveled by camel for about an hour and that the route had contained many turns, but she was not certain that she was correct. The possibility also existed that her captors might have backtracked to confuse her so that she would not be able to lead anyone to their camp.

Shaking her head sadly, Sallie had to admit that she was not much help to any of them. As the tears trailed down her cheeks, Ben tried to console her by saying, "You have been more help than you can ever know. Your descriptions of the area and the overall appearance of the cabin narrow our search to a half dozen possibilities rather than to the hundreds of tiny villages and compounds that dot the desert. My people are fairly nomadic in their tendencies and have been known to travel in search of a better place to live quite frequently. A village on the map today might not be there tomorrow. Your information will help the police greatly."

Smiling through her tears, she accepted his kind words but wished there were more she could do for her friend. She was terribly worried for Ashley's safety even though the leader had promised that she would be safe. Some of his men looked as if they were fairly tightly wound and eager to sample the pleasures of a Western woman even if she were not a willing participant.

After Sallie left the room, Ben and the captain of the Egyptian police force on special assignment to the pyramids sat down to strategize. They knew that the telephone call from Ashley's captors would be coming soon, and they wanted to be prepared to respond quickly. Already they had installed the wiretapping equipment. They did not want to miss the chance to catch her kidnapper on the first contact. Her life and the security of the treasures rested on their success.

Putting their heads together, the two men labored for more than three hours revising their security plans. They ordered all work in the pyramid halted and the structure locked and guarded around the clock until Ashley returned. All of the archaeologists had been instructed to stay in the compound until further notice. Reporters from all the major international news organizations waited for the latest news and swarmed around the parking lot. Leaving their watch for only a few minutes, they ran back and forth between their temporary broadcast stations relaying whatever they heard to the listening world. They drank coffee by the gallons as they paced anxiously in their sweat-spotted white shirts.

Kasim could barely contain his worry as he waited in Ashley's cubicle. His first instinct was to rush into the desert in search of her. However, Ben had convinced him that his actions could result in her death. He felt completely helpless as he paced the floor. Looking at the tiny bedside table, he lovingly fingered the work gloves she had carefully folded and placed inside her safety helmet. Slipping his hand under the pillow, he pulled out the nightshirt she had stored under it that morning as she had hurriedly dressed and joined the others. Burying his face in the sweet smell of her, he cursed himself for his inability to protect her.

Yet, Kasim knew that there was nothing he could have done. The security measures had failed. The kidnappers had foiled their best efforts to protect the archaeologists and the treasures. Now all they could do was wait until the men telephoned their demands.

Stretching out on her cot, Kasim tried to sleep. He stared at the metal frame of the structure's ceiling and listened to the soft swishing of the ceiling fan. At the opposite ends of the long row of cubicles, he could hear muffled voices of expedition members and Ben. He knew that he should join them, but he could not. For the moment, he needed time alone to think and plan.

But as his frustration and anger mounted, Kasim rose

and walked to the conference room. Ben and the police captain turned from the sketches they were drawing on the board as he entered. Offering him a cup of strong Egyptian coffee, Ben said, "We have not heard anything yet. They should be contacting us very soon."

"Good. I will stay here, if you do not mind, until he does. I cannot rest anyway," Kasim replied accepting the offered cup. He settled himself in one of the hard chairs, crossed his legs, and sipped his coffee without waiting for a response.

As they sat in silence, the jangle of the telephone sounded, breaking the solitary nature of their thoughts. Waiting until the captain gave him the nod, Ben breathed deeply to calm his nerves and slowly answered the demanding ring saying, "Amad, here."

The sound of nothing but the humming of the battery-powered wall clock in the room was almost overwhelming as Kasim stared anxiously at Ben's tense face. The police captain, wearing headphones and staring at the second hand of his watch, waited as the minutes ticked away. He motioned for Ben to speak slowly and deliberately. They needed time to trace the call.

"Ben," the voice on the other end replied, "listen carefully. Ashley is safe and will remain so as long as you cooperate with me to the fullest. I have no intention of hurting her. All I want is the treasure. I will be generous and share it with you, if you would like. I have preselected specific items that I want delivered to me before I will set her free. I will not repeat my request. Get it correct the first time, please. Her freedom depends on it."

"I am ready. What is it you want?" Ben requested in a controlled voice that belied the turmoil in his mind. He knew that nothing was as important as human life and that he would do anything to obtain Ashley's freedom. However, the thought of relinquishing the treasures tormented him. They had worked so hard and overcome so many obstacles to acquire the wealth of the tomb that he hated to part with it.

Ben listened attentively, scribbling hurriedly on the white board as the caller listed everything he wanted from the pyramid. Kasim watched as the list of unbelievable treasures increased in length before his eyes. Gold bracelets, emerald and diamond earrings and necklaces, gold encrusted vases, and rings of all description appeared. Ben did not stop writing even when a cramp seized his hand and caused him to wince in pain. The blue ink flowed until he had covered the entire surface.

And then the caller hung up.

"Hello?! Hello?! Are you there?" Ben repeated into the silence. Turning to Kasim with frustration, worry, and helplessness playing over his face, he put down the phone and sank utterly exhausted into the nearest chair.

"Well, what do we do next?" Kasim asked, impatient to spring into action. In his concern for Ashley, he totally ignored Ben's discomfort. "Is Ashley safe? What did he say?"

"From what I can tell, she is safe and in no apparent danger. I did not speak with her since he hung up too soon. The caller was obviously aware that the police were tracing his call. When he calls back later, I will ask for her. We should hear from him at two o'clock this afternoon. He is giving us time to collect the items from his list of demands. This man is certainly comfortable with the tomb's inventory," Ben responded, wearily wiping his forehead.

"And then what?" Kasim demanded. His worry was heavily tinged with anger. He believed in making things happen not in waiting peacefully for events to fall into place. It bothered him to sit around while someone else called the shots. For Ashley's good, he would have to control his impulse to start hunting through every little village in the vicinity of the pyramids for her.

"He will outline the rest of his plan. Come help me get these things together. Mohammed must have been detained at the university this morning, and I need another pair of hands for this project," Ben concluded, grabbing up his hat and gloves.

As they reached the door, the police captain entered shaking his head. "Sorry, gentlemen, but we were not able to trace the call. He hung up too soon. Next time, we will have more success, I hope. From the sound of that list, the man we are looking for is very knowledgeable about the contents of the pyramid."

The three men looked at each other as they wrestled with their thoughts. The kidnapper had demanded jewels for Ashley's release, but he had already stolen something more precious from them. He had robbed them of their belief in each other.

Ben had tried desperately to push his suspicions about Mohammed from his mind as he listened to the caller's demands. His muffled voice had sounded very familiar. He did not want to think that his longtime colleague and friend could possibly be involved in a kidnapping and theft. Mohammed had such promise as an archaeologist and historian.

Kasim's thoughts had centered on the kidnapping as a form of extortion in which an American would be held as ransom until someone paid the demanded price. He fumed at the notion that the kidnapper so blatantly put the woman who had captured his heart at risk of death. He wanted to inflict his own form of justice on the man. No pain was too great for such a betrayal.

The police captain considered it yet another crime to discourage foreign tourists and investors from coming to Egypt as the dissatisfied anti-government groups worked to topple the country's economy. He worried that the foreign press would play up an already disastrous event. If they turned it into a media circus, the kidnapper might panic and kill Ashley.

They walked in silence toward the pyramid as the sun warmed their slumped shoulders. Each was too occupied with his own thoughts to feel the pain of the other, yet, they all had the same concern for Ashley's safety. Ben and Kasim felt confident that the kidnapper would keep his word and not harm her; his plan hinged on her safety. The police captain was not as sure. He had seen too many kidnappings go awry.

The guard on duty at the pyramid's opening snapped to attention as they approached. Muttering instructions to him, the captain followed Ben and Kasim into the darkness and down the rope-lined path to the chambers below. Breathing the stuffy air and following the bobbing beam from their flashlights, they made their way to the treasure room where Ashley had worked only a day ago. Already the whirling dust had covered their footprints and reclaimed some of its own.

Filling the straw-lined crates they had brought with them, Kasim and the captain worked silently under Ben's skillful direction. They recorded, wrapped, and packed every requested item until they grew weary from the constant bending and lifting. When they had finally finished, Ben straightened his stiff back and looked around him at all they had accomplished. On the pyramid floor at their feet sat six large pine boxes filled with the most exquisite treasures offered up by any pyramid other than Tut's. They hoped that this would not be the last time they or the rest of the world had a chance to behold such beauty.

Balancing the boxes on the hand carts left behind by the others, they looked around the massive room. Even with all they had taken from its stores, indescribable wealth still remained filling gold and jewel-encrusted chests. Figurines of cats and women in gold and ebony sat silent beside ornately carved thrones and vases. This was clearly no woman's burial site or that of a secondary and unimportant family member. Only a pharaoh would have commanded such wealth in the afterlife.

Hoisting first one hand cart and then the other to the surface, the men squinted into the afternoon sun. It was almost time for the kidnapper's call; they would have to hurry to make it back to the compound with such a heavy load. As they struggled under the weight of their burdens, each one again thought about the role he was about to play in negotiating Ashley's safe return and the protection of the treasure.

The ringing of the telephone greeted them as they hurried into the building a little past the appointed hour. Rushing to answer it, Ben puffed, "Amad, here."

"I was afraid you had not returned from the pyramid. I gave you a little extra time knowing how heavy those crates must be," the muffled voice replied.

"So, you have been watching us. Somehow that does not seem quite fair. You know who we are and what we're doing, but we do not know anything about you. We do not even know if Ashley is safe," Ben cajoled, settling into his chair and wiping the sweat of exertion and the dust from the pyramid from his face.

"And that is the way we are going to keep it. As long as you do what I ask, she will remain in my protection. It is not in my plans to harm a woman. She is merely a pawn as are you in my larger plan. Now, you are to bring the crates to the little van parked at the edge of the parking lot. After loading them inside, you are to drive it into Cairo and leave it in the lot of the Empress Hotel. Leave the key in the locked van. We will pick it up at our leisure. Do not arrange to have us followed. Ashley's life depends on your total cooperation. We will return her to you tonight after we verify the contents of the crates and are sure that we are not being followed in any way. Any questions?" The voice stopped, allowing the silence to fill Ben's ears.

"None, except how do I know I can trust you to keep your end of the bargain?" Ben asked.

"The same way I know I can trust you. I believe that we are men of honor," the caller answered and hung up.

As the men worked feverishly to load the van, the kidnapper and his colleagues readied themselves to accept its delivery and expedite Ashley's return. They knew the police would have the van under surveillance from the moment it left the compound until they picked it up. Their hope lay in a successful switch of vehicles that would throw their pursuers off track. When they were in possession of the treasure and safely out of Egypt, they would release the woman. Until then, they had plans to rehearse.

Ashley sat quietly munching on the sandwich one of the men had provided. She had slept surprisingly well due to the sedative her kidnapper had given her. She had eaten a light breakfast of yogurt and fruit, and taken a leisurely shower in the makeshift stall behind the cabin. None of the men had bothered her despite the obvious interest that shone in their eyes every time they looked at her. To them, she was a Western plaything to be traded as the American boys exchange baseball cards and comic books, nothing more. She was not worth giving serious consideration, so they mostly ignored her.

All of them, that is, except the leader, who was painfully aware of her presence. Even in her stillness, he could feel her eyes on him, imagine her lips on his, and breathe in her fragrance. She filled the little room without trying and made it difficult for him to keep his mind on the greater task at hand. He wanted her as he had never desired any woman, Western or Egyptian.

Sending his men out to ready the transfer vehicle, the leader moved his chair closer to Ashley's and sat gazing at her. He was grateful for the handkerchief that covered his face and prevented her from reading his expression. He knew that she would have realized the power she held over him if she had seen it, and he could not afford for anyone to control his destiny. Too much depended on the successful completion of this endeavor to allow a woman to compromise it now. Too many people needed the money he could fetch from the sale of the treasures.

Watching her nibble on her lunch even under the weight of his stare, the leader found it difficult to disguise the feelings he had for her. Her elegance even in the soiled jeans and shirt and her composure in captivity made him want her even more. He longed to take her into his arms and press his lips against hers.

Unable to tolerate her closeness any longer, he stood and crossed the short distance that separated them. Ashley slowly raised her eyes to his as he towered over her. Taking the sandwich from her hand, he untied the rope around her waist that bound her to the chair and pulled her to her feet. Her eyes never left his as he slowly eased his arms around her slender body. Her expression never changed as his hands explored her back and shoulders, easing downward to her curved buttocks before returning to the full, roundness of her breasts. His fingers slowly caressed her nipples as his eyes drank in the wonder of her.

At first Ashley stood rigidly at attention. Externally, she appeared calm and removed, but inside she steamed at the violation of her person. She did not fear him; she hated him. Her only thought was to find a way to pay him back for this insult.

And yet, Ashley could not hate him. Something about this arrogant man was too familiar. She decided to play along with him until she could uncover his identity.

Turning up the bottom of the handkerchief, the bold man lifted her face to his and pressed his mouth against hers. Breathing deeply of her sweet perfume, he sank into the softness of her lips and tasted the tenderness of her kisses. His knees grew weak as desire tingled every nerve of his body.

The smell of him, the touch of his lips, the sweetness of his breath were so familiar and comforting that Ashley was caught off guard. Her determination faded and she melted into his arms as his warmth mingled with the heat in the room. She knew from the feel of his muscular chest and the smell of his body that the masked kidnapper must be Kasim. Rather than being furious with him for frightening her, she clung to his strength and enjoyed their togetherness.

"Kasim!" Ashley whispered as they separated and looked into each other's eyes. "Why? The artifacts belong to everyone. You can't possibly expect to get away with stealing them. You'll get caught or shot. You have to turn yourself in."

With a soft chuckle her kidnapper untied the handkerchief, removed the cap that covered the top of his face, and smiled at the puzzled expression that played across hers. "Not Kasim," he replied, "Omar, his twin brother. He never would have had the courage to pull this off. He is too busy chronicling treasures for the art and history worlds rather than thinking of himself and people who really need the money. Get caught? Me? Never. I have worked out a foolproof plan. If anyone takes the blame

for this, it will be my wonderful, brilliant brother the professor."

Ashley stepped back as if slapped. Standing before her
was an exact copy of Kasim, the man for whom she cared
so deeply, the man whose embrace had confused and upset
her mind.

"Omar? Kasim never mentioned a twin brother," she
sputtered, unable to believe her eyes. Yet there was something in the tilt of his head that was different. Omar really
was the twin and not the man himself. She was relieved to
believe that this man was not the one she had come to
know and trust.

With a shrug Omar returned to his seat before answering
smugly, "I am not surprised. He never does. None of his
snooty colleagues know anything about me. I am the black
sheep of the family, if you will. Everyone has a doctorate
in some lofty high-minded academic field except for me.
They all have 'meaningful' jobs. They are all giving back
to the world, to society. I am the only one still trying to
find myself. They think I have wasted my talents, that I
have not made the most of my opportunities. At least that
is the excuse my parents give for my failure to live up to
their expectations and when they feel sorry for my failures.
I cannot possibly tell them what I do with most of the
money. Well, at least I will be rich when all of this is over.
I will be able to escape from this valley of dust and despair
and make a life for myself somewhere.

"What they have never understood about me is that I
am a free thinker. I refused to be tied down to a nine-to-
five job, to grading papers, to lecturing, to the 'publish
or perish' mentality of academia, and to a boring life of
conformity. Sometimes I think my loudest critics, my father
and uncle, are actually jealous of my lifestyle and wish they
could join me in my freedom, but it is too late for them
to change. At this stage in their lives, they certainly cannot

break loose from the bonds of conventionality. It is I who feel sorry for them.

"And do you know the good part of all this? Since my wonderful, productive brother never mentioned me, everyone will think he and that missing assistant of his named Mohammed are the thieves. No one knows that he has a twin, therefore, no one will suspect his carbon copy of committing the heist. The cops will spend all of their time trying to prove that Kasim and Mohammed stole the treasures. With the exception of a few insignificant papers, I have left no trace of my existence. I will be able to get out of this country without anyone looking for me. Not bad for the black sheep of the family."

Ashley watched as Omar limped to his chair and folded his arms across his chest. Looking at him now, she could see that he really was different from Kasim. Omar had none of Kasim's gentleness and none of his sophistication. Omar might be Kasim's identical twin, but the corners of his mouth did not crinkle in an easy smile; they turned downward in an angry frown. His eyes did not laugh, they burned. His lips, though sensuous like Kasim's, barely disguised the coldness that filled his heart when they smiled a joyless grin. Even the slope of his shoulders was different. Kasim stood proudly and glided when he walked as if mindful of the treasures his world protected, whereas, Omar appeared to dart between the shadows as if always aware of being the hunter.

Yet this man had a certain spark that Kasim did not possess despite his limp. Omar's step was like that of a tiger who prowled the earth as if it belonged to him. His gaze was straight and unwavering. His manner was direct and compelling. He was used to being taken seriously and insisted on being heard. He was dangerous. He was exciting. He sparkled . . . like champagne. Omar was a man with a purpose that was grander than himself. He stole, but he helped others with the money he made from selling the items. Like Robin Hood, his deeds would have been more admirable if he had earned the money himself, but he did more than many who never shared with those less fortunate. Still, Omar knew that no one would have any sympathy for him if he were ever apprehended. No one would see the good he did, only the bad.

"What have you done with Mohammed?" Ashley demanded now that she believed the identity of the man who had boldly taken her into his arms.

"Don't worry. I have not harmed him. I need him too badly for that. No, Mohammed is safely stashed out of the way where no one will find him. He is tied up in an apartment in town out of the way, calmly resting. I will set him free as soon as Ben and Kasim deliver the treasure," Omar replied. With a crooked smile he added, "Funny, is it not . . . I cannot even pull this off without his help. Well, after this, it is no more little brother status for me. All my life I have had to walk in his shadow. Now, at last I will be free. I will have more money than any man or woman could ever spend in one lifetime. I will do work that will give back to the people of Egypt more than the contribution of my poor misguided brother who locks his treasures away in the museum. I will sell them and share the money with the poor."

At that moment, one of his men entered the cabin. Without waiting for Omar to look in his direction, he blurted, "The van is in place. Ben should arrive in about half an hour. We will be watching. I am leaving with the other men and will call you as soon as I spot them."

"I will be waiting. As soon as I hear from you, I will make the call," Omar replied as he returned his attention to his attractive hostage. Again, he thought that it was indeed a shame that he would not have time to get to know her better. His brother certainly had a good eye for treasures, especially women. Like Kasim, Omar could understand their father's love of an African-American woman after meeting this one. Ashley was a real beauty, and she was brave like their mother, who left everything she knew behind her in the States to make a life with their father in Egypt. She had not shown any sign of fear even after discovering his true identity. Ashley would make a great partner for him. Too bad there was no time. Otherwise, he would make Kasim prove that he was the better man. Unfortunately, Omar would have to leave this treasure for his brother.

"What makes you think you can get away with this? Don't you think the police will be looking for you? Eventually they'll believe Kasim or find birth records . . . something," Ashley asked.

"We are from a nomadic family, so there are no birth records. Unlike my brother, I have not left a paper trail of degrees to mark my journey through life. Besides, by the time the law finishes bumbling along at its usual slow pace, I will be long gone," Omar responded confidently. There was little doubt that he had planned his efforts with as much attention to detail as Kasim mapped out their excavation schedules.

"And Kasim and Mohammed will be left holding the bag. Their reputations will be ruined," Ashley retorted angrily.

"I really do not think that will happen. You will be able to convince the authorities that Kasim really does have an evil twin who held Mohammed captive and you for ransom. After all, we have shared some intimate moments. You will be able to tell them some of the less well documented differences. Besides, I will take care of my brother's well-deserved reputation. He will not get hurt. I have a plan that will clear his name and Mohammed's," Omar replied with a smile as he tried to reassure Ashley of his good intentions.

Ashley was not sure how she felt toward this man. Omar might look like Kasim, but he was nothing like him. His arrogant demeanor kept the resemblance from going any further. Ashley knew that when questioned by the police, she would quickly tell them that the man she knew to be Kasim, the coleader of their expedition, in no way resembled this monster. Kasim could never be so cold, calculating, and unfeeling.

Yet, Omar exhibited a spirit that Kasim did not, and Ashley found that fire intriguing. Even when uncovering the grandest of treasures, Kasim remained calm and subdued, as if he were holding his emotions in check. When they embraced, he seemed slightly distant. Ashley had thought it was his conditioned deference to woman that made him hold her slightly away even as the electricity passed between them. Meeting Omar told her that Kasim's reserve was not a cultural difference as she had thought. He was simply a reserved type of person, someone who held himself in check, someone in control of his emotions. She could not help but wonder if he even felt strong passions. Perhaps he had conditioned himself out of feeling or maybe Omar was the twin who listened to his inner self and responded to the voice within him.

Still Ashley could not forgive Omar for what he planned to do. Yes, Omar wanted to do something for people who needed his help. Ashley understood the need for treasures to be protected safely by museums, and sometimes she felt that the money spent would help the poor so much better. Often she thought that some or all of the worth should be used to educate and house those who needed help. However, Ashley could not accept the premise that this modern-day Robin Hood was a virtuous man. He would always be a thief and a kidnapper to her.

Glancing at her watch, Ashley saw that it was now four o'clock. From what she had overheard while Omar made his demands of Ben, she knew that the treasures would be arriving at the drop-off point at any moment. After that, it was simply a matter of time before she would be free. Ashley did not think for a moment that Omar would hurt her. She could tell that, as determined as he was to live outside the confines of the expected norm, he had some sense of honor. All Omar wanted was the money that the treasures could bring him and a chance to experience the benefits of wealth.

"How did you learn so much about the contents of the pyramids?" Ashley asked. Considering the separation between the brothers, she doubted that Kasim had told Omar about their discovery. Much had been written about its potential value in the papers and covered by international television, but Ben had been careful not to disclose any specifics. Someone inside must have shared the information with him.

Stretching and lightly tapping his nails on the telephone, Kasim answered, "Most of the guards are my men. He has been reporting back to me with all the details since the first day your group entered the pyramid. I know everything that has happened to you. He told me about the rock, the winds, and the ants. I even have pictures of the treasures, if you would like to see them. There's nothing I do not know. He made the camel ride look so appealing that you and Sallie could not help but want to experience it. I told you, I am very careful when it comes to making plans. I do not leave anything to chance. I had to have an inside man so that I would not risk my freedom on useless junk. After he reported the great wealth of the dig, I decided to strike. I certainly cannot be of help to myself or anyone who needs the money the treasures will bring if I am in jail, now can I? I had to know what to expect and how to get my hands on it quickly."

"You have photographs? I didn't see anyone with a camera who did not also have a sketchpad. Might I see them?"

"Of course. I am sure you will find them quite informative," Omar replied with a sneer.

Reaching into the saddle bag on the table, Omar produced a large leather portfolio containing a photographic record of the excavation of the pyramid. As Ashley flipped through the photos, she saw captured on them every treasure they had uncovered. Nothing had been missed. No item had been too small. Now she understood how he had been able to make his selection from among the myriad of discovered artifacts when he had not entered the tomb.

Looking more closely, Ashley found that she had not been ignored by the photographer either. She saw herself bending over the overflowing chest, brushing ants from her legs, dusting sand from an ornately gem-studded bracelet, and sitting next to Sallie drawing sketches of the throne. Whoever it was who had taken the photographs had carefully selected shots of her that could make her easy to identify even in a crowd of people. No wonder Omar had been able to kidnap her with such success.

Returning the photographs to him Ashley said, "I suppose your assistant told you when I usually took my exercise and when I planned to go on that camel ride. You certainly were thorough in your work."

"We had hoped to grab you that first time, but we had not counted on your strength and stamina . . . or your bravery. We had hoped the spiders would run you away. The wind turbulence we did not arrange, but I thought the arachnids would be a nice extra touch. You certainly stopped that effort. It was much easier yesterday with you on camel," Omar agreed.

"Your men put the spiders in the tomb to scare us off?

You really will go to any length to get that treasure. Someone could have been bitten. How did you train them to stop at the doorway?" Ashley inquired both furious and fascinated with Omar's determination.

"That did not poise a problem at all for my men. The spiders were not poisonous. The most anyone would have experienced was a rash. A light sprinkling of salt at the entrance stopped them from crossing into the corridor. I knew that no one would see the grains mixed in among the sand. Ingenious do you not think?" Omar answered with a smile.

"So, what's next? How do I figure into your plans now?" Ashley asked growing tired of his confidence.

Although he was as handsome and exotic in his looks as his twin, Omar's arrogance made his presence almost unnerving in its forcefulness. Ashley was anxious to get away from him. If she could only escape, she could warn Ben of his plans.

"I will retie you and make my last phone call to Ben. I am enjoying your company dearly, but the longer I stay here, the greater the chance for discovery. It is time to pick up the van and return you to him," Omar replied as he tightly wound the rope around her wrists and the chair. At least for the moment, Ashley had to put aside any thought of escape.

Dialing the number he knew by heart, Omar gazed almost tenderly at Ashley. He would miss her company. If only the time and place were different . . . but they were not. He could not afford emotional involvement now. Nothing must stand in his way.

"Ben," Omar said into the phone. "It does my heart good to know that you were sitting there waiting for my call. I am glad to know the van has been delivered. Now, if you have followed my instructions and loaded it properly, we'll make the switch. If you have not, Ashley will be lost

forever. Some of the desert nomad groups would love to
have a slave to do their menial labor for them. An English
speaking one would be most helpful. This will be my last
call to you. If all goes according to my plan as I outlined
it to you, she will be back in the arms of the men who love
her by midnight.''

As he hung up, Omar took one last look at Ashley and
walked out of the room. He had pushed all thoughts of
romance out of his mind. All that mattered to him now
was a successful mission and escape . . . at least for the
moment. There would be time enough for the pleasure
of a woman's company when he had the treasures safely
tucked away. Decoding this woman's brave front would
take time that Omar, unfortunately, did not have at present. Omar knew instinctively that if he put his plans on
hold for even one extra day, he would not be able to escape
the trap that Ashley's luminous eyes, soft skin, gentle voice,
tender lips, and sensuous body would offer him. Omar
could tell that he would have no trouble losing himself
and his purpose in her arms forever.

Ben and Kasim looked at each other as the phone line
once again went silent. All they could do now was hope
that the kidnapper was an honorable man in his own way.
They had kept their part of the bargain by parking a van
filled with the required treasures in the designated spot.
They had to trust that he would soon release Ashley. All
anyone could do at this point was to wait until the thieves
made their next move.

CHAPTER SEVEN

As Ben and Kasim nervously paced the office, Kasim's voice came in a near whisper from the strain that filled his heart as he asked, "Where's Mohammed? I thought you said he'd return shortly, but we haven't seen him all day."

"I know and I'm quite concerned. It is not like him to stay away this long. He is never out of touch for more than a few hours. He did say, however, that he had to attend a meeting at the university. Perhaps he has been detained," Ben replied, stroking his chin.

"Do you think he could be involved in Ashley's kidnapping?" Kasim asked, giving voice to a thought that had plagued him since her disappearance.

"Never. He would never do anything to bring shame and dishonor on his family. Mohammed is too dedicated to the search for antiquities to ruin his reputation with something like this," Ben said, bristling at the thought that his colleague could be implicated in this sordid affair.

"That is an awful lot of treasure. Any person would be

tempted to pocket a few trinkets with so much unrecorded wealth lying about. Historians and archaeologists do not exactly make huge salaries, unless you are holding out on me," Kasim continued, ignoring the stiffening of Ben's back.

"I was not aware that you were engaged in this line of work for the money, Kasim. I will forgive this outburst knowing that you are concerned for the woman's safety. But, we have known and worked with Mohammed for a long time, and we know he is beyond suspicion. I am confident that he will have a good accounting for his time," Ben responded, firmly hoping to end the conversation.

With that, Kasim changed his line of questioning since he did not want to anger Ben further by inferring that their colleague would do anything dishonest. Kasim remembered that Mohammed had been a friend of Ben's since their university days together. Continuing, Kasim said, "I am terribly sorry that I impugned Mohammed's character, but everyone does have his price. There have been highly placed government officials who had been persuaded by just the right offer to divulge security secrets. I am not saying that Mohammed would bend under pressure, but he might be experiencing unknown financial difficulty that would cause him to do something quite out of the ordinary."

Ben took a deep breath before answering and then responded very deliberately, saying, "That is your American side talking. I will forgive your inherent skepticism and mistrust of your fellow man. I would never swear to the loyalty of another without first walking in that man's shoes, but I sincerely hope that I have not misjudged Mohammed all these years. I have only known him to be above reproach in all of his dealings. I think, for the time being at least, we should cease any further speculation as to his whereabouts and his guilt or innocence in this matter. Our most important task is Ashley's safe return followed by the retrieval of the ransomed jewels. We will think about Mohammed later.''

"Very well," Kasim conceded. "What is our next move? I cannot just sit here doing nothing until something happens. I have to help get Ashley back."

"The police are in control of the situation. Unfortunately, there is nothing we can do right now. We know that our actions are being watched by the kidnapper as closely as his van is being monitored by the police. The only thing we can do now is sit tight until we get the call that she has been released," Ben responded with resignation.

Rising and thrusting his hands deep into his pockets, Kasim responded, "At least I can take a walk around the perimeter of the compound. This endless sitting and waiting is getting on my nerves."

Ben's eyes followed him out the door. "Youth!" he muttered to himself, pouring another cup of coffee. He was not content to wait either, but there was nothing else he could do.

Kasim needed the stroll around the grounds to clear his head. He had been cooped up in the building for far too long. He had sat staring at the telephone, the lifeline to Ashley, for as long as he could. He needed some time alone to think, and he needed to be away from Ben's watchful eyes. Kasim knew that the tired man could only do what his superiors at the university and the police instructed, but that knowledge did not contain the irritation and anxiety brought on by Kasim's need to do something to bring Ashley back.

Not seeing any guards along his route, Kasim became bold and decided to venture out of the compound. As he walked through the tourist-filled parking lot, adjacent to the Great Pyramid, a flicker of a plan darted through Kasim's mind. Mingling among the throng of visitors, he was all but invisible from the watchful eyes of the men who held Ashley captive. Being no taller or fatter than the others and dressed in robes identical to those of the guides and the local Egyptian vendors, Kasim could blend into the mob scene at the pyramid entrances, the kiosks, and the camel rides without drawing anyone's attention. If someone did single him out for inspection, he would only appear to be another Egyptian mixed in with the crowd.

Immediately, Kasim knew what he had to do and headed toward the camel rental sign. He would ride at the back of a Western tour group as if he were one of their guides. When they reached a village at about the distance Sallie had mentioned, he would then drop away from them and explore it. If it turned out to be the wrong one, Kasim would resume his travels alone, maybe even follow at a respectable distance behind them. Kasim was aware of the danger in entering the little settlements; many of the people feared and hated outsiders and people from Cairo. He hoped that the influence of his father's genes in his face would at least buy him enough time to look around and get out unharmed. He was happy that he had inherited his father's Egyptian features rather than his mother's lighter brown hair and eyes. At this point, his own safety did not mean as much to him as freeing Ashley from her captors.

Taking his place among the guides and climbing atop the resting camel, Kasim waited for the leader to give the instructions for the animals to rise. Casually looking around, he did not see anyone who looked especially intent on watching him although he realized that they would try not to make their presence known. Not one head turned, and no one tried to detain him.

As the animal began its lumbering walk into the desert, Kasim took a deep breath. So far his impromptu plan was working. He tried to find a comfortable position in the hard rocking saddle with its coarse, scratchy blanket. Work-

ing in the city at the university, Kasim seldom ventured
into the desert on camelback. The lumbering gait
reminded him of his childhood and the trips he took with
his family to different oases.

Scanning the sandy, flat horizon for a spot he thought
might fit Sallie's description of a village about an hour's
ride from the pyramids, Kasim tried to compose his
thoughts. Now that he had put the first part of his plan into
action, he needed a second step. Kasim had not considered
what he, an unarmed man, would do if he found Ashley
and her kidnapper. He would need to figure out a way to
overpower him.

If Kasim had not been so tense, he would have found
the gentle swaying and the monotonous landscape quite
relaxing. He might even have dozed off in the warm sun
as several of his companions had done. Even those who
managed to stay awake were now silent as they marveled
at the splendor of the ancient desert.

Approaching the first little village, Kasim noted how easy
it would be for him to part company with the others. Even
the leader would not notice him as he snoozed at the head
of the line. His only concern was whether the camel would
heed his instruction since it was so accustomed to following
the others. Kasim was not sure that the animal would willingly break from its pack.

With the entrance to the village in sight, Kasim nudged
his ride to veer off in its direction. At first the beast ignored
him and appeared to be walking in its sleep. Giving it a
sounder kick in the side and a harder pull on the reins,
he turned its head to the right and applied steady pressure
to its left side as he would have to a horse in order to
change its direction. Slowly and reluctantly the animal
obeyed and the gap between Kasim and the next man
increased until he finally rode alone.

As he approached the small cluster of makeshift houses,

Kasim knew instinctively that Ashley was not among the
poor men, women, and children who squatted on the
ground cooking over fires of pungent smelling stews. Their
eyes searched his face without either curiosity or malice
as he approached. Even the young men in the village
looked at him with only the slightest interest. They were
too tired and poor to concern themselves with a stranger
when their bellies cried out for food.

From where he sat atop his camel, Kasim could see into
each one of the four open huts. They were very small and
furnished with nothing more than cots, a table, and a few
stools. These were not the headquarters of a kidnapper
and his men. No cars or vans littered the open spaces
between houses, just an occasional clothes line and some
scrawny chickens scratching in vain at the sand in search
for a bug to eat.

Turning his mount around, Kasim headed out of the
village and back to the vanishing tracks of his companions
who were now far ahead of him. He did not rush to catch
up but allowed the camel to set its own pace. As it lumbered
along, Kasim searched for signs of yet another village. Sallie
had been wrong once about the distance and she might
be again. He wondered on how many other false turns her
memory would lead him before he found Ashley. With a
shudder Kasim pushed from his mind the thought that he
might never find her in the endless sand and heat of the
desert.

Entering another village, Kasim again felt his hopes of
quickly freeing Ashley slip from his fingers. This time
instead of being greeted by indifference, he found open
hostility. The young men brandished their rifles and the
children threw stones and spat at him. Even the women
rejected him as they shouted curses at him as an intruder
into the privacy of their village. He tried to explain that
he was Egyptian and on an important mission, but they

would not listen. His perfect speech and prosperous appearance further alienated them. Undaunted, Kasim peered into their homes as he warily rode down the main and only street around which the ten cabins were arranged. Still there was no sign of modern communications equipment or vehicles. Giving up amid the hail of rocks, Kasim nudged his camel into a run and quickly departed, leaving them to wave their fists at his retreating back.

As his camel settled into its customary unhurried gait, Kasim began to wonder if he would be able to find Ashley. Sallie had been badly shaken by the kidnapping experience and might have failed to notice the landmarks and the sounds correctly. She might have been confused in her concern for her own safety and that of her friend. After two unsuccessful attempts, Kasim could understand why the police had been so reluctant to trust her memory.

Nearing another town, Kasim knew he had to try again. Even if he uncovered nothing, Kasim could not return to the expedition site and simply wait for a call. He had to do something to get Ashley back.

Pointing the camel in the direction of the rows of cabins, Kasim was surprised to find that several did not have the usual run-down appearance he had come to recognize as typical of the desert. The three newer looking buildings stood out among the others, and appeared out of place amid the weather-worn structures that surrounded them. Their wood plank sides and freshly shingled roofs did not match the appearance of the sun-bleached, weathered cabins. Equally improbably in this setting were the Mercedes and the van that sat partially obscured by the torn blankets, straw, and assorted rags that someone had piled on them as camouflage.

Kasim rode unnoticed down the deserted streets. Every nerve in his body was alert to the slightest movement at the windows and doors as he passed the dilapidated cabins.

Children whispered and peeked out the open doors before their mothers silently pulled them back and scolded them with silent hand motions. No one ventured out, no one greeted him, and no one seemed to want to know anything about the stranger among them.

Passing one of the newer houses, Kasim thought he saw a slight movement behind the soaped window. A shadow passed behind the impenetrable screen so quickly that he almost doubted that he had seen the motion at all. Yet, Kasim knew that his presence had not gone unnoticed. Someone inside this one cabin wanted to know more about him.

Easing his camel into the resting position, Kasim dismounted and walked the short distance up to the larger of the new cabins along a sandy path that led from the unpaved road to the wood-slat porch. As he carefully picked his way through the rocks and litter in the front yard, the toe of his shoe caught in something, causing him to stumble. Righting himself and brushing off the dust that clung to his robe, Kasim carefully dug into the sand to uncover a brush. Lifting it into the sun, he examined it and discovered that it was the same one that Ashley always used. He could read the last traces of her name on the handle Kasim now knew with certainty that she was nearby.

Shoving it into his pocket, Kasim knocked on the door without taking his eyes from the windows. When no one answered, he tried the knob only to find it locked. Walking to the window, he tried to peer through the thick coating of soap, but he could see and hear nothing. With a casual shrug of his shoulders, he walked away trying to make it look as if he were a lost tourist only looking for directions.

Remounting his camel, Kasim slowly and deliberately retraced his path out of town. He did not want to appear in a hurry, but his mind was quickly noting everything along the way. He knew he had stumbled onto something important. The silence of the town and the deserted appearance of the new cabins spoke loudly of something sinister in their midst.

Kasim stopped about a half mile out of town. Before he could return to the expedition site and the police, he knew he had to have more proof than a well-worn brush that could have been picked up by any number of children and carelessly discarded. He needed proof that something was amiss in the cabin. But for that, he would have to see inside.

Quickly walking back in the warm sun, Kasim sneaked into the village using a footpath down the road from the new cabins. As he approached from their windowless side, he moved stealthily through the silent sand. He could not afford to disturb anything or frighten the people inside with his approach.

Easing up to the building, Kasim pressed himself almost flat against its wall. Moving almost without breathing as the perspiration glistened on his face and ran down his neck, Kasim approached as if on cat feet. His breath barely flowed through his parted lips as he struggled with his natural desire to throw himself against the door.

As he stepped onto the small porch, the door opened wide. "May I help you, sir?" asked the man in a flowing white robe very similar to his own.

"I am afraid that my camel has thrown me. I remembered seeing a car here when I rode through the town. I was hoping I could obtain a ride back to the Great Pyramid from someone," Kasim responded.

Looking him over the man replied, "I am terribly sorry, but we have no car. We have only a poor horse. We are not wealthy people here, sir, only teachers and trades people. Maybe one of the trades people would give you a ride if they are going that way, but petrol is very expensive, you know."

"No, thank you, but that will not be necessary. I'm sure the animal will return shortly. I will simply sit and wait for it. However, I could have sworn that I saw a car parked behind the house when I rode through here earlier. I am terribly sorry to have bothered you. I must have been mistaken," Kasim answered as he eased his way down the path and away from the house. From the man's demeanor and his tightly folded arms, Kasim could tell that his presence was definitely not wanted. A slight bulge under the man's left arm as if a holster rested there showed through the fabric of his gown.

Looking behind him, Kasim saw that the place where the car and the van had occupied was now empty. Only the rags and the brush remained as reminders that the vehicles had once been parked there. Tire tracks left behind in the sand had been hastily covered over by a broom, yet he could still make out the faint squiggly tire treads.

As Kasim began his walk back to where he had left his camel, he had the strangest feeling that someone was watching him. With each step, a new piece of discovery fell into place. Suddenly, he realized that the man had appeared even before he had time to knock at the door, almost as if someone had ridden ahead of him to inform the man that he was coming or leaked information from the expedition.

Hurrying along, Kasim told himself that he had to reach Ben and the police as quickly as possible. He knew in his heart that Ashley was inside that house. The man, dressed so out of keeping with the rest of the poverty of the village, had become suspicious of him when he first rode through the village and had suspected that he would return. Kasim was frightened at the prospects of what the man might do next if Ashley were still in his care.

Finally reaching his sleeping camel, Kasim coaxed the reluctant beast into a trot. Covering the distance between the cabins and the archaeological dig in half the time it had taken him to make the outbound journey, Kasim's heart pounded in his chest with each tooth-rattling thump of the animal's hooves. Entering the area of the pyramids at a run, Kasim was surprised to see many police and security people rushing around in great excitement. Wiping his sweaty brow with his handkerchief, he entered the building to find Ben and Mohammed in a serious discussion. Standing over them was the police captain and his secretary, who scribbled furiously to write down all that the man said.

Looking up as Kasim entered, Ben gestured for him to take a seat, saying, "While you were away, Mohammed joined us. It appears that he has just escaped from where he was being held captive by the same people who have kidnapped Ashley."

Looking at Mohammed's battered face, Kasim eased into the chair and said, "You are a very lucky man. I just left a village in which I believe I have located the house where the kidnapper is holding Ashley. Do you have any idea who he is?"

Looking first at the floor and then at Kasim, Mohammed replied softly, "I have some very unfortunate information for you, my friend. The kidnapper is your brother Omar. I have seen him with my own eyes and spoken to him. I have no doubt about his identity."

"That is not possible. I thought he was in Europe somewhere. The last time I heard from him, Omar was lounging by a pool on the French Riviera. Besides, you have never seen him. I have kept his identity far from my professional life and have seldom spoken of him," Kasim replied with great sorrow and anger.

"It is Omar alright. The man is your identical twin. The only difference between you is the limp. I have seen it and I know the man to be Omar," Mohammed rebutted softly.

Seeing Kasim's agony, Ben added, "Omar had Mohammed bound and gagged in an empty apartment in Cairo until about an hour ago. Mohammed came here as soon as he broke free." He could see that worry and fear for Ashley and the shame of his brother's deeds had reduced Kasim to a tightly wound coil.

Kasim could hardly believe his ears and certainly not his eyes as he stared at Mohammed. But the man was proof of his brother's disrespect for their family name. Mohammed sat beside him with dirt and dried blood on his face and rope burns on his wrists and ankles.

"It is amazing that despite all my best efforts, Omar has appeared to torment me. He always was the rebel of the family. He inherited none of our mother's love of order and decorum. Instead, all he ever wanted was to wander the world with his belongings on his back. I suppose now he wants to travel in style. I am sure that you are right and that the man was my brother. We are indeed identical except for the limp he still carries from a riding accident," Kasim muttered, sinking deeper into the chair.

"It is more than that; it is astounding. I have known Kasim all these years and only met his brother on one occasion. If I remember correctly, you rushed him out of the university as quickly as you could so that no one would see him. I would not have either if I had not been in your office at the time of his visit. And to think that he held Mohammed captive and appears to have Ashley," Ben added. He, too, was suffering from the impact of discovering that Kasim's twin could be engaged in the kidnapping and theft of priceless treasures.

Walking toward the stunned police officer, Kasim directed, "We must not let my kinship with the kidnapper interfere with the investigation. Ashley's life is at stake. We will continue along the prescribed course of action regardless of the consequences to my career. The only thing of importance at this time is safely freeing her from Omar's grasp."

Nodding in agreement at Kasim's bravery, the officer replied, "I understand and will keep you informed of our investigation. However, I am afraid that there is little we can do until your brother contacts us. I will dispatch someone to the village, but I can do little else for fear that Omar will harm the woman."

Placing his hand on Kasim's shoulder, Ben said, "He is right. Omar is in control now and there is nothing we can do."

While the men at the expedition cite waited for the call and pondered their next move, Ashley watched Omar pace the floor of the small cabin. His limp grew more pronounced as fatigue and stress weighed heavily on his shoulders. The muscles of his broad shoulders flexed against his robes with each step he took. His fists clenched and opened repeatedly under the strain of his thoughts. His eyes darted restlessly with the need for action.

From his man's reaction to seeing Kasim at the door, Omar knew that they had to move quickly. He did not for a minute think that his brother had accidentally stumbled upon his location. Now that the hideout had been discovered, they had to abandon it before the police heard Kasim's story and came hunting for them.

Turning to Ashley, Omar shook his head as he approached the chair where she sat muzzled and bound. She did not struggle; she had already tried all the ropes while Omar was eavesdropping on the conversation between his man and Kasim and had found them securely tied. There was nothing Ashley could do except wait until Omar made his next move or heard from his men who were watching the expedition site. From her calculations, Ashley assumed it was almost time to trade her life for the treasures. She needed to conserve her strength in case the opportunity to run away appeared.

Ashley had spent a great deal of time studying Omar, too. He was always thinking and planning, never patient and relaxed. His mind always seemed occupied with the task of solving an unspoken puzzle. From the quick restlessness of his stride, she could tell that he was a man who enjoyed being constantly on the move. He would not be content to remain in one place for long.

"Well, Ashley, if my man was correct and our visitor was my brother, Kasim, we must get under way immediately. I am not going to wait for him to lead Ben and the police to us. We are leaving now," Omar said through clenched teeth as he freed her from the chair and removed the gag. "Remember that I will be right behind you. Please do not try to run away. One of my men has pulled the van around front and will be watching it at all times. Besides, the desert can be very unfriendly to those who do not know her. We will climb into the back together. After you are safely tucked inside, we will drive away from our little cabin. I have come this far; nothing is going to stop me from finishing this transaction. Not my well-intentioned brother, not Ben, and not the police. Get up, please. It is time for us to leave. My only regret is that I did not have time to get to know you better. Under different circumstances, I could have encouraged you to join our little band."

Rubbing her wrists, Ashley allowed Omar to guide her toward the door. All the time she had been held captive, she had tried to formulate an escape plan for just this moment. Now, with the weight of his hand on her shoulder, she knew that this was not the moment. With patience, the right one would present itself.

The interior of the van was hot and smelled of stale cigars and cigarettes. Ashley did not relish the idea of spending any time in this foul vehicle with Omar's equally offensive men. She hoped that the kindness he had shown toward her would be her shield. Omar had kept the other men away from her when they looked at her with disrespect in their eyes. Omar had been willing to fight to protect her from him. He had drawn a sinister looking knife and placed himself between Ashley and the man. She had watched as the two men squared off. Her heart pounded in her chest, knowing that if the other man won, she would be his prize. Omar was all that had stood between her and humiliation and rape. The expression on his face convinced the other man that Omar meant business, forcing him to back down and leave the cabin.

After that, Omar had not left her side for even a moment. Ashley had not been sure if he was protecting his possession or if the warmth she saw reflected in his eyes came from a genuine concern for her welfare. Considering the alternative was to align herself with the men who called him their leader, she decided not to question his intentions and simply accept them. Besides, she could not fight for her safety against his men while she struggled with her emotions against him.

As the van moved out of the sleepy village and headed in the direction of Cairo, Ashley tried to peer through the curtained back windows. Nothing but desert greeted her straining eyes. Giving up, she settled into the tattered seat and tried to make herself comfortable as the van bumped over the poorly maintained road. She would have to wait for the opportunity to escape.

The heat and the stuffiness lulled Ashley to sleep as the

hum of the road infiltrated the van. Leaning her head
against the dirty seat cover, she allowed her eyes to close.
As usual, images of her phantom man filled her dreams.
The desert, Cairo, and the kidnappers were far away as
she dreamed of being on the beach with him.

Ashley could feel his strong arms around her as he pulled
her against his broad chest. His fingers tangled in her hair,
pulling her face back, lifting her lips to his. His mouth
pressed against hers as she gave herself up to his caresses.
Her hands tightened on the swell of his shoulders and
hungrily played in his hair. She welcomed his tongue as
it darted around hers, sending chills down to her toes and
warming her insides. Her hot fingers burned the tips of
his ears and the nape of his neck, making him moan with
desire.

As they sank onto the hot sand, their bodies intertwined,
and the gentle breeze fanned their moist skin. Gently blowing the dust from her skin with feather-light kisses, the
man buried his mouth in the soft space between her
breasts. Freeing them from the confinement of the bikini
top, his teeth and tongue teased the tender nipples until
they stood erect. His hands burned along the length of
her thigh as he searched for her tender recesses. Finding
the bikini strings, he unwrapped the precious package she
offered him. Then he tugged off his trunks freeing his
manhood to stand erect and ready.

Ashley moaned softly as his hands tantalized her body
and cupped the pulsating wetness between her legs. She
eagerly reached for him and pulled the phantom's weight
over her until he filled her emptiness. Arching her body
to meet his, she moved in rhythm with his thrusts and
drove toward the rapture that would soon overtake them
both. As their perspiration mingled with the salty spray
from the sea, they clung to each other and rode their own
tide of emotion and release.

Lying spent on their sandy bed, Ashley snuggled into the sexy warmth of his body. His arms circled around her as protection from the wind, blowing sand, and prying eyes. All was calm and tranquil in their world as they dozed on their deserted stretch of sand.

In her dream as Ashley turned on her side to smile into her lover's tranquil face, she discovered that that of Omar had replaced his face. His dark laughing eyes appeared to delight in her confusion as she struggled to free herself from his arms. The laughter rose from deep in his throat as she hastened to a sitting position covering her nakedness with her hands and quickly pulling her abandoned clothing around her.

"It is a little late to cover up now, do you not think?" Omar asked with a sultry grin as he folded his arms behind his head. His manhood signaled that the sight of Ashley's naked body had aroused his passion . . . again. Before she could answer or run away, his hot kisses burned into her flesh.

At first, she struggled against him, detesting the closeness of his body and the yielding of her own. Soon, however, she found that her will power began to dissolve as his tongue traced a path down her stomach to the areas beyond. Her eyes fluttered closed as his tongue tasted her sweetness. Ashley shuddered and moaned as the warmth spread throughout her body. Pulling him close, she called his name, begging him to release her from the passion he had awakened in her.

Just as he was about to pull her into his arms, the van pulled to a stop and jarred Ashley from her dreams. She could hear Omar's voice in the distance but could not make out any of his words. She sat erect as she listened, hoping to catch a sound that would tell her where they were. Ashley was instantly embarrassed that her thoughts had betrayed her in such a vivid manner. She hoped that he would not be able to read her responses on her face. She had thought he meant to take her to Cairo, but, after falling asleep, she could not be sure of his direction. He might have doubled back, driven farther into the desert, or taken the main highway to Aswan.

As the door opened and Omar climbed into the back with her, Ashley heard the familiar sounds of Egyptian music and the honking of horns. Relieved, she knew they were in a large city and judging from the lack of stiffness in her body, she was fairly sure that they had not traveled far. From the contented expression on his face and the overall relaxed posture, she decided that they had reached Cairo without their movements being detected.

"Okay, my dear, it is time to get out. It looks as if we have outsmarted old Ben and your friend. With any luck at all, this enterprise will still prove profitable to both of us. Let us go, please. I am sure you will feel more comfortable inside this apartment than in the back of this hot van," Omar stated as he unbound her feet so that she could walk with him into the building. He slipped the kind of dark glasses worn by the blind over her eyes as he untied her hands and helped her leave the vehicle.

"Just in case," Omar added. "I cannot have you recognizing anything around here, and I do not want anyone to ask any questions. Anyone seeing us together will think that you are simply a beautiful blind woman in my care. Remember, your safe return is in your hands. Please make sure that you follow my instructions precisely."

They strolled through the busy lobby to the elevator with Omar holding firmly onto Ashley's elbow. Although she could not see through the glasses with their black lenses and wrap-around sides, she could hear the voices of the people they passed. No one spoke to them, although she sensed that many people looked in their direction. They rode up a few flights alone and walked down the empty, silent hall on their way to the apartment. No distinguishing sounds or smells greeted her, and no one approached them. With so little to use as clues to her whereabouts, Ashley could have been in any large city in Egypt.

Even the apartment smelled of nothing in particular—just the aroma of fresh paint mingled with that of a thousand meals. Omar guided Ashley to the chair in the middle of the room, securely tied her hands and feet, and removed the glasses. Gazing around, Ashley could see that there were only two other chairs, a couple of sleeping bags, and a telephone on a little three-legged table in the large living room. She guessed that there was probably no other furniture in any of the adjoining rooms either. The apartment did not contain anything that would indicate anything about the personality of the person who rented it.

As if reading her mind, Omar pulled up one of the chairs and sat down opposite her. Taking a deep breath, he folded his arms across the back of the chair and explained the reason for their move to this particular location with an edge of irritation in his voice. He spoke saying, "No one lives here. There is no connection between this place and me or any of my men. We only recently rented it for the purpose of holding you here until the treasures could be transferred to us. When the transaction is completed, we will call the apartment's manager and tell him that you are tied up here. He will be a hero when he finds the American amateur archaeologist and teacher. The papers will rave about him when he sets you free. He will probably become a national icon for his role in international relations. Good idea, do you not think? Anyway, the call from my men should be coming in soon. My brother's bumbling onto our hiding place only forced me to put our plan into action sooner. He did not upset anything. I regret that he found you so soon. He deprived us of our opportunity to become better acquainted. I had hoped for more time with you.''

As they sat looking into each other's eyes, Ashley could feel the tension building between them. This man was so like his twin brother but in many ways very different. Staring into the sultry half-closed eyes, she saw the single-minded determination that drove Omar. Kasim's expression was far more gentle and almost playful. Omar's eyes exuded the will to possess everything in his path. Right now, he had decided to make her the center of his attentions.

''When this is all over, I will vanish into the masses of people who fill Cairo,'' Omar continued. ''I will become a memory of your eventful excursion into the Egyptian desert. You thought you had come to unearth ancient treasures, but instead you have discovered Robin Hood. After you finish telling the police and friends about me, I will fade from your mind in the same way old photographs lose their impact after a while. You will remember that you knew me, but you will no longer feel the sensation of our encounter. That is, unless you have decided that you would rather have a life with me than with my brother. Do not look so surprised. I have known for quite some time how infatuated with you he has been, and I think you have had feelings for him. Ashley, put him out of your mind and come with me. I will show you a good time. We will travel, help people, and live like kings.''

''We'll live on the run, you mean. No, Omar, there's no way I'd go with you. Kasim is a good and honest man. He deserves better than my defection. It is not possible for me to leave him for the life you offer. Besides, I can't be the partner of a pirate even if his intentions are praiseworthy. The money you make by selling the treasures helps people, but the antiquities don't belong to you any more than the Sheriff of Notingham's money belonged to Robin Hood. I'm not Maid Marion. I need security in my life.

Moving all over Europe from one hotel or villa to the other in the fear that someone will find us is not my idea of a life. Sorry, this is one adventure I'll pass up. I wouldn't think of abandoning Kasim that way. He rode out to the cabin to find me, risking his own life and safety for me. He's probably beside himself with worry right now," Ashley responded. Although Omar was certainly exciting in his own way, nothing he said or did would ever convince her to give up her peaceful, predictable life for his life of crime. Also, she admired Kasim too much to run away with his twin brother without a word of explanation.

Shrugging his broad shoulders Omar replied, "Life for us will not be difficult. With the money I will have from selling the artifacts, we will be able to live exactly as we please. Our days will be fun and filled with adventure. We will travel to places most people only dream of seeing. We will tour the palaces of kings, eat in the restaurants of the greatest chefs in the world, and frequent the opening nights of opera and theater dressed in black tie and riding in chauffeured limousines. There are countries and people who will never ask about my origins and would never think of looking at the wanted posters hanging in post offices and government buildings. But you must follow your own heart. I would not think of forcing you to betray your conscience. If you change your mind between now and the time that I must leave you, you have only to say the word and I will take you with me. I would love to have you beside me in everything I do. We could have such times together. I would make you forget all about Kasim. I know that something already exists between us. I can feel the tension in your body every time I come near you. When you moan in your sleep, it is not good old reliable Kasim who disturbs your dreams."

Stiffly, Ashley replied, "Perhaps it is not Kasim, but it is not you either. I could never find a thief like you attractive.

You might look like Kasim on the outside, but your soul is dark and twisted."

"That is exactly what you might find appealing, if you would only give me the chance," Omar smirked.

Before Ashley could answer, the telephone in the corner rang, stopping any further conversation. Rising quickly Omar covered the distance in two long strides. "Yes?" he answered without taking his eyes from her face. "Good. we will meet as planned."

Hanging up, Omar asked one last time, "The time has come sooner than I had imagined. Will you come with me? You will not regret it, I promise."

"No, I can't. Thank you for asking me. I'm not that adventurous. I'm more the white picket fence type," Ashley responded with sarcasm in her voice.

"Too bad," Omar said with an almost sad shake of his head as he replaced the gag in Ashley's mouth. "We would have been so good together. Very well, I am off. The building manager will find you shortly. I regret having to tape your beautiful mouth, but, sadly, it is necessary. I believe that you would not betray me, yet, I must keep up appearances. Have no fear, you will not be uncomfortable for long. I hope to see you again before you leave Egypt, Ashley. Do not worry if you do not recognize me. I do not expect you to greet me."

As if driven by a force greater than himself, Omar strode across the room. He untied Ashley's hands and pulled her into his arms. Lifting her lips to his, he covered her mouth with his. His hands hungrily explored her body as if to memorize every curve. His breath came in hard gasps as her fingers intertwined in his curls and held him fast. All thoughts of anyone or anything left them. For a moment, Omar put aside his plans of wealth and infamy and thought only of her.

"You are a villain and nothing like your brother," Ashley spat angrily.

"This is a fine time for you to mention the obvious," Omar chuckled as he released Ashley's slender frame and stepped back. Gently, he eased her back into the chair and retied her hands. Their eyes never left each other's faces. For the moment, they were locked in silent combat.

A horn sounded impatiently outside in the street below the window. Looking into her upturned face, Omar put his thoughts to words. "Some other time, some other place," he whispered.

"Not in your lifetime," Ashley replied through clenched teeth.

With that, he quickly bound her feet and loosely applied the tape to her kiss-swollen lips. Turning, he opened the closet door and snatched up a single well-worn, ordinary looking duffel bag. Throwing it over his shoulder and without a backward glance, Omar strode out of the apartment, locking the door behind him.

The click of the latch sounded like the closing of a prison door to Ashley's ears as she wondered if the manager would find her and if she would ever be free again. She listened as the retreating sound of Omar's sandals grew fainter and fainter. She doubted that any intercontinental police force regardless of its ability would find him either. His theft of the ancient treasures would go down in the annals of history as one of the greatest heists and probably win a spot beside the great train robbery in England.

CHAPTER EIGHT

Omar had been right . . . Ashley was not alone in the empty room for long before she heard the jangling of keys at the door, the pounding of fists, and the sound of rapid, angry voices. Rushing into the apartment with their weapons drawn, the police quickly searched for signs of Omar and then returned to untie her.

As they freed her from the uncomfortable seat, the officers asked if he had given any indication as to his next move. From their line of questioning, she could tell that he had given them the slip at the van, too. "No, he was careful to say nothing that would give me any indication of his plans. Is Mohammed safe? Did Omar release him? I've been very worried that something might have happened to him," Ashley replied as she wiggled free. She had no way to know that Mohammed had joined Kasim and Ben in their efforts to find her. She hoped that Omar would keep his word and clear Kasim's name and reputation from any connection with the kidnapping and the theft.

"You don't need to worry. He escaped and his identification of the man is what helped lead us to you. His brother, Kasim, did his part, too," the officer responded.

Rubbing her stiff wrists, Ashley listened to the police officers' conversation as they discussed Omar's flight from justice with their commanding officer at headquarters. She wondered what plans Omar had in mind that would help him continue to slip through their fingers.

When they had finished, one of them turned to her and said, "We will take you back to the pyramids now. There is nothing more we can do here. That bugger took everything that might have proven to be evidence against him. The chair and the rope will not do us any good; they are both too rough to hold fingerprints. From the looks of them, I would say they were handmade, probably in the desert somewhere, so there is no way to trace them. He is a crafty one for sure, but, rest assured, we will catch him."

The ride to the camp site through the crowded streets was noisy but wonderful. Ashley peered at every man along the way and wondered if he were Omar. He could not have gone far in such a short time and in the teeming traffic of Cairo. He was probably still in the city, watching and laughing as the authorities tried to track him down.

Kasim and Sallie greeted her as the police car pulled up to the compound's door. She ran to his arms as soon as the car rolled to a stop. Ashley could feel the tension fade from his body as he held her. She stole away from him only long enough to hug her friend Sallie, who stood anxiously waiting to greet her. Tears of happiness at their reunion flooded her cheeks. Sallie had thought she would never see Ashley again.

Reaching into his pocket, Kasim pulled out the brush. "You dropped this," he said handing it to her. "I found it in the sand in front of the cabin where Omar held you captive."

"Yes," Ashley replied almost dreamily as she stuffed the brush back into her back pocket, "I hoped someone might come looking for us. I wanted to leave a clue that Sallie and I were inside, but I didn't want it to be something that Omar's men might think of as a deliberate attempt to alert the police. I guess it worked."

"Then you should keep it as a reminder of the gift the heavens have given you and me. I will never let you out of my sight again," Kasim replied as he led her inside.

Everyone in the compound expressed relief at her return as Ashley walked toward the dining area and office. She needed to see Mohammed and to know that Omar had kept his word about freeing him. She found Mohammed sitting at the table with Ben going over the transcript of his interview with the police.

Mohammed stopped reading as she approached. Rising, he bowed from the waist and said, "I hope that your ordeal has not been too dreadful. As for my own, I can only say that I am most grateful to be free and among friends."

"I am so happy to know that you are safe, too. Although Omar did not hurt me, I do not want to experience a kidnapping again," Ashley commented.

Standing beside her, Kasim said with sadness in his voice, "I am glad my brother did not hurt either of you. Omar is not always the most considerate of people. I hope that he has not changed your mind about my people or my family. My brother is very impulsive and hot-headed. Rather than working for what he wants, he takes it. Even when he was a little boy, he felt no need to ask permission, thinking that he had a right to everything . . . even things owned by others. His attitude was an embarrassment to our parents and to me. However, I never thought that he would come to this. Stealing antiquities from the government, the citizens of Egypt, and the world is an unthinkable act of selfishness and a shame that my family will have to carry forever.''

Ashley was immediately struck by the differences between the physically identical twins. The weight of Omar's wrong-doings lay heavily on Kasim's shoulders, making his somber personality even more noticeable. There was none of Omar's sparkle or hint of mischief in Kasim's eyes or the tilt of his head. There was also none of the arrogance and disregard for the happiness of others. Now that she knew both of them, she was grateful for the opportunity to forge a bond with the gentle one.

"You're not to blame for your brother's actions. I'm sure everyone will understand that you had no part in any of this. You're a dedicated archaeologist not a thief. Omar said he would issue a press release that would free you from any responsibility for his doings,'' Ashley replied, hoping to ease Kasim's mind and make him feel better.

"That might help some, but, in this country, my brother's sins will stick to me as well as to him. He has ruined all of my work and my family's reputation. I do not know if we will be able to salvage it,'' Kasim lamented.

It made Ashley's heart ache to see him so dejected, but she understood the importance of family honor. She watched him as he turned his concentration to the papers on the table with drooping shoulders. She hoped that one day he would be able to undo the impact of Omar's deeds. Until then, there was nothing she could do to lighten his load. Besides, there was still the unfinished business of her phantom man that separated them. Until that was resolved, Ashley would continue to have questions of her own.

Allowing Ben to seat her at the conference table, Ashley sank into the offered chair and began to explain her days of captivity to the officer. He listened attentively and took copious notes as she relayed the information regarding her treatment at Omar's hands, any plans she might have overheard, and the location of the places in which he held her captive. As she spoke, Ashley realized that she really could not tell the police much about him. He had carefully kept her from seeing any of his men; the only one she recognized was the one who had tried to snatch her in the parking lot. Except for the interior of the cabin, she had learned nothing of its location either. Kasim's and Mohammed's descriptions were actually more helpful. Kasim knew more about the hideout than she did, having seen the outside of the cabin and the village.

Ashley could only say that Omar had treated her with respect; she did not mention his suggestion that she accompany him. In her mind that was never an option for consideration. Kasim did not need yet another pain heaped onto what he already carried. When Ashley thought about her time in captivity, she really did not have much to offer. She had seen nothing and heard nothing that would help discover the whereabouts of the ancient treasures.

When the conversation ended, Ashley retreated to the privacy of her cubicle. She needed a shower and change of clothes desperately. She needed time away from Kasim's sadness and constant attention to think about her future with him in peace. Despite all that had happened, or maybe because of it, Ashley knew that any relationship with Kasim would only be fleeting. She would not be able to settle down with someone whose lifestyle and culture were so different from her own. She had to compose her thoughts and come to grips with the reality that she would never see him again after the expedition ended regardless of how much she might want him in her life. Their backgrounds were too different.

As the warm water washed over her body, Ashley hummed a simple tune and allowed the tension of captivity to flow from her being. Thinking about Omar, Ashley was surprised that she could ever have mistaken them. As identical twins, they were physically matched in every way except for Omar's limp, but their personalities were totally different. Kasim was an intellectual and Omar was an adventurer. Kasim preferred solitude and quiet evenings with a few friends, whereas Omar craved excitement. She could never see Kasim living the carefree life of the libertine, and she could never imagine Omar as the studious professor of antiquities at a university. She was strangely happy to have known both of them and sadly wished they could meld into one terribly exciting man who possessed the best qualities of both.

Toweling off the water droplets that glistened on her skin, Ashley sadly admitted that she probably would never have what she searched for in a man . . . he existed on the run, in fiction, and in her dreams. Besides, it was not fair to expect anyone to live up to the expectations she had set for the man who would join his life with hers.

When Ashley rejoined the men in the conference room, the police officer had left Ben and Kasim drafting a press release that would explain the steps the authorities were taking to retrieve the precious artifacts and bring the thieves to justice. All four of them had decided that Omar would never be found; he had planned the theft too carefully and left no telltale traces. Even Kasim had to admit that his brother had pulled off the perfect robbery.

Excusing themselves from the conference room, Ashley and Kasim strolled the grounds hand-in-hand and looked at the light show on the Great Pyramid. As they sat among the newly returned tourists, they marveled at the grandeur of the ancient structure and the skill required to build it. Slipping his arm around her shoulders, Kasim whispered, "Let us leave this place and its curses. We will get married and settle in the States or somewhere in Europe or even here in Egypt if you would prefer. I do not wish to take a chance on losing you again. I just need you with me."

Taking him by the hand and leading him away from the pyramids, Ashley replied, "I can't do that, Kasim. My thoughts are all confused between you and the mystery and magic of Egypt. I need time to sort out my thoughts. Right now, I can't tell if it's you I love or your country. Let's be realistic. Neither of us can simply turn our backs on the discoveries of this pyramid. You have your entire career tied up in these digs, and I still have two months left on my work here. Omar might have taken a large chunk of what we've discovered and catalogued, but there's so much more waiting for us. I can't desert the group."

"No one would blame you. You have been held prisoner, ransomed for treasure, and left tied up in an empty apartment. Everyone would understand if you left," Kasim persisted.

"Maybe they would, but I wouldn't. I came here to work on this dig, and I'm going to see it through to the end. Don't worry about me. The worst should be over. How much more can there be? I've already experienced a runaway boulder, ants, and a tornado. I'll be home in no time," Ashley replied, giving Kasim's cheek a discreet peck.

"Does it not matter at all to you that I need you with me? I love you, Ashley. Is there nothing I can say to change your mind?" Kasim asked, his frustration showing in his face in the moonlight.

"I'm sorry, Kasim, but I have to finish what I've started. That's just the way I am. I think I love you, too, but I have to do this for me. I have to be sure before I commit to you. We only have two more months on this dig. If you still feel the same and if I've worked out my confusion, then we can find a place that would be good for both of us. By then, I'll be ready," Ashley replied with a smile, trying to cheer him up. She saw no reason to tell him about the phantom of her dreams.

"I can see that nothing I say will change your mind. You are one stubborn woman, but I guess that is what attracted me to you. I just hope when the time comes and you have sorted out everything that you want me in your life. Well, I guess it is good night then. I do not know about you, but the excitement of the last few days has all but done me in," Kasim answered with a shrug and a chaste kiss to her forehead. Her rejection had only added to the layers off unhappiness that weighed heavily on him. He was not happy with Ashley's decision, but he knew there was no point in trying to convince her to abandon her plans. She was determined to see the expedition through to the end.

Returning to the compound, Ashley and Kasim found everyone excitedly discussing a television broadcast. Easing in among them in front of the set, she listened to the announcer as he played a recording bearing a message in a very familiar voice. Listening closely to the scratchy tape she heard Omar's voice saying, "Good evening ladies and gentlemen. By the time your hear this recording, I will be far away. I am leaving you this message in an attempt to clear my family's reputation. I want everyone to know that neither my brother nor any other member of my family was in any way involved in my theft of the antiquities. Believe me when I say that I will put them to good use. I alone engineered the plan and executed it. No one in my family even knows where to find me. I hope that all of you will believe me and accept the fact that in these modern times a family should not bear the burden for the acts committed by its singular members.

"To my family, I would like to say goodbye, for I will never see any of them again. I will never return to Egypt and will never contact you in any way. Trying to find me will be futile since my identity will be known to no one and my face to even fewer. I pray you will find peace in the years to come and that Allah will be merciful toward you. Goodbye.''

As Ashley watched, Kasim straightened his shoulders for the first time since finding out the identity of the kidnapper. Omar's message had liberated him from his responsibility for his brother's actions or at least had tried to set him free. There would always be people with small minds who would not believe him. Now he could once again walk with his head high. He hoped that his brother would find happiness wherever his travels took him.

The next two days passed in a whirlwind of excitement as the international and local press filled the compound interviewing Ashley, Ben, and Kasim. Not since the initial discovery of the worth of the treasures had there been so many cameras and reporters recording every action, every conversation, and every memory. At first, Sallie and the others weathered the interruption in their lives with good grace, but, after the novelty of their celebrity status wore thin and the press became pests, they grew impatient for the return of their daily routine and the sand of the pyramids. Now that all of the team members were safely back in the compound, everyone wanted to return to the excavation.

The group found that they could not even go out to dinner together without being recognized. Kasim, who wanted to put the incident and his brother's behavior behind him, hated the attention. He withdrew into himself when the other diners recognized Ashley from the press coverage and broke into spontaneous applause at the sight of them. Ashley blushed and waved as they followed the waiter to their table. All eyes were on them as they ordered and tried to share their last few hours together. Unable to talk in private and feeling very self-conscious with the watchful faces absorbing every exchange, the little group of friends left before dessert.

Happily, Ashley found that the expedition site was once again a place of productive excitement with everyone readying their supplies for a day in the pyramids. The cameras and reporters had finally left them alone to continue their archaeological exploration. She shook her head at the behavior of the press since they should have been equally as excited by their discoveries as by her kidnapping. She considered it amazing that the great treasures had caused so little stir when first unearthed compared to the flurry of activity generated by the ransoming of them.

"Let's go!" Sallie called from the opening of Ashley's cubicle. Looking up, she saw her friend standing with filled arms waiting for her to gather her tools. "Come on, the others are waiting for us."

"Ready," Ashley replied tucking her brush safely into the waistband of her jeans. Picking up her flashlight and case, she joined her friend as they walked out of the compound and into the bright sunlight. She was ready to return to the quiet splendor of the pyramid.

"Gee, it's good to be back in action again," Sallie remarked as they unloaded their things and began the task of cataloguing the items in the throne room. Everything except the artifacts taken by Omar was in exactly the same place as when they had left the treasures a week ago. A fine coating of sand had drifted over them obscuring their beauty, but, otherwise, everything was the same.

"It's comforting to be in a place where time stands still," Ashley commented, brushing away the dust and beginning to tag and record items already pulled from the chest at her feet. She felt relaxed and ready for a day in the dusty silence. The routine would do her good, help to quiet her emotions, and provide her with a place for reflection. She needed to compose her thoughts before talking with Kasim. Ashley knew that she had to close out that chapter of her life before she could move forward into the future. She had given it a lot of thought in the last few days and knew that she had to tell Kasim about her feelings for him and why she could not marry him. Regardless of how hard she tried, Ashley could not put the feeling that she had not yet met the man for her out of her mind. He still visited in her dreams of the phantom lover.

As she worked, Ashley slowly became aware of someone watching her. She looked up to find Kasim's dark eyes staring intently at her. He had put down his pen and clipboard and sat on a three-legged folding stool gazing at her. She could almost read the concern, the pain, the affection, and the guilt he still carried written across his handsome face. She longed to hold him but knew that she would only confuse both of them if she did. She would always consider Kasim to be a good friend, but nothing else.

Realizing that Ashley had discovered him, Kasim smiled and shrugged before returning to his work. Sadly, he could think of no words that would ease the rift between them. Kasim was resigned to loving someone who would never have him. His brother's antics had seen to that. If only Omar had not kidnapped Ashley, he would have had more time with her. He would have been able to erase any thoughts of their differences from her mind. The only thing Kasim could do was forget the pleasure of holding Ashley in his arms and return to the lonely life of academia. Even without her telling him, Kasim knew that it was only a matter of time before Ashley put an end to his futile hopes.

Kasim never guessed that his brother had done more

than simply kidnap Ashley. He had confirmed her belief that a relationship between a man and a woman could be more than peaceful evenings before the fire, candle-lit dinners, symphony tickets, and opening night at the opera. Although she did not believe in his apparent lack of principles, he had shown her that passion could exist. A passion so consuming that all other thoughts paled in the glow of its heat. Ashley wanted that fire in her life and in her relationships.

Every night Ashley saw the phantom lover who embodied all that she craved again and again in her dreams. She felt his arms enfold her. She inhaled the spicy sweetness of him as she lay against his strong chest. His words of passion echoed in her mind as she felt his hands caress her body until she moaned at the pleasures enflamed by his touch. She relished his closeness as she titillated his flat, taut stomach and firm thighs with her teasing fingers.

When they could tolerate the waiting no longer, they locked their bodies in the timeless dance of lovers. She arched her back to receive his sexuality. She locked her ankles behind his buttocks to hold him tightly against her. She lifted her hips to match his thrusts. At the height of their desire, she wordlessly called out his name. She clung to him as if he would fade with the rising of the sun. And, when the music stopped, they slept warmed by their shared love.

That night as the members of the group sat around the conference table recounting the day's finds and displaying their sketches, Ashley once again felt Kasim's eyes on her. When she looked at him, he smiled sadly and looked away. She hated to see the pain on his face, but there was nothing she could do until they had a chance to be alone and talk. Unfortunately, they were all so tired after the hours of unaccustomed work that everyone turned in as soon as the meeting ended. Any conversation between them would have to wait until the morning.

Just as Ashley began to fall asleep, she felt someone's hand lightly resting on her shoulder. Looking out of the tiniest slit between her heavy eyelids, she saw Kasim standing silhouetted in the light of the small lamp beside her bed that she kept on as protection against things that prowled in the night. Never had she thought that he would be one of them.

Quickly sitting up she said, "Kasim, you surprised me. Can't this wait until morning? I'm awfully tired."

Even before Kasim replied Ashley could read from the tormented expression on his face that he felt a sense of urgency in his need to talk with her. Drawing up the chest that served as table and extra seating, he wearily perched on it before answering her. "I will not be but a few minutes, if you do not mind. I need to clear the air between us. It is too painful working with you and having unspoken words hanging between us. I have felt so miserable these last few days that I have even considered abandoning the expedition and returning to the university. The only reason I have not left is that my thoughts would torment me anywhere I go. I would not accomplish anything by running away."

"I'm glad you didn't leave. Omar's betrayal must have been hard on you. You've worked very hard to establish your identity and to make a reputation for yourself in the field only for him to put a black smudge against it," Ashley said softly. She hated to see Kasim's tortured face.

"The blessing is that people will soon forget what he did. His audio tape did more for me than I had anticipated it would. But I was not thinking only of him. I was talking about us. We seemed on the brink of something when he kidnapped you. I feel that we need some resolution to it. It has been very hard on me to work so closely with you and not be able to touch you. I do not know where I stand with you. Do you think ill of me because of my brother? Does that mean that there can be nothing between us? I would hate to think that Omar's brash behavior ruined everything. I know that initially you could separate him from me, but I need to know if you can still see us as two distinctly different people," Kasim replied in a soft, broken voice.

Listening to him and seeing the slump of his shoulders, Ashley could clearly make out the difference between the brothers even in the glow of the dim bulb. She wondered how she would ever have missed the wonder of Kasim's gentleness and wished that she did not still see their differences.

"I don't hold you in any way responsible for Omar's actions; besides, he was a perfect gentleman. If I had met him under different circumstances, I would have found him quite charming. He has a certain undeniable flair. However, kidnapping is not the way to make an impression on someone. I don't feel any animosity toward him at all. I've wanted to speak with you all day but never found the time. I cherish the memory of what we had and hope that we can build a lasting friendship on its foundation," Ashley responded. She hoped that her tone would convey the message that their past affection had moved to a more congenial level in her mind. She was quite content with the new direction her life had taken.

Taking a deep breath and straightening his shoulders, Kasim smiled weakly and said, "I am glad for that, Ashley. I would hate to think that the time we shared together had been tainted. I could use a good friend. Good night. I will see you in the morning."

She watched his retreating back as he slowly made his way toward his cubicle. Ashley knew that Kasim wanted more, but she could not give it to him. He was sweet and dedicated and a wonderful historian, but they were worlds apart in culture and upbringing although he had learned much about American women from his African-American mother. If she were able to forget the cultural distance that separated them, Kasim would be her first choice for a meaningful love, but she could not.

Snuggling into her pillow, Ashley silenced the thoughts that galloped noisily through her mind. Over and over she asked herself what she would have done if she had met Kasim in the States rather than in the mystic sands of Egypt. She wondered if she could have looked at him for the man under the robes rather than as a vital component of the majesty of the pyramids. Ashley remembered the feel of Kasim's lips on hers and the fire that coursed through her body when he held her. She felt that so much more could have existed between them if they had come to know each other in a less enchanting environment. She would have been able to separate the man from the driving sands, the sun-drenched marvel of the pyramids, and the danger of the expedition.

Kasim was all the passion and excitement that she had always dreamed of finding in a man, but she wondered if a relationship with him would last. Maybe the fire would grow dull after familiarity set in. Maybe he would need the constant conquest of exploration to feed his flames. He might never be able to settle down and live in that little white house she had always wanted, and she was not sure that she had the personality for a life without roots. Omar had said that their family lived as nomads. Perhaps that was why Kasim enjoyed traveling from one dig to the other with only periodic stops at the university. As she dozed off to sleep, she admitted to herself that finding out would have been half the fun. Unfortunately, Ashley did not think that she would ever be able to give herself the opportunity for discovery.

As she drifted into the world of dreams before the darkness begins, Ashley saw the pyramid wall and the words, "Remember me." The man stood with his arms open as he reached toward her. Slowly his bearded face faded into nothingness as he backed away from her. His hands returned to his side, and he was gone.

CHAPTER NINE

The last months of the expedition passed quickly. Every morning they made the short walk to the pyramid in which they spent their days uncovering unbelievable treasures and recording them before shipping them off to the University of Cairo. Every evening they returned to the compound to debrief, shower, eat, socialize, and rest. No other phenomena greeted them when they entered the tomb. Everything went according to schedule. Everyone including Kasim was happy and excited about the day's work.

A team of men had managed to dislodge the boulder from the main entrance making it unnecessary for them to use the rope entry and giving them a great deal of freedom during the day. They often lunched in the compound instead of inside the dusty pyramid now that they could easily come and go during their workday.

Ashley marveled at the serenity of the tomb. Other than the powder of new dust on the artifacts they had recently uncovered, there was no sign of the old turbulence or of any unexpected danger. Actually, to the untrained eye, the

burial room looked as if no one had ever penetrated its
protective shell.

Unfolding the little seat she carried with her, Ashley
pulled out her brush, opened her notebook, and began
the day's work of dusting and cataloging artifacts. Although
she had already spent countless hours laboring over the
overflowing trunks and baskets, she was constantly over-
whelmed by the beauty of the jewels, the craftsmanship of
the pottery, and the intricacy of the gold work. Holding
one exquisite article after the other in her hand, she felt
awe at the artistry that had survived unharmed over the
ages.

Ashley was so engrossed in her work and lulled by the
tranquillity of the tomb that she did not notice the subtle
changes that were occurring around her. She did not see
the slight shifting of the sand in the walkway between her
workstation and Sallie's. She did not feel the eyes that
periodically stared at her from around a case of freshly
catalogued artifacts. She did not hear the almost impercep-
tible hissing of air as it escaped from the slim bodies that
glided soundlessly under the sand.

If she had looked up from her examination of the intricately carved gold and enamel necklace, Ashley would have
seen the soft beige sand come alive with hundreds of tiny
slithering snakes. They coiled around the base of vases,
up the sides of unopened trunks and cases, and over the
shoulders of golden statues. Fearlessly, the army of reptiles
took up its sentry duty in an effort to protect the possessions
of the tomb from being removed by the intruders. Confident that its members had been properly stationed to
guard the artifacts, it now moved forward in ordered rows
under the sand. Moving slowly but methodically so as not
to attract attention, the snakes glided toward the members
of the expedition with only one thought in mind . . . to
kill the invaders.

"Darn, what a klutz!" Ashley proclaimed, fussing with herself as she dropped her brush into the fine powdery sand at her feet.

Reaching down to retrieve it, her fingers closed around something cold and oddly flexible. Thinking she had only picked up a misplaced treasure, Ashley peered at the article with mild curiosity. To her surprise, staring back at her was a small, scaly, brown snake. Its tongue flickered rapidly as it scented the air.

Chills ran down her spine as Ashley realized what she held in her unprotected hand. One of the things she had been taught to recognize and fear during her preliminary sessions on Egypt was the appearance of predators, sand storms, and snakes. This seemingly docile specimen that curled the lower portion of its body around her fingers and raised its top section had been high on the list of creatures to avoid. Instantly, Ashley recognized it as a member of the asp family . . . the same kind of snake that had killed Cleopatra.

Not wanting to move too quickly or to scare Sallie, Ashley looked around for a safe place to throw the reptile. The spectacle that greeted her eyes was even more frightening than the one she held in her hand. Everywhere she looked, she saw asps covering everything. There was not a single container, vase, statue, or box, including the one at her feet, that had not been transformed into a pulsating, squirming mass of snakes. They even crawled over her sturdy sandals.

"Sallie," Ashley whispered fearing a loud voice or sudden movement might frighten the asps into attacking them. "Don't move! We've been surrounded by snakes. They look like asps to me."

"What? You've got to be kidding. Damn, they're everywhere. And today of all days I didn't wear my boots," Sallie replied with real fear in her voice.

"Don't panic and don't move. I didn't wear mine either. I'll call to Kasim. Maybe he'll have a suggestion. One thing's for sure. We have to get out of here," Ashley responded, trying to keep her voice level as the taste of panic began to fill her mouth.

"Make it quick. They've started to crawl toward me. If I move even an inch, I'll step on one of them," Sallie whispered sounding desperately afraid.

Still holding the little asp in her fingers, Ashley called to Kasim in a loud whisper saying, "Kasim, can you hear me? We're surrounded by asps. Sallie and I are wearing sandals. What do we do?"

"What? Snakes? Stay perfectly still. I will be right there. Do not panic or make any sudden movements," Kasim instructed from his perch on top of a ledge. He had spent the morning examining the details of the paintings around the treasury walls. Archaeology was such a solitary occupation that little interaction occurred between the members of the group after they arrived in the tomb. He had been so preoccupied with his own work that, even as the leader, he had not noticed the advance of the snakes.

Looking down, Kasim saw that the potentially lethal asps had surrounded him, too. They crawled in and out of his chalk sticks, among the sketch pad sheets, and over the toes of his boots. Glancing at Sallie, he could see that she was indeed in a very precarious predicament as she sat with snakes approaching her bare feet.

Seeing him look in her direction, Sallie whined softly, "Kasim, what should I do? I'm too afraid to run and besides I'm scared that one of them might bite me. Damn, I wish I had worn my boots."

Turning ever so slightly, Kasim glimpsed Ashley sitting with her right hand in the air. A squirming little snake dangled from her fingers. Following her eyes, he saw that another one had crawled up her leg and now sat perched on her bare knee just below the hem of her walking shorts. After studying her face for a minute, it slithered back down as if awaiting further instructions from a higher source.

Stepping from the ledge, Kasim carefully eased his foot among the slippery asps. He moved slowly, trying not to disturb them with his motions. Barely lifting his feet, he virtually skated on the surface of the snake-covered sand until he stood beside a whimpering Sallie.

Grasping her by the shoulders, Kasim pulled Sallie to her feet and quickly lifted her into his arms. She clung to him with her eyes wide with fear as he began to slide toward the door. As he passed Ashley he called over his shoulder, "I will be right back for you. Do not move until I return."

Ashley watched Kasim and Sallie slowly make their way to the chamber's opening. Depositing her in a sobbing heap on the other side where she was safe from the crawling reptiles, he slowly reversed his direction until he once again entered the burial room and began the slow slide to where she sat. Ashley involuntarily held her breath as he approached. One misstep and Kasim could suffer an extremely painful and perhaps mortal bite.

Kasim's progress was slower this time. The snakes had not liked having him move among them. Many of them had raised their bodies into the strike position. He waited until they resumed their slow deliberate crawl before he carefully eased his feet forward. He knew that his ankles and legs would be safe from their bites, but he worried that Ashley's bare skin would become a target for their attack.

Ashley sat motionless. She barely breathed for fear of disturbing the snakes that crawled around her seat, over her bare toes, and dangled from her outstretched fingers. She watched Kasim's progress with fear and awe as he slowly pushed his way through the massing bodies of warriors determined to defend and protect the contents of the tomb.

When he reached her seat, Kasim spoke softly and slowly, "Ashley, I am standing directly behind you. Hold tight to your materials. Be sure you do not drop anything. Turn around very slowly without lifting your feet. Try to disturb as few snakes as possible."

Ashley did exactly as Kasim instructed. She moved so slowly that at times she felt as if she were standing still. Facing him with her snake-filled hand still extended, she waited for his next set of instructions.

"Now, I am going to pick you up fireman style. As soon as I give you the signal, drop the snake. I will hoist you up and run for the door. Are you ready?" Kasim asked with a crooked little smile that tried to make her feel better.

"Ready. I hope this works," Ashley replied in a voice that quivered with skepticism.

"Do not worry. We will be okay. Let us go for it," Kasim responded as he placed his hands on Ashley's waist.

With one swift movement, Kasim lifted Ashley and threw her over his shoulder. Immediately, he spun around to face the door. "Drop it!" he shouted tightening his grip on her body. Taking several long strides, he charged through the teaming river of snakes until they stood on the other side of the doorway in the quiet sand. Sallie, Ashley, and Kasim breathed heavily now that they were safe.

Looking into the burial room, they were amazed at the sight that met their eyes. Every snake in the room had raised its head in anticipation of the united strike against the intruders. Thousands of pairs of eyes stared after them. The angry hissing of the reptiles broke the silence of the room as the marching line waited in well-formed rows of venom-armed soldiers. Yet, not one crossed the line into

the corridor. Their job was to protect the treasures not
pursue the retreating archaeologists.

"Impressive," Ashley remarked checking herself for
bites. "Thanks for rescuing me. If they had attacked, we
wouldn't have stood a chance."

"Have you ever seen so many snakes in one place in all
your life?" Sallie asked with a shudder. "Of all the things
in the world, snakes are the scariest. They are the only
creatures I fear when on an expedition. Kasim, I owe you
more than I can ever repay." She gave Kasim a brave smile
and a hug, which appeared to embarrass him greatly.

"I have never seen anything like this. I thought our
other experiences were unusual, but this attack of snakes
is even more bazaar. It is uncanny the way they know to
stay within the burial room and not cross this line. I will
get some of my men to round up as many of them as
possible. It looks as if our work is over for the day," Kasim
said as he gingerly rubbed his arm.

"I hope I wasn't too heavy," Ashley said noticing the
grimace on his face.

"No, not at all. However, I think your little friend bit
me," he replied. Kasim rolled up his sleeve to expose a
red, puffy spot on his arm. With close examination, Ashley
and Sallie could see two tiny pin pricks at the center of
the swelling.

Exchanging looks of horror with Sallie, Ashley immediately began searching through her fanny pack for the snake
bite antitoxin she carried with her at all times. Seeing the
perspiration sparkling on Kasim's strained face, she pulled
the vile from her bag. Working quickly as the venom spread
through his veins, Ashley expertly plunged the loaded
syringe into his exposed arm. Then she and Sallie lowered
Kasim to a sitting position on a nearby boulder.

Ashley watched with a worried expression as the color
continued to drain from Kasim's pinched face and his

shoulders sagged under the weight of poison that threatened his life. Ashley and Sallie exchanged worried looks over his head as they gently wiped the perspiration from his clammy skin. She hated to see her friend looking so ill. He had saved her life and risked his own. Ashley felt absolutely dreadful.

Kasim lay back into the sand with his arms folded over his chest. His breathing was shallow and frighteningly irregular. His eyelids and lips had turned a grayish-blue shade. Periodically, his body convulsed as the antitoxin and the venom did battle for control of him.

"Sallie, go get Ben. I'm so worried. The shot should have worked by now. Hurry!" Ashley instructed as she lay her hand lovingly on Kasim's. Its cold lifelessness frightened her greatly.

As Sallie rushed to get help, Ashley gently cradled Kasim's head in her lap. His eyes fluttered open, and he smiled bravely as she kissed his moist forehead. "Kasim," Ashley cried, "you have to fight the venom. You have to get well. The expedition needs you. I need you. Please!"

Summoning all of his strength, Kasim whispered through parched lips, "I love you, Ashley."

Before she could respond, his eyes closed again. Kasim appeared to sleep in her arms.

"What is it? What happened? Sallie was so hysterical that I could not understand a word she said," Ben demanded as he joined them. Sallie followed behind him nervously wringing her hands and sobbing.

"Kasim has been bitten by a snake. I gave him the antitoxin, but it doesn't seem to be working. I think it was an asp. Look inside the tomb. It's crawling with them," Ashley replied as she cradled Kasim's body against hers.

Looking into the room in which the snakes still stood guard, Ben exclaimed, "Asps!"

Immediately, Ben extracted another vile from his bag

and injected Kasim with the serum. "He will need another. One is not enough to counteract the strength of the venom. He should be all right in a few minutes, but we will take him to the infirmary to be safe as soon as he can walk."

Gradually, Kasim's complexion began to improve, the perspiration ceased to flow, and his breathing returned to normal. Looking thankfully from Ashley's eyes to Ben he whispered, "Thank you, that was certainly a close one. I have never been bitten by an asp before. Now I understand how Cleopatra committed suicide with one. This one was tiny and it made me feel this dreadful. I can imagine what the poison from a full-grown snake would do."

"It was all my fault," Ashley cried, "If I hadn't worn sandals and shorts, you wouldn't have had to carry me out of the treasury room. And, if I'd remembered to drop the snake I was holding, it wouldn't have bitten you. In my petrified state, I just didn't think. Are you feeling well enough for us to return to camp? I want the doctor to check you over."

"Of course, I can make it just fine. All I need is a little rest and some cool tea. I will be restored at a few sips of that elixir," Kasim answered, rising unsteadily to his feet.

"We'll help you," Sallie said as she and Ashley positioned themselves on either side of Kasim. Resting his arms on their shoulders, he used them as crutches to make his way out of the pyramid and into the heat of the Egyptian afternoon. Ben brought up the rear pulling their two crates of supplies.

Walking slowly, Ashley and Sallie aided Kasim into the cool protection of the building. As they walked Ashley shouted, "Dr. Freedman, we need you. Kasim has been bitten by an asp."

The doctor immediately met them in Kasim's cubicle. Examining the bite and taking Kasim's vital signs, he clucked his tongue like an old woman. Satisfied, he turned to Ashley and Sallie and said, "Your quick thinking saved Kasim from even greater illness. If you had not used that antitoxin, he could have lapsed into a coma or worse. Good work, ladies."

"Ashley and Ben are the ones who saved him. All I did was help her bring him back here," Sallie volunteered, smiling proudly at her friend.

"It was all my fault in the first place. I should have been more careful," Ashley replied. She felt awful that her actions had caused a problem for someone else.

Kasim, lying quietly on his bunk, reached up and took her cold hand in his. "Do not blame yourself. Snakes and spiders are hazards of the job. I am fine. Now, leave me for a while so I can get some rest. I will see you at dinner. Besides, we were forewarned about everything that has happened to us in the tomb in the hieroglyphics on the walls. We were too scientific to believe that ancient prophecy and omens could come true. Even the betrayal of my brother was foretold."

"Yes, but it's hard for me to feel otherwise," Ashley replied softly.

"My love, you saved my life. What more could a man desire than to have a woman at his side who really cares for him? Perhaps now you will put aside your concerns about our differences and look only at our similarities. We are made for each other," Kasim commented, squeezing Ashley's hand affectionately.

Not wanting to upset him as he recovered, Ashley replied, "We'll talk about that later, Kasim. For now, you need to rest."

Ashley, Sallie, and Dr. Freeman quickly left Kasim to his much needed sleep. As they parted company in the corridor, Dr. Freeman said, trying to console Ashley, "Don't worry. Kasim is a strong, healthy man. He is doing fine. Your quick thinking and the medicine saved him.

Now, go get some rest, both of you. You have had a real shock today."

Sitting in the conference room sipping tea, Ashley let the tension of the day drain from her body. She had joined the expedition for the purpose of unearthing antiquities. She had not expected spiders, tornadoes, sliding rocks, snakes, kidnappings, Kasim, and the phantom of her dreams. Ashley had certainly unearthed more than she had originally planned. Yet, she did not regret a single minute of the time spent in the desert of Egypt and would miss everyone terribly when she returned to the States. Ashley had found sharing strategies and expectations to be among the most rewarding experiences in her life.

Turning to Sallie, Ashley said, "This has certainly not been a routine expedition. Not only did we unearth treasure far greater than originally anticipated, we woke up an assortment of long forgotten tomb gods. This sabbatical will certainly make interesting lecture material."

"I can hardly wait to see my husband's face when he reads my journals. He has always been the one to participate in the exciting, unusual, or prestigious digs. This time, I'm the one. It feels great despite the scare of the snakes," Sallie agreed with a great deal of pride in her voice.

Kasim joined them at dinner that night looking almost his old self. Everyone chatted excitedly about the latest escapade in the tomb. None of the veteran archaeologists had ever participated in a dig like this one. Jokingly, someone said that one of them must have brought out the wrath of the gods. With good-natured teasing written on their faces, they looked toward Ashley and laughed.

* * *

The next day, Kasim's men reported that they had removed all of the asps and had returned the tomb to a reasonable state of safety. During the last few days of cataloging, no other incidents or disruptions interrupted their progress. It looked as if they would finish their work despite the repeated interference by the ancient gods. Ashley wondered if Omar had arranged the snakes, too. She wanted to tell someone about his expertise in arranging deceptions, but she had to remain silent. No one must know what he had done. Ashley was not sure that Kasim could stand another scandal involving his brother.

No one had heard anything from Omar in quite some time. At first, sightings often appeared in the foreign press. People had reported seeing him or uncovering artifacts in places like New York and Paris. When the police investigated, they found the rumors to be untrue. Omar had vanished with the treasures just as he had told Ashley he would. Ashley was far too busy with her work to think about him often, but when she did, she wondered if he were happy. Ashley did not think that anyone could live with contentment while on the run from the police.

Her friend Toni had called every day since the frightening news of her kidnapping had appeared in the paper. She was almost hysterical with worry. When Toni discovered that Ashley was safe, she made her promise again to be home in time for her wedding. She was busy making preparations and wanted to share everything with Ashley. Using a fax and the Internet, Ashley helped her work on the details of the ceremony, arranging the catering, ordering the gown and the invitations, and arranging for the flowers from the shadow of the pyramids. The two of them could not have been busier or happier. Ashley found herself caught up in Toni's excitement and was counting the days until the expedition ended and she could return home to the States despite her affection for Kasim.

Seeing the new excitement in Ashley's life, Sallie asked, "What happened to the mystery man in your dreams? Have you given up on finding him? Have you decided that Kasim is the one for you? He's an awfully nice guy. You could do worse, you know."

"I guess my phantom isn't as important as I used to think he was," Ashley replied with a sigh as she lifted a full box of cataloged artifacts and walked to the conference room. "Besides, dreams don't always come true. I suppose he was one of the ones that should just fade from memory. I'm still not sure about Kasim. I know I care deeply for him, but I can't put aside our differences no matter how hard I try. I guess I'll have to let time settle that one."

"Let's hope something happens soon. Time is something we don't have in abundance," Sallie commented to herself as she folded some of her clothes into the boxes for shipping home.

Sallie was excited about the trip to the States, too. She had not been home since she married her Egyptian professor and had happily announced one afternoon as they worked in the pyramid that she would accompany Ashley on the return trip. Sallie had not realized how homesick she was for the sounds of New York and Washington until a reason for returning presented itself. Now, she was almost as impatient as Ashley to return.

Kasim and Ben made more frequent trips to the university than before as the work of discovery and cataloguing slowed down. They gave televised lectures complete with slides that showed the treasure lying on velvet cloth or inside glass cabinets. They seemed to be enjoying the life of historian and archaeologist. Kasim was especially relieved that his reputation was still intact, despite the efforts of his twin. With a few exceptions, almost no one

asked him about Omar. He seemed to have been forgotten.
There were reports about money that seemed to appear
when the poor needed it, but no one ever said who supplied
it. Since the stolen jewels never materialized, no one connected the two events.

A few days before their scheduled departure, the teams
crated the last of the treasures and packed up their personal belongings before moving back to the hotel in Cairo.
Their last outing as a group was to one of the many
delightful oases in the desert. The expedition's cook
packed a feast of cheese, olives, cold roasted lamb, cous-
cous, thick-crusted bread, and fruit for them to eat in the
shade of the trees. As the gentle breeze fluttered the leaves
and rippled the water in the little spring, they spread their
meal on woven mats and they made themselves comfortable on the lush carpet of grass. For the first time since
arriving in Cairo, they had no schedule to keep and no
treasure to unearth. They were totally at leisure.

Lying on her back and looking up at the sky through
the canopy of leaves, Ashley did not for one minute regret
coming on the expedition. Perhaps because of the spiders,
snakes, tornado, and Kasim, she had experienced much
more than she had ever expected. She had not dreamed
that such adventure awaited her. She had hoped to see
the majesty of the Great Pyramids about which she had
read, but instead of only seeing Giza, she had met wonderful people, eaten sumptuous food, and lived a life that she
had never thought existed. She had been kidnapped and
released by a handsome rogue, had ridden into the desert
at night on camel, had read hieroglyphics that were still on
a pyramid wall, and had catalogued a fortune in treasures.

Nothing at home could ever compare to her months in
Egypt. Words could not begin to describe the beauty of

the desert at night when the stars twinkled overhead or at sunset when the red of the sun turned the sand the color of blood. Ashley doubted that she would ever be able to make her students understand the sense of expectation that filled her heart every morning when she awoke knowing that more of the glories of ancient Egypt lay waiting for her to discover them.

Ashley had arrived in Egypt with the expectations of discovering breathtaking treasures and artifacts. The tomb had proven to be a great storehouse of all that and more. She had enriched her understanding of the ancient civilization and had broadened her knowledge of herself at the same time. Despite the dust, thirst, and hardships, she had found that she was a daughter of the Nile in spirit as well as in historical understanding and grounding.

Now on the last day in Egypt it occurred to her that it was entirely fitting that she should be lying in the shade of the trees on a lush little oasis. As the breeze fanned her face, Ashley dreamed of one day returning to this country and its many mysteries. She knew that she had uncovered only an insignificant number of those that lay buried in the sand.

"What will you tell your sponsors about your sabbatical?" Sallie asked as they lay side-by-side on their blankets watching the clouds float across the sky.

"I guess I'll begin with the usual lecture on antiquities and the process of unearthing them. I never realized how painstaking the process actually was until I joined the expedition. After that, I'll show them some slides of the pyramid and the compound. They usually think of pyramids as pointed. Seeing this one will come as a real surprise for many of them. I guess I'll finish my talk with a question-and-answer session. No matter what happens, I'll find someone who will listen to my stories about this expedition. The directors of the university that funded the grant will probably want a full accounting of my time. Too much has happened to me here to keep the news to myself. I've had experiences about which most people only dream," Ashley replied with a tinge of longing in her voice. Although the dig had officially ended when the last of the crates had been loaded onto the truck, they had made such good friends that parting was very bittersweet. Everyone said that another expedition would definitely be part of future plans. They all hoped to work together again.

"Well, when I return after Toni's wedding, I'll try to convince my husband to take a little vacation from the university. He hasn't been on a fun expedition in a long time. Most of his trips are highly structured. Ben said that another group is forming to work on the sister pyramid to this one. Who knows what we'll find this time," Sallie commented as she munched contentedly on a handful of grapes.

"No matter what we do in the future, I don't think anything can ever compare with this adventure and these good friends," Ashley said, growing sentimental about the camaraderie she had enjoyed. When she left the States almost seven months ago, she had been apprehensive but excited about this trip, now she wished it were only beginning rather than ending. That night for the first time in months, Ashley would sleep in a real bed not a hard cot, dine on china plates not chipped industrial-strength ceramic, wear a dress and not shorts, and shower in a lavish bathroom not a makeshift stall with a temperamental bent shower head.

Later that day, the group climbed aboard the same bus that had brought them to the Valley of the Kings. This time as they watched from the windows, a heavy sadness fell over them. As the massive pyramids gradually grew smaller in size, Ashley said a silent farewell to the desert she had learned to love. She wondered if she would ever see it or its people again.

As she dressed for their final dinner together, she experienced such mixed feelings that Ashley felt almost paralyzed by emotions. She was both happy to be returning to the States, Toni, and her friends and sad to be leaving the company of people who had grown to mean so much to her. They had experienced some pretty scary adventures together and had formed an indelible bond that was every bit as precious as the treasure they had unearthed. In particular, Ashley knew that she and Sallie would continue their friendship for many years to come. She was still unsure about her relationship with Kasim. That was the one unresolved element of the expedition.

Over paté, champagne, truffles, oysters, roast beef, chicken, luscious vegetables, and juicy fruits, the assembled team listened as Ben praised them for their hard labor and recapped the value both in money and in archaeological importance of their efforts. They had unearthed a king's pyramid, which had obviously lain undiscovered over the centuries while historians rushed to record the wealth of more elaborate structures. Believing the shorter pyramid to be that of a lesser queen or a faithful servant, they had ignored it in favor of the treasures of Tut and others. Now, according to Ben, their discovery proved that the ancient pharaohs often used the tombs of others as hiding places for their wealth to protect their riches from thieves who would keep them from making a smooth journey to the afterlife. What Ben and the university had originally thought would be an informative but fairly commonplace discovery had proven itself to be one of the most enlightening and valuable in recent times. Lifting his water glass for one last toast, Ben thanked them and wished them a safe trip home.

* * *

After dinner, Ashley and Sallie walked arm-in-arm through the courtyard catching a breath of air before returning to their rooms. They were both exhausted but too excited to sleep. The expedition had been everything they could have possibly hoped and then some. Neither of them had expected such high adventure and so much drama. Ashley had thought she would have the suspense of uncovering artifacts from the past, but she never imagined that she would be held hostage for those same relics. She actually found herself regretting that she would not have a classroom of eager or sleepy faces with which to share her hundreds of photographs, her souvenirs, and her memories. Already requests had begun to find their way to Egypt via her e-mail address. This adventure had opened many opportunities and created many possibilities from speaking engagements and teaching to writing.

Before she could leave Egypt the next morning, there was still one more thing Ashley needed to do. She had repeatedly tried to catch a few minutes alone with Kasim during the last months on the dig, but the pace at which they worked and the constant crush of people around them had prevented her from finding the right time. Now that she had booked a flight out the next morning, she had to find him. Despite their earlier talk in his cubicle, he never seemed happy these days. Ashley could tell that he was waiting for her to make up her mind about him.

Bidding Sallie good night at her door, Ashley quickly returned to the lush lobby and dialed Kasim's room on the courtesy phone. When he did not answer, she went looking for him. She did not have to search long, for he had taken refuge in the tea bar. Sitting slumped over a delicate rose-patterned cup, he looked as if the troubles of the past months still rested heavily on his shoulders.

"Kasim," Ashley said softly as she gently placed her hand on his white-robed shoulder, "I'm glad you're still here. I wanted a few minutes alone with you. Do you think we might talk for a while?"

When he turned toward her, Ashley could see the deep circles of exhaustion and the frown lines in his previously unmarred skin. Her heart lurched at the heaviness in his voice as Kasim replied, "Of course, I would be delighted. Let us take that table over there. Another pot of tea, please," he called to the waiter.

Sitting across the cozy table from him, Ashley did not have to prod for information. As soon as the waiter left the teapot and fresh cups before them, Kasim unloaded his heavy heart. Pulling a letter from his pocket, he handed it to Ashley who studied it as he poured the tea. Reading quickly, Ashley saw that it was from Omar.

"Dear Brother," the letter read in a neat script, "I hope this letter finds its way to you. I wish you well in the knowledge that I am safe. It is my sincere hope that my actions have not caused you any difficulty in your archaeological or academic endeavors. It was never my intention to harm you or anyone else. Take heart in the fact that they will soon forget me if they have not already. They will never know the good I do with the treasures, but I trust that one day you will. I will not write to you again but know that you are often in my thoughts. O——"

When she had finished, Ashley refolded the letter and returned it to him. Pushing aside her tea she said, "He's not what I wanted to speak with you about, although maybe Omar is part of it. I've tried to talk with you almost every day, but something always got in the way. There were always so many people around you."

"I know. They were all trying to make me feel better after what Omar did. He is not a bad person really . . . just a bit misdirected. Anyway, he seems happy wherever he is.

That envelope came to me by way of someone who got it from someone else who met someone on a train who handed it to him. I do not even know where he is now. I trust that he is well. He alludes to doing good deeds; I hope they give him satisfaction.''

"Well, I'm sure he'll be just fine. I didn't want to leave Cairo without telling you that I meant what I said that night when we spoke about our relationship. Omar's actions in no way influenced my decision about returning to the States. He did not affect my feelings toward you in any way. I still value you as a dear and cherished friend, but I cannot stay here with you.

"If anything, he opened my eyes to a number of things. Our worlds are too different for us ever to make it as a couple. I can't settle here and wouldn't make a very good Egyptian wife even if I tried. I saw the way men on the street looked at me when I ventured out alone. I'm too liberated to return to a life of subservience for women, and you wouldn't like some of the harsher sides of living in the States. Prejudice based on skin color is still alive and well. As a nation we can't seem to shake that old heritage. As much as I'd like to think that we could have been more to each other, I know that our worlds are too far apart.

"I know it sounds selfish, but I have to live where I'm comfortable and where I can feel at home. I realize that in many ways I'm taking the easy route, but it's the only thing I can do right now. I'm not strong enough to face a life of uncertainty. Maybe the time will come when I'll have a reason to be more daring, but, until it does, this is the best I can do,'' Ashley said with sadness and longing in her voice. She still found Kasim to be an incredibly attractive and appealing man, perhaps even more now that she would never see him again.

Placing a light kiss on the back of her hand, Kasim

replied, "I understand, Ashley. It would be difficult, maybe even impossible, for me to adjust to another home and a different way of life. Our mother tried to teach us about her country, but to me the United States is still very far away and very big. I am just relieved to hear that Omar's behavior in no way changed your mind about me. You know, I am not like my brother at all. We are twins, but our personalities are totally different. I like peace and quite and a healthy dose of routine. I do not think, however, that I will ever get over my love for you. I will bury myself in my work, but you will always be with me. Perhaps some day we will meet again."

Finishing the last of their tea, the two friends chatted about the expedition and their plans for the future. Now that Omar had cleared Kasim's name, Kasim was free to join other expeditions in the quest for the story of the Egyptian kings and queens buried in the sands of the desert. He had already been contacted by several firms in search of an archaeologist with his talents. He had already been contracted by the museum. Cataloguing the artifacts and helping with the design of a permanent display would consume much of his time over the next months and perhaps years.

Rising from the table, Kasim walked Ashley to the elevator and bowed deeply over her hand as the door opened. He waved good night as it closed, taking his hopes of a future together with him.

The next morning, the team assembled one final time for a photography session in the temporary workroom at the museum. They smiled and posed for the camera as the curator's staff snapped their last official photo. For a moment as she stood among the others, Ashley thought she saw someone with Omar's laughing eyes. Her skin

momentarily prickled with fear. He was carrying one of
the overflowing trays of coffee, tea, juice, and Danish. He
had paused to stare at her, and a slight smile of recognition
had crossed his lips. Then he inclined his head toward her
in greeting and turned away. When the photo session had
finished, Ashley looked again, but the man had vanished
into the kitchen.

When Ashley saw the man again, the slope of his shoulders told her that he could not be Omar. He could have
altered his face, but nothing could change the strength of
his massive shoulders. There was no way he could camouflage his muscular frame under the thin white waiter's
jacket. It was possible that this man was Omar wearing an
extra large jacket to disguise the bulk of his muscular arms,
but he was probably simply one of the many strikingly
handsome men who lived in Cairo and who possessed the
same penetrating dark eyes. Finally, brushing him from
her mind, Ashley followed the others to the waiting taxis
and the ride to the airport.

As the taxi pulled away from the curb, Kasim ran forward
waving madly. Ashley rolled down the window and waved.
Shouting above the noise of the street, Kasim called,
"Remember me!"

"What?" Ashley whispered as she clutched at her throat
in disbelief. But it was too late to turn back. The cab had
pulled into the busy street, leaving Kasim standing on the
curb as clouds of smoke and dust enveloped him.

" 'Remember me.' He said 'Remember me,' " Ashley
muttered as she sank into the seat.

"Did you say something?" Sallie asked as she glanced
at Ashley's stricken face. "Do you feel okay? You look
horrible."

"I'm fine. It's just the heat," Ashley replied, turning for
one more look at the hotel. All she could see was the
distant pyramids through the dust.

Ashley suffered from mixed feelings as she rode through the crowded streets. She loved the sights and smells of this exciting country and had enjoyed the company of its stimulating people, yet, as a modern Western woman, she knew that she would never quite fit in with the more conservative views of the roles of the sexes. She had thrilled with each uncovered artifact, but she could not bury herself in the sands of the past forever. The time spent on the expedition had given her the needed space to breathe, to think, and to discover herself. Ashley had learned quite a bit about her love of exploration, both of self and of others. She was ready to return home and getting on with her life. Still, the memory of Kasim would live with her for many years to come. Ashley would always wonder how her life would have been if she had given in to the love she felt for him and agreed to marry him.

It was only a matter of hours before she would arrive in the States and find herself embroiled in Toni's wedding plans. With thousands of miles between her and the mysterious land of the pharaohs, Ashley would be able to find peace and happiness. Toni would be waiting at the airport for her. They had so much to do before the wedding at the end of the week, but with Sallie's help everything would get done on time.

Ashley and Sallie chatted animatedly about the wedding and the expedition until the hum of the plane lulled them to sleep. As she napped, Ashley dreamed not of Toni's wedding but her own. She saw herself walking down the aisle of her family church to meet her groom in his morning coat. His face was shrouded in a mist, but Ashley could feel his happiness. Yet, despite her rapture and the big grin on her father's face, she felt that something was not quite right. The closer Ashley watched herself come to him, the less he looked like himself until finally his face vanished completely. In its place, she saw the face of her dream man at the pyramid and finally Kasim's face.

Reaching out to her, his fingers closed around hers and pulled her to him. His arms encircled her and drew her against his strong chest. She buried her face in his shoulder and allowed the smell of his cologne to seep into her pores. She thrilled to the feel of his body against hers. The people in the church stood with their mouths open, but Ashley did not see them. They faded from her mind as she held on tightly for fear he, too, would vanish.

Sensing her concern, he lifted her face to his and slowly pressed his lips to hers. The taste of his kiss quickened her breathing. The pressure bore into her soul. Clinging to him, Ashley moaned softly. She belonged to him and he to her. Not even the stunned faces of the congregation could tear them apart.

Bending ever so slightly, he scooped Ashley into his arms and began to carry her down the long aisle of friends gathered to witness her marriage to another man. Passing each row of pews in slow motion, they made slow progress toward the back of the church. Hands reached out to her along the way, but they did not stop. Voices called out, but they did not hear.

When they reached the door, he lowered her to the ground and looked longingly into Ashley's face. Seeing confusion written there, he gently eased her to the carpet. Taking both of her hands into his, he lifted the palms and kissed each one. Then he bowed and said, "Remember me."

Ashley watched as he turned and walked out the church door. Running to catch him, her heel caught in the hem of her flowing gown, causing her to lose her balance and fall. Rubbing her bruised knee and walking gingerly into the sunshine, Ashley scanned the street for him, but she did not see him at first. Searching the distance, she finally saw him turn and wave before vanishing into the crowd on the sidewalk.

"Ashley, wake up. We're almost home. I thought you might like to watch the descent over Washington," Sallie said, shaking her shoulder and pointing out the window with a childlike excitement born from years of absence from the States. The lush green of the Virginia farmland stretched beneath them as the plane banked and slowed for the landing at Dulles Airport.

Rubbing the sleep from her eyes and shaking herself awake, Ashley gazed out the window. Everything looked as it had when she left except that the light snow that had covered the ground that winter day had long ago melted. She wondered if she was as unchanged. Somehow, she doubted that she returned as she had left.

After being away for almost seven months, Ashley found herself surprisingly happy to be back. She had not realized how much she had missed the sights, smells, and sounds of Washington. Now that she was home, the first thing she wanted was a thick steak smothered in mushrooms and onions and a glass of red wine.

Walking through customs, Ashley's eyes anxiously searched the crowd of people for Toni. In the crush of waiting families, she almost missed her until she heard Toni's voice calling to her. Turning in its direction, Ashley finally spotted Toni standing at the back of a group of students waving a gigantic banner of welcome. On it was written in huge red letters, "Welcome home, Ms Stephens!!" Suddenly Ashley realized that the beaming faces belonged to about fifteen of her students. She could hardly believe that they had remembered her and taken time from their summer vacation to gather at the airport.

As Ashley beamed with happiness and hugged each of them, Toni and Sallie stood quietly by watching her. Ashley had a natural way with teenagers that caused them to seek her company. Seeing them reaching out to touch her and to be embraced by her confirmed that Ashley belonged in the classroom despite her desires for adventure.

Laughing and trying to out-talk each other, the kids told Ashley of the newspaper coverage of her kidnapping and the success of the expedition. "You're a celebrity," gushed one young woman who gazed lovingly at Ashley.

"Believe me when I tell you that I didn't plan any of it. I would have been just as happy to have gone through my time there without being noticed. Wouldn't you, Sallie?" Ashley asked including her friend in the warmth of the children's affection.

"Without a doubt. I never want that experience again," Sallie agreed.

Allowing themselves to be led to the baggage claim area, Ashley and Sallie mingled with the happy children who continued to tell them everything that had happened while Ashley had been away. In the few minutes since landing, the students had brought her up to speed on the happenings of the past few months. She had learned about the teen romances and heartbreak and the marriage of two of her colleagues who she had not suspected of having a relationship with each other. The kids had told her about the retirement of the music teacher who had been the member of the faculty with the longest tenure in the school.

Looking on, Sallie smiled at the loving reception from Ashley's students, reading in their faces the contribution Ashley had made to their lives without even knowing it. It was clear that she had missed them as much as they had longed for her return. The friendship between them was obvious.

As the teenagers drifted away to their own cars, the three adults seized the opportunity to share confidences. Toni had just completed the rehearsal dinner arrangements and helped her parents put the finishing touches on the

wedding details. Opening the gifts was the next task that
awaited them, but that could wait. Now that everything
had been done, they could relax a bit until the festivities
of the weekend. Heading the car out of the parking lot
and toward Virginia Beach, Toni drove the weary travelers
to her beach house where they planned to do just that.

This year the warm water was without a trace of the
troublesome jellyfish that usually plagued August vacations. The hot sand and sun relaxed Ashley's flight weary
body as she stretched out on the towel beside Toni and
Sallie. They had so much to share that they did not know
where to begin. Despite the expensive telephone calls,
Ashley realized that she had not told Toni everything that
had happened while she was away. They chatted happily
for hours.

Ashley felt the fatigue of the long flight ease from her
body as she listened to the waves lapping on the shore. She
had always loved the beach and found its voice comforting.
After the excitement of the last months, she welcomed its
deep, mellow rumble even more. She planned to lay a
towel on the sand and not move from that one spot after
Toni's wedding. For the time being, she had experienced
enough excitement and celebrity; she longed for peace
and routine.

Water droplets glistened on Ashley's soft brown shoulders as she lay in the summer sun. The two piece shocking
pink swim suit accentuated her glowing complexion. The
book, the one she had promised herself that she would
read during the lull in activity on her sabbatical, lay
untouched on the sand next to her. A half consumed can
of warm soda sat in the shade of the umbrella that had
long ago ceased to shelter her from the late afternoon
rays. Laurie, the late afternoon rays . . . Laurie, their ever-

faithful dog companion, slumbered peacefully at her feet. Her ears twitched as she dreamed of past adventures with Ashley and Toni. Music from Ashley's boom-box played softly in her ear mingling with the voice of the waves and the cry of the gulls circling overhead.

Turning onto her back, Ashley refused to get up. There would be time tomorrow for all the last minute arrangements Toni wanted to share with her. For now, all she wanted was to rest far from the shadows of the pyramids, the dreams, and the memories.

Even Laurie had given up trying to get Ashley to play and had decided to take a nap. Since returning from Egypt, Ashley had been content simply to lie on the sand, walk in the waves, sit on the porch, and watch the sun set over the ocean. She did not want to think of doing anything that required more than a minimal amount of movement. At the moment, sleeping was the perfect activity for her. There would be plenty of time for swimming and games. Now was the time for doing nothing.

This was the peaceful life Ashley always loved when she spent her summers at Toni's beach house. She would come here after a brief trip to a Mexican archaeological dig, while Toni was on honeymoon in Hawaii. She would not miss the smell of the Atlantic, the crab feasts, the fireworks on the barge in the bay, and the good times with good friends who dropped-in during the summer to spend whatever time they had with them.

As much as Ashley complained about the loss of solitude once friends starting arriving, she actually looked forward to the companionship of people with whom she spent time only once a year. They were together long enough to keep their friendships alive but not too long to get on each other's nerves or become too familiar.

They all enjoyed the charming house that sat directly on the beach. Winding wooden stairs led down the hillside to the sandy shore. In thunderstorms, Ashley always commented that she could feel the surf moving the pylons that held the side porch and the deck above the churning water. Toni said it was her imagination, but Ashley's opinion never changed. Considering that the house stood barely two feet away from the highest point of the water line at high tide, it was entirely feasible that Ashley did feel something when the angry sea pounded the shore.

Although she loved the free-flowing interior of the house, the deck was one of Ashley's favorite spots. She felt as if she were an expert in all of its physical properties since she had spent her time equally divided between here and the beach. It had one of the best views of the water, was sunny from morning until night, and made an ideal place to sit during her vacation months. It was great fun to watch the tide roll in while feasting on Maryland blue crabs, corn on the cob, and garden fresh string beans.

Forcing her relaxed body to sit up, Ashley looked at the waves lapping at the shoreline. The sight of such power was frightening and exhilarating at the same time. She could feel the energy of the sea seeping into her bones. After a few days of soaking up the sea breezes and the salt air, Ashley always felt as if she could face anything.

Toni shared the same feelings, which was probably why they had been best friends for so long and had gone into teaching at almost the same moment. Sharing a dorm room had led to sharing the beach house, which had led to sharing an apartment in town. They would always be best buddies regardless of the roads they traveled.

Ashley's sabbatical had been hard on both of them. Even daily electronic communication had not dulled the pain of separation. When Toni read about Ashley's kidnapping, she had become frantic with worry. Hearing Ashley's voice during the daily calls had made her feel better, but it was not until Toni saw Ashley at the airport that she really felt that her friend was safe. Both of them knew that Toni's marriage would prove to be a test of their friendship, but they were determined not to allow the presence of a husband to pull them apart. One day when Ashley married, they would make a happy foursome for card games and vacation trips.

Until it happened, Ashley and Toni never talked about the inevitable distance that would come between them when they married and moved away from each other. It was almost as if they understood that the summers would continue to be their time together. Ashley hoped that no matter where life took her that she would always come home to Toni and the beach. Toni was not only her best friend, she was her other self. She understood Ashley's emotions even when Ashley could not express them herself. There were so many things between them that went unsaid because they were already understood without being spoken.

Ashley smiled at the memory of those carefree days of being a beach bum. She had been so happy as they sailed the rickety little boat they rented on a whim. She had loved cooking barbecues and making clam bakes on the beach. Ashley chuckled when she thought about the time she and Toni had practically destroyed the kitchen preparing crabs one night. They had rolled with laughter as the escaping crabs skittered around the floor. They ran toward the safety of the back porch and chased the cat that hissed and swatted at the outstretched, snapping claws. She had scooped up the runaways and tossed them into the pot filled with seasoning and the other snapping crustaceans. Twenty minutes later with the kitchen properly cleaned to Toni's satisfaction, they sat down to a delicious feast. After that, they had done all of their crab cooking outside even if it meant holding an umbrella in a downpour. Her life was always overflowing with fun whenever Toni was around.

She remembered their last trip to Boston for a seminar designed for teachers of U.S. history. Ashley had resented having to go over her winter break, but, when she arrived and saw the city blanketed in fresh snow, her spirits soared over the Charles River itself. Boston at night with the city lights subdued into stars reflecting off the snow, the Charles moving slowly along its path that divided the town from Cambridge, and the silence of crisp air created a visual and auditory memory she would never forget. Even when her nose, fingers, and toes felt as if they would fall off from walking along the waterfront, Ashley had been ecstatic that Toni had convinced her to take the trip. As Ashley nibbled on butter drenched lobster and scarfed down the renowned baked beans, Boston quickly became one of her favorite cities.

The lobby of the hotel was a treat in itself. The gold-swirled marble floor and pillars had glistened in the light of the massive chandeliers. The mahogany reception desk and mailboxes shone from the careful attention given by devoted hands over the years. Ashley could almost see the legendary technicians who lovingly polished the wood with soft clothes until they could see their reflections in the shine. The Turkish carpets and wall tapestries echoed the colors of the sofas and chairs that invited fashionably dressed patrons to linger as the pianist played for their enjoyment. Gold clad porters waited to carry their bags to the well-appointed room that continued the opulence and elegance of the famous hotel.

Stepping aside as he opened the door, the bellhop dangled the two gold tasseled keys in his outstretched hand as he pointed out the amenities of the massive suite. Terry cloth robes with the hotel's crest waited for them in the bathroom. A whirlpool bath beckoned to Ashley promising to soothe and calm her tense body; slippers stood ready to caress her feet. Bath oils and lotions in the most luxurious of fragrances and textures occupied the counter between the double marble sinks. The gold faucets sparkled brightly in the light of the miniature chandeliers, and fresh floral arrangements added a splash of additional color to the decor. Placing their luggage on the waiting rack, the porter thanked them for the tip and discreetly left them to enjoy the sights of Boston from their window.

On their short stay, they visited all the tourist attractions. At Toni's insistence, they walked the Freedom Trail with the winter winds making their eyes tear. Ashley allowed her imagination to recreate the Boston Massacre, Paul Revere's ride, and the sight of the lanterns swinging in the windows of Old North Church. She could almost hear the anti-British speeches that inspired the Boston Tea Party ring out from the Old South Meeting House and the shouts of triumph as the colonist fought for their liberty. Despite the cold, she never regretted a minute. She knew that her classroom discussions would be enriched by the thrill of her experiences.

Now, shading her eyes as she looked at the ocean, Ashley felt a tug of sadness. She knew that those days with Toni would end as soon as they left the beach for Washington and Toni's wedding day. She was determined to soak up as many memories as she could before that happened.

At that moment, Toni and Sallie ran past on the way to the water with Laurie suddenly awake and following on their heels. Sallie had missed the thunder of the ocean waves after adopting Cairo as her new home. Ashley watched as they laughed and played in the surf. The two women had quickly become friends themselves. Fortunately, Toni and Craig planned to settle in the area. Life would be different with him in the picture, but Toni would still be around for conversation and laughs.

Leaving the others to play in the waves, Ashley pushed herself to her feet and began the short walk up the hill to the house. Pampas grass grew beside the flagstones of the walk, bending in the breeze as she passed. Laurie joined her, frolicking happily beside her like the puppy she had been years ago. Running up the porch steps, Ashley stopped only long enough to wash the sand off her legs and from the dog's thick coat.

"Hey, stop that!" Ashley scolded Laurie with a laugh as the big, old puppy shook water and fur all over her. "Enough of that. Be still. Now, I have more hair on me than you do."

Showering quickly, Ashley lathered her still short hairdo. After almost seven months away from home, she had managed to keep her short style despite the difficulty in finding someone to cut it for her in a country that believed that women should have long, covered hair. She finally gave up and cut the black curls herself whenever she needed a trim, although she did allow it to grow long enough to gather into a trim French twist for special occasions.

That night the friends feasted on steak, Maryland crabs, and white corn on the cob on the back porch overlooking the ocean. They talked into the night until they finally had to retire. Jet lag and excitement won out as they turned off the lights and went to bed. The pyramids and the adventures mingled with the memories of a far away place in her heart.

The week sped by with Ashley and Toni showing Sallie the historic sites of nearby Virginia. When they finally tired of Williamsburg, Busch Gardens, and Monticello, they returned to the beach house and its delightful solitude. Every night they sat under the stars and discussed their plans and their futures. As the weekend approached, Toni's need to see Craig increased. She talked about nothing other than her wedding day. Ashley and Sallie looked at each other and laughed uproariously at her eagerness to settle down to married life.

To take her mind off the big event, Ashley suggested that they clean out some of the old junk stored in the attic. Plopping a baseball cap on her head, Ashley said, "We've been planning to get to that horrible job one day. This is the day. Grab a trash bag and follow me."

"But I'm getting married in a few days. This is hardly the time for exploring and cleaning the attic," Toni objected as Ashley shoved a cap on her head also.

"What better time than before you start your new life? You won't want to do this once you're married," Ashley responded with a chuckle.

"I don't want to do it now!" Toni complained as she followed Ashley and Sallie into the attic.

However, in only a few minutes, all three of them were laughing their heads off at the collection of stuff from years past. Old dolls, party dresses, lamps, tables, and enough bric-a-brac for a dozen yard sales soon filled the trash bags for donation to a worthy cause. The three friends laughed so hard at some of the discoveries that they almost choked on the dust that filled the attic.

Clutching one of the old dresses to her body, Toni exclaimed, "Mother must have kept these here for summer parties back in the days when people dressed to go to each other's houses. I love the rustle of this one. Take a look at the bow on the back of that one you're holding, Ashley."

Ashley pirouetted so that Sallie could see the gigantic bow at the waist of her lime green dress. "Well," she said, holding her purse by its tiny strap and giving Toni a critical but playful look, "at least it's not dandelion yellow."

Sallie laughed, "I don't know which is worse, the color or the ruffles."

"Oh, look, it's Mother's wedding gown. Gee, she was tiny. Her waist must have been seventeen inches," Toni exclaimed, pulling the yellowed satin from the battered box. Fitting the veil on her head, Toni pretended to walk down the aisle as she held her mother's dress in front of her.

Looking fondly at her friend, Ashley remarked, "You'll make a prettier bride than she did. Your gown is very simple yet sophisticated without all those layers of fabric."

Digging into other boxes, Sallie mused, "I wonder if any of the bridesmaids dresses are in here. I bet they were something else."

"I'm sure they were full of ruffles and bows. The one I've selected for Ashley to wear is a lovely pale rose. She'll look heavenly in it," Toni gushed as she refolded the gown and secured the top to the box.

The friends continued to search and clean without much luck in finding the gowns. By the time they finished, they were tired and dirty, but the attic at last was clean. Tossing the last bag on the pile of fifteen for giveaway, they retired to their bedrooms for showers before going to a local crab house for dinner.

Dinner was fabulous. The waiter heaped mounds of steamed Chesapeake blue crabs on the plastic-covered table, gave them mallets, and left them to crack claws and open backs to their hearts' content. Ashley, Toni, and Sallie barely spoke as they replaced the mound with a pile of empty shells. Finally, they devoured the delicious Silver Queen corn and thick slices of chocolate cake that rounded out the meal.

Pushing away from the table, Ashley commented, "That was delicious. The food was good in Egypt, but nothing like this."

Raising her glass, Toni offered a toast saying, "To friends, old and new, to happiness, to memories, and to wonderful times."

Sallie added, "To great beginnings."

"To people and places remembered," Ashley contributed with a tug of sadness at her heart.

They spent the rest of the evening in small talk as they walked home along the beach. Toni chatted enthusiastically about her wedding. Sallie reminisced about her home and husband in Egypt. Ashley shared anecdotes about Kasim and the joy she had left behind. She tried not to allow her memories of the man in her dreams to enter her reality. Now that she was back home, she wanted to forget about him and move on with her life.

In the last days before Toni's wedding, they sat on the sand and watched the stars play in the sky. They sipped champagne and ate strawberries as the soft tunes from the CD player mingled with the thunder of the waves. They laughed and sang along with their old favorite songs, and they shared their dreams for the future. Egypt, her phantom man, and Kasim seemed so far away.

Finally the time came to end the blissful days on the beach. Driving back to Washington the day before the wedding, the three friends rode in hushed silence. Each was preoccupied with personal thoughts. Ashley thought about Kasim and wondered for the millionth time if she had made a mistake. Toni mulled over the last details of her wedding day, although everything was ready. Sallie was homesick for her husband and Egypt and looked forward to the flight home in two days. None of them felt the need to explain the silence.

CHAPTER TEN

On the way to Ashley's parents' house in the suburbs from which they would leave for the wedding celebrations, they drove into downtown Washington so that Sallie could see the city she had longed to visit but had never found the opportunity to visit before moving to Egypt. Tourists packed the streets as Ashley eased the car along the wide thoroughfares from one museum and monument to the other. Passing the crush at the Lincoln Memorial on the way out of town, Sallie sat in stunned silence at being back in the States and in Washington, D.C. Although Cairo's traffic was maddening and often moved at a snail's pace, she had forgotten just how aggressive American drivers could be. She marveled that they managed to maneuver through the crush without losing a fender or worse. Sallie was quite relieved when they reached the quiet of the suburban streets.

Fortunately her friends did not guess that Ashley's silence had anything to do with the pyramids and Kasim. She found it hard to believe herself that she could be so hopelessly smitten with a man she would never see again. She had decided of her own free will to put an ocean between them, and now she wondered if she should fly back to Cairo with Sallie. Ashley was afraid to make that move for fear that Kasim would not want her. She could not call him to test the idea because she would not be able to tell if his response were polite or genuine. The only option was to pop up on his doorstep at the university and hope that his reaction was favorable. Not being one to take risks, Ashley decided to stay in the States.

Ashley realized that some of her reaction to Kasim was a direct result of her former feelings about Toni's wedding. Now that her lifelong friend was getting married, she was ready to take the step herself. The only problem was that she did not have a man in mind to marry. Inwardly, Ashley chuckled at her own folly for falling in love with a man she would never see again. Worse still was her continued infatuation with a man who no longer visited her in her dreams. She had been quite silly to allow the excitement of the archaeological dig to transfer to her thoughts about men.

Yet, despite her self-criticism, Ashley knew that it had been necessary for her to leave Egypt and Kasim. Their relationship had progressed too quickly without her having the time to assess what she really wanted and the depths of her affection. He had started speaking of marriage before she even became accustomed to the idea that her reaction to him was more than the effects of moonshine bouncing off the pyramids.

Now with only a few hours left before Toni's wedding, Ashley had no regrets either about rejecting Kasim's proposal. She was happy that she had decided on the more familiar path. Still, Ashley could not help but wonder what would have happened if she had chosen the other route. She knew it would have been peppered with exciting places, people, and sights that would make her think that she was living the legends of Sinbad and Ali Baba. She was also aware that Kasim would have filled her heart with words of love from exotic poetry and music from distant lands. He could have given her treasures and jewels, if only temporarily as they explored yet another tomb. Ashley would have had everything the nomadic life of the field archaeologist could give except the security and sense of permanence she needed.

Helping Toni open wedding gifts that filled Ashley's parents' dining room, Ashley carefully recorded each one in a white-leather-covered log. She shared Toni's excitement and appreciation for each toaster, juicer, piece of silver and china place setting as they waded through the stacks of boxes. As they worked, the doorbell rang constantly with delivery men dropping off still more packages. They laughed and wondered how they would ever fit all the presents into Craig's house and joked that the young couple would have to buy a new one even before they started having children.

When they reached the last gift, Toni handed it to Ashley and said, "This one's for you. I wonder who sent it. That's odd, don't you think, that someone would give the maid of honor a gift for my wedding? Hurry up and open it."

Pulling off the white embossed paper, Ashley searched for a note before opening the box. Finding none, she carefully lifted the lid of the black velvet jewel box to find a replica of one of the treasures from the pyramid lying on a bed of satin. Running her fingers over the enamel and gold, she carefully lifted the pillow and looked underneath. Finding a card, she slowly eased it from its envelope. On its white surface the sender had written, "Remember me."

The unsigned card fluttered to the floor as Ashley sank into the nearby chair. Only five people on the expedition had seen the scarab necklace of inlaid emeralds and rubies

before it had been included among the items ransomed
for her return. Kasim had access to drawings of the original
which Omar had probably already sold. Looking at her
friend's face, she knew they shared the same thought.
Kasim was in Washington!

"Why do you think he hasn't come to see you?" Toni
asked.

"Who?" Sallie asked, returning from the kitchen with
a tray containing soup and sandwiches Ashley's mother
had prepared for them.

Without answering, Ashley handed the box to her and
waited to hear her response.

"Kasim must be in town. I guess he followed you here.
That man must really love you," Sallie remarked as she
returned the necklace.

Ashley commented, "I don't know how I should feel. I
thought it was over between us, but now he's here. Only
he isn't really because he hasn't come to see me. Why
didn't he stay away and leave me to my memories?"

"Well, it seems rather obvious to me that Kasim still has
feelings for you. I'd say that it's up to you now. He has
come all this way, but he isn't pressing you. He went to a
great deal of expense having this necklace copied. I guess
you have to decide what you want to do," Sallie interjected.
She had secretly hoped that Ashley would decide to marry
him. She enjoyed Ashley's company and would have liked
to have her join the university wives.

Smiling at her friend's counsel, Ashley said with perhaps
a touch of melancholy in her voice, "I don't even know
how to get in touch with him. Besides, it's probably too
late now anyway. I can't imagine what I'd have to offer
him after leaving him in Egypt like that."

"Only your love," Sallie answered, reading her emotions.

Caught off guard by her friend's astute observation, Ashley tried to speak but could not find her voice. She could not tell them that her thoughts were divided between the man she thought she loved and the one who had captured her heart and filled her dreams. She was ashamed of her lack of control and her inability to remove both of them from her thoughts. Ashley knew that Kasim should be a memory of a great sabbatical experience and nothing more, but she could not bring herself to relegate him to the ashes with the other antiquities.

Ashley could not explain how she felt, and she doubted that her friends would understand if she tried. She was confident that in time and with distance, she would forget the feel of Kasim's hand, the softness of his lips, and the smell of his skin . . . If she tried hard enough, she would forget the way he looked when his eyes lingered on hers. She would learn to ignore the sound her soul made as it cried out to his.

So, she let the silence speak for her as the three of them munched their grilled cheese sandwiches.

Finally finding her voice, Ashley continued as if the break in their conversation had not taken place. She returned her partially eaten sandwich to its plate and said, "We don't know for certain that Kasim sent this. It could have come from a practical joker who read the account in the paper. Any number of people who know my interest in archaeology could have purchased this gift from any little shop. I remember seeing a necklace very similar to this one in the mall yesterday when we went shopping for stockings."

"Ashley, give it up. You know that you and I and a few other people are the only ones who ever saw that necklace. Kasim's here and you know it. It's up to you to decide how you'll react when you see him again. I just hope you'll be ready. It's not often that we get second chances in life," Sallie commented, looking deeply into Ashley's eyes.

"You're right, but I can hardly prepare myself if I don't know when he'll appear," Ashley replied, turning away from her friends.

Toni asked softly, "Have you forgotten about the man in your dreams? Are you over the need to search for him?"

Ashley responded with a soft, dreamy tone in her voice, "You know, at first, I thought that finding him really mattered to me, but after meeting Kasim, I'm not so sure. It really doesn't matter. He was just a fleeting passion, and you know what they say about passions."

"No, what do they say?" Toni asked.

"You're supposed to enjoy your passion but never have him and certainly never marry him. It was silly of me to spend so much time fantasizing about someone who doesn't exist. I threw away the opportunity to make a life with Kasim because of a phantom," Ashley lamented sorrowfully.

Sallie interjected with the purpose of making Ashley see the truth about Kasim. "Would you have given yourself to Kasim? Don't forget all those differences you noted. Were you ready to give up all you know to live in his world? I'm not sure that at the beginning of the expedition you were ready for that level of commitment with Kasim. Remember, I've been there and done that. Turning your back on everything you know isn't easy. You get awfully lonely for home at times."

"I probably wasn't ready then, but Kasim does have more charm than the law allows. I'm ready for the challenge now, not that it makes any difference. Unless he appears as more than the giver of terrific gifts, I'll never know if we can make a go of it. I really blew this one big time," Ashley said, sadly returning to the white-leather-bound notebook in which she noted the description and giver of each gift. Fortunately, she did not have to describe Kasim's necklace. If she had been the bride, she would not have

known what to write about the reproduction of the priceless treasure.

Toni and Sallie looked at their friend's face and understood the decision and the doubt that still lingered. It was
awfully hard to decide which road to travel and which to
pass by. Ashley had chosen one, but she longed for the
other. Putting their arms around her, they held her close
as each remembered painful decisions and forgotten
dreams. In their hearts, they hoped that she had made the
right choice and that Kasim would leave her alone if she
had.

At a posh hotel in downtown Washington, Kasim paced
the floor of his room. He had taken a calculated risk in
sending Ashley that necklace as a token of his continued
affection for her. He hoped that her thoughts were as
filled with him as his were of her. When he delivered the
package to the door, he was disappointed that her friend
Sallie had opened it. He had counted on seeing her. He
had dreamed that she would rush into his arms and run
away with him. Not wanting Sallie to recognize him by the
sound of his voice and sound the alarm before he could
see Ashley, he had pretended to be a deliveryman and left
the gift with a simple bow of his head. His cap had been
pulled down so low on his face that Sallie had not been
able to make out his features.

Now more than ever he had to see Ashley. Fearing that
she would turn away from him, Kasim realized that the
only way he could get near her was to appear at the church.
He carefully made his plans to rent a car, buy an inconspicuous black suit, and make his presence known at the appropriate time. He would have to wait until just the right
moment, but, if he could convince her to go away with

him, all of his effort and planning and patience would be well worth the risk of rejection.

Picking up the telephone, Kasim ordered airline reservations for Egypt for both of them. He would propose to her as soon as he managed to get her away from the rest of the wedding party. He could not imagine continuing to live his life without her. He needed Ashley in his life. He would have to make her understand how important she was to him. She was the only person who could make Kasim feel complete.

Closing the door behind him, Kasim went out to make his arrangements and do his shopping. He had much to do and little time in which to do it. He had an important date to keep . . . probably the most important one of his life. After all, it was not often that a man convinced a woman to marry him, leave her country, and take up residence in a foreign land.

The rehearsal dinner the next night was a great success. The hotel staff had decked the intimate banquet room in white and yellow flowers as Toni had requested. White and chamois bunting gently waved in the breeze. Crystal bowls with yellow roses floating in sparkling water mirrored the reflection of the chandeliers that glistened overhead and the candles that flickered on every table. The meal of lobster Newburg, shrimp cocktails, prime rib, string beans almondine, baked potatoes au gratin, and chocolate torte had been sumptuous and plentiful, and the band had played with gusto.

The guests spent a fabulous evening mingling from one table to another and seeing old friends. Everyone ate, drank, and danced until the wee hours of the morning before collapsing in the rooms that Toni had reserved for them. They all said they had never had a better time or attended a more joyful rehearsal dinner party. It was really more like a family reunion or a gathering of old, long-separated friends than a prewedding feast. Everyone, including the bride and groom, was relaxed and jolly. Seeing everyone having such a good time, Toni and Craig knew that they had made the right decision in selecting the most expensive hotel with the most renowned chef in town for their special night. After the success of the evening, they wondered if the wedding reception at Toni's family's country club would be as much fun.

As the maid of honor, Ashley did everything she could to make the evening a success. She smiled at all the guests, danced whenever she was asked, and in general sparkled through the evening. No one would have guessed that her heart ached for a man who she was not sure she would ever see again. She was so charming that Craig's best man, Brandon, never realized that she was not totally engrossed in his somewhat boring anecdotes from his legal practice. They made the perfect couple.

A quartet led by one of their oldest friends played the cool jazz for dancing after dinner. Martin tickled the ivories as only he could do. Moving around the room in Brandon's arms, Ashley found herself searching the faces of the musicians and waiters for any sign of Kasim. Her heart pounded in her chest as she scanned the crowd until with disappointment she acknowledged that he was not there. Ashley scolded herself for thinking of him rather than forcing him into the recesses of her mind. She convinced herself that her fascination was a flaw in her character not a sign of love for him. He was part of the past, of a glorious adventure. He belonged in Egypt with her other memories of pyramids, temples, and unexplained mysteries. Still, he could be anywhere in the crowd of laughing faces. She wanted to see Kasim. She needed to be near him, and she was afraid of her actions if she had the opportunity. Finally, she gave up looking for him and surrendered to the music and Brandon's skillful dancing. Ashley remained on edge and waiting, but for what she did not know. The only thing she knew for certain was that she had to have a few minutes alone with Kasim if she were to be truly happy ever again.

They were the last to leave the hall when the music stopped and the tired musicians and waiters packed away the remnants of the festivities. Walking side-by-side, Ashley and Brandon sleepily made their way to their rooms. They chatted gaily about the wedding the next day and the bunch of old shoes Brandon would tie to the back of the getaway car. Ashley's feet hurt from all the dancing, and she carried her three-inch heels rather than wearing them.

Leaving her at her door, Brandon bade Ashley goodnight. With a big grin he said, "This was a great party. If tomorrow is even half as good, Toni and Craig will have pulled off the wedding celebration of all times."

Stifling a yawn, Ashley replied, "It was a wonderful evening. They are certainly lucky people to have found each other. They looked so happy as they danced together. I'll see you at church, Brandon. It was a lovely party."

As she leaned against the closed door, Ashley heard Brandon whistling softly as he walked down the hall to his room. She wished that she were as carefree as he was. Despite her fatigue, Ashley could not stop the thoughts of Kasim from coming to her tired mind. Watching Toni and Craig had been especially difficult. They had looked so happy and sure of their commitment to each other. Ashley could not stop thinking that if she had not allowed a phantom dream man and her fear about the differences between her culture and Kasim's to interfere in her life, she might have been the one dancing away the evening in the arms of her love. The only thing about which she was totally sure was that Kasim had to become a memory . . . quickly. If he did not make contact with her soon,

Ashley knew that she would have to go on with her life. She would not allow this unrequited love to stand in her way forever. She would not allow herself to be plagued by two phantoms.

Throwing her key into the tray on the dresser, Ashley hardly noticed the floral arrangement that sat on the bedside table. Smiling at the sight of the dainty, blue flowers, she picked up the card. She was so sure that they were from Toni as a way of thanking her for being her maid of honor that she almost threw the card away without reading it. From habit, Ashley eased the card from the unmarked envelope thinking it was strange that the florist had not used the usual embossed card bearing its address. Maybe Toni had slipped out and purchased the flowers herself. Turning the card over in her hand, Ashley read the name on the plain white card. "Kasim" it shouted in bold, black handwriting. Kasim had sent the forget-me-nots that adorned the table.

Once again Kasim had reached out with a gift to tempt her rather than appear in person. Under the circumstances, Ashley realized that she probably would have done the same thing. After all, she doubted that he would want to endure many more rejections. She had been very firm in turning her back on him in Egypt. Ashley realized that he must have cared deeply for her to have gone to this much trouble.

Sinking onto the bed for fear that her wobbly legs would not hold her, Ashley sat with the card clutched between her trembling fingers. Kasim was so close and yet so far away. He must have been in town to have sent both the necklace and the flowers, yet he could be almost anywhere in the country. She longed to see him and wondered when he would make himself known.

All kinds of thoughts flooded her mind. Maybe Kasim had left the flowers himself after finding her room empty, or perhaps he had paid someone to deliver the necklace and the flowers to let her know that he would soon be with her. Ashley did not know where he was or what he planned to do. She only hoped that he would make his move soon.

Pulling her favorite old T-shirt over her head, Ashley picked up her diary to make one last entry before turning out the light. This would be the final passage dedicated to her life with Toni and, appropriately, it would occupy the last pages in this notebook. Tomorrow, her best friend would enter a new and exciting world of marriage, leaving Ashley to dream of her own future.

At first Ashley wrote about the usual prewedding events such as the rehearsal dinner, the final fitting on the maid of honor's gown, the food, and the hotel accommodations. Next, she moved to a discussion of finding the flowers from Kasim in her room and, of course, the necklace. Then she allowed her thoughts to flow into areas that Ashley needed to discuss but that she could not share with anyone. Not even her best friends, Toni and Sallie, would understand exactly how she felt. Ashley was not sure that she understood herself.

Toni had warned her against going on the expedition. Now, Ashley knew that her premonitions had been correct, but not for the reasons Toni had thought. The natural and planned events in the tomb were enough to fill several diaries themselves. The dreams of the phantom occurred with sufficient frequency to warrant special treatment. And then there was Kasim, whose face never left Ashley's mind and whose impact on her filled reams of paper.

Ashley had not told Toni about the depth of her feelings toward Kasim, although she thought that her best friend knew that she was still pining for him despite her efforts to appear casual about the possibility of seeing him again. Ashley would never tell her how difficult it would be to remove him from her thoughts if he did not appear. Ashley knew Toni would have encouraged her to get over whoever he was and get on with her own life. There was little point in loving someone she could never have . . . someone who was part of a dream.

She had also not shared the depth of her feelings with Sallie, who Ashley assumed had guessed the truth about them. Ashley thought that Sallie knew that Kasim had made an undeniable impression on her from the first moment they met. Ashley had seen her watching them at dinner the first night. She had seen the sparks that flew across the table. Sallie had witnessed Ashley's loss of composure whenever Kasim stood near her. Sallie knew the difficulty Ashley experienced in separating the mystery of the pyramids from the true impact of the man. After all, Sallie had fallen for a handsome man of the desert as soon as she arrived in Cairo and had never regretted her decision to leave her parents and country for him.

Ashley was aware that Sallie would have advised her to leave her thoughts of Kasim in Egypt where they belonged until she was ready to make the commitment he requested. Sallie completely understood the attraction, but she knew that Ashley was not sure that she would be able to make the sacrifice of rarely seeing her home and friends again. Sallie also knew about the phantom of Ashley's dreams.

Scribbling away with the pen she kept attached to the spine of the notebook, Ashley let her emotions flow onto the paper just as the tears rushed down her cheeks. She wrote about the feel of Kasim's arms when he held her and about the clean spicy smell of his skin. She relived the taste of his lips and the strength of his hands on her body. Once again she caressed the massive shoulders and felt the muscles tighten under her fingers. She felt him press her firmly against him and rejoiced at the response of his body to the nearness of hers.

Allowing her imagination to take her to a place she had never visited with him, Ashley slowly eased her arms and legs around his body and encouraged him to enter her soft wetness. Yielding her very soul, she melded to him and moved in tandem with his thrusts. They were like one being designed for each other from the same sturdy substance. As they matched their strokes, she imagined that she could hear him whisper her name through the fog of her own passion. Her body trembled as he thrust into her, taking her to heights of passion she had never experienced. Finally, their hands grasping and their lips burning, they struggled with the flames no more. Instead, they lay spent and exhausted in each others' arms.

Ashley remembered the strength of his arms when Kasim caught her when she fell. She heard the sound of his voice in her ears as he spoke of love. She saw the expression of hurt in his eyes when she refused to marry him. As the tears blinded her, Ashley closed the book and put down the pen. She saw no point in continuing to torment herself.

Aching from the desire her imagination had caused to burn in her body, Ashley shivered not from cold but from the build up of emotion and yearning. She allowed her fingers to finish what her thoughts had started. She tried to force the last pictures of Kasim from her mind forever. The faces of the forget-me-nots made it difficult for her to stop remembering him.

Picking up the pink satin ribbon, Ashley retied it around the mauve binder and buried it at the bottom of her carry-on luggage. Her fingers touched something strangely familiar as she nestled the diary under a pair of tennis shoes. Pulling it out, Ashley smiled at the forgotten brush she had used on the expedition. She had used it so often that its bristles were worn and bent. She remembered uncovering vases and coins with it. She had unearthed the necklace Omar had demanded in ransom for her with it, too. It reminded her of the replica among the wedding gifts in her parents' house. Ashley knew that she would never wear it and probably never look at it again. It held too many memories. Looking at the faded inscription on the handle, she tossed the brush into the trash can. It was now just one more piece of the past that she had left behind.

Then, she turned out the light and tried to sleep. As her eyelids grew heavy and she sank into the fog of dreams, once again the images of Kasim and the bearded man at the pyramid melded together as he beckoned for her to follow him into the desert. Reaching out her hands to him, Ashley felt her fingertips lightly touch his. The joy of shared intimacy flooded over her body as the warmth of his fingers transferred to hers.

Throwing a blanket onto the still-warm sand, they snuggled against the slight breeze that fluttered the silent sand. Kasim gently lifted Ashley's nightshirt and tenderly stroked her breasts until the nipples stood erect and hard. His lips burned a path from her neck to her belly as he helped her remove her clothing. Then he covered her nakedness with the extra blanket he had brought. Ashley helped him ease out of his boxers and T-shirt as her fingers mischievously traced tantalizing paths from his shoulders to his eager manhood.

Pressing their bodies together, he probed her moist recesses as she caressed the head of his penis. Their breath came in simultaneous gasps as they struggled against the passion that filled their bodies and blocked the thought of anything and anyone from their minds. Their lips and tongues drank hungrily of each other's mouths. Their bodies joined when the need for release became almost unbearable.

Sliding under his moist body, Ashley spread herself wide and pulled him deep within her. She would arch her body

to meet his thrusts, her hands clinging to his buttocks
and directing the position of his movements. She would
shudder under the fire that burned hot within her as she
matched his movements with those of her own.

Kasim drove into her, searching for the release from
passion that they both craved. He probed for the spot that
gave her the most pleasure and made her cry out his name.
Clinging to her trim body, he pulled her rounded hips
higher to meet his thrusts and mingled his kisses with hers.
Deep within his very being, his voice rose to call out her
name as they clung together.

Spent and satisfied, they lay quietly on their blanket
atop the burning sand. Together they pulled the forgotten
blanket over their sweaty bodies as they lay intertwined on
their sandy bed. They dozed until the chill of the night
woke them and drove them back inside the little cabin
where they quickly washed the sand from their bodies and
crawled between the sheets. They slept locked in each
other's embrace until the first rays of morning light penetrated the shades and woke them from a peaceful night's
rest.

As his hands were about to close on hers, the sound of
a distant bell broke the spell. She reached for him, but it
was too late. His face became dim until he faded from
sight, taking the warmth with him.

Reaching across her body, Ashley turned off the insistent
alarm clock and peered through sleep-heavy lids at its
numerals. "Unbelievable," she said aloud to the empty
room. "I just went to sleep. I must be crazy. It must have
been the combination of the wine at dinner, the fatigue,
and the flowers."

Throwing her T-shirt into the open bag and bounding
to the bathroom, Ashley forced her stiff body to move
quickly. It was already ten o'clock, and she had to be ready
by eleven-fifteen. She hoped that skillfully applied makeup

would cover the darkness under her eyes that six hours of sleep had not erased. With any luck, a quick shower and cold compresses to the forehead would revitalize her.

Ashley took particular care as she dressed for her friend's special day. Her hair and makeup had to be perfect, and she knew how to work with her often disobedient curls and oily eyelids better than anyone else. Ashley smiled as she combed her no longer short locks into a tight French twist that would compliment the garland of flowers that Toni had ordered to adorn her hair. Her fingers trembled as she added a sprig of Kasim's "forget-me-nots." The bobby pins would slip out easily enough when she changed into her casual clothing after the reception. She almost decided to wear it down but thought that twist would show off the neckline of the dress in all its glory. Unlike other weddings at which she had been a participant, Toni had carefully selected dresses that her maid of honor and bridesmaids could wear again with only the slightest alteration.

As she rushed around the room, Ashley was grateful that Toni had already painted her finger and toenails with a soft rose-beige color that perfectly complimented the rosy hue of her gown. She would not have had time for such luxury this morning. Munching hungrily on a piece of toast and a strip of bacon, Ashley open the box that housed her bouquet and marveled at the way the white roses and calla lilies contrasted beautifully against the hue of her skin and clothing. Toni's flowers contained the same mixture only in larger abundance and with a streamer of ribbons and white tea roses.

Gulping down the last of her cranberry juice, Ashley surveyed the rose lingerie that lay on her bed as she slipped out of her hot pink terrycloth robe. The silk bra and panties matched the gown perfectly. She would feel especially beautiful in such lovely clothing.

Only yesterday she had helped Toni pack her honeymoon finery including the sexy nightie and matching teal blue slippers and knew that everything was ready for her friend's trip. Craig had not told Toni exactly where they were going, although she knew that they would spend their time on one of the Hawaiian Islands. Toni had confided in her that she hoped that Craig had remembered that she had once said that Kauai would be the perfect place for them to visit one day.

Ashley and Brandon had driven to Baltimore Washington International Airport before the rehearsal dinner to stow Toni's bags safely away in a locker so that they would not be forgotten in the madness accompanying their departure. One of his other friends had the task of collecting the carry-on bags and loading them into the limousine at the last minute. After all of Toni's planning, it would have been very upsetting for her not to have some of her special purchases for the honeymoon night.

As for Ashley, she tucked her single luggage key into the back pocket of her shorts for safekeeping. She did not need to lock this bag since it would be with her on the plane. Before fastening the button, she shoved her passport inside also, remembering that having one made for speedier customs clearance. While her friend honeymooned, Ashley would be in London delivering a speech on the artifacts unearthed on the expedition. Not having anything in particular to keep her at home, Ashley decided to leave immediately following the reception.

Fingering the delicate lacy bra, at the last minute Ashley decided against wearing it. Lingering over the open suitcase, she pulled out the old white eyelet shirt and the pair of well-worn comfortable white shorts into which she had just stowed her things for safekeeping. With a shrug, she slipped into the soft shirt and buttoned it up the front.

Since her gown had a high neck and long sleeves, no one would notice what she wore underneath anyway. Ashley decided she might as well be comfortable. Besides, she would not have to spend as much time changing clothes if the reception ran overtime if she were already dressed for her trip under her gown.

Pulling on the shorts, Ashley stepped to the full-length mirror and surveyed the outfit. Smiling, she acknowledged that she already looked dressed for a vacation trip. She wiggled her toes in the thin-strapped rose satin sandals and almost laughed out loud. Opening her carry-on bag, Ashley threw the lace finery inside. She decided that she might need it when dressing for dinner some night while on the lecture circuit.

Stepping into her gown and adjusting it over her shoulders, Ashley pulled up the satin ribbon she had attached to the zipper and stood back to admire her reflection in the mirror. She had to admit that the gown was fabulous. Toni certainly had wonderful taste. Even while Ashley was on sabbatical, Toni had managed to select a maid of honor gown that Ashley would have chosen for herself if she had been at home. The puffy sleeves added dimension to her thin shoulders and the slim skirt accentuated her height.

Buttoning the matching belt, Ashley thought she looked pretty good in her apparel. At least she would be able to wear it again, unlike Toni who had spent so much money on a gown and veil that she would wear for only a few hours. Ashley decided that, if she ever married, she would select something practical—perhaps a cream silk suit and a rose blouse that she could wear to dinner after the wedding became a memory. Better still, Ashley thought that shorts and tennis shoes would be more useful especially considering her hobby of unearthing forgotten antiquity.

* * *

At eleven fifteen exactly, Ashley received a call from the concierge. The pearl-gray limousine had arrived for the drive to the church and the high noon service. Rushing to Toni's room, she helped her gather her veil and train and make her way to the waiting car as the bright sunshine beamed down on them. "Oh, you look stunning!" Ashley gushed at the sight of Toni standing in the puddle of white satin in the middle of her hotel room.

"How will I ever get through this day? I'm so nervous that my knees are knocking. If you weren't here, I don't think I could do it. Craig and I would have to elope," Toni lamented as she clasped Ashley's hands.

"Everything will be just perfect. Don't worry about your knees. No one will hear them over the sound of the organ," Ashley consoled with a laugh.

"Thanks," Toni said, giving Ashley a crooked smile. "I needed that reality check."

The intensity of the sun's rays reminded Ashley of Egypt and the wonderful months she had spent there. And, of course, her memories found their way to Kasim. Once again, Ashley could hear the deep rumble of his voice, feel the strength of his hands, and see the laughter flash in the steadiness of his gaze. Pasting a happy smile on her face, Ashley giggled as she helped Toni climb into the limousine. She did not want anything to spoil her best friend's wedding.

Ashley did not realize that she stood transfixed on the hotel sidewalk until Toni interrupted her thoughts saying, "Hey, are we going to a wedding or simply planning to stand here all day? These flowers are becoming quite heavy and they're starting to wilt. Actually, they're not the only thing that's fading fast. I can feel my makeup beginning to melt. I thought I was the one who supposed to dawdle and get cold feet."

Shaking herself at the sound of her friend's voice Ashley responded, "Don't mind me. I was just back in Cairo for a minute. Strange how little things can spark memories. It must have been the glorious sunshine. Let's go. I'm starting to get a little wilted myself."

Ashley had initially objected to riding in the car with Toni and her parents. She was perfectly content to share the second limousine with the bridesmaids, but Toni had insisted that she would not be able to survive the morning without her friend at her side. Now, seeing how nervous her friend was, Ashley was glad she had agreed.

Climbing into the cool interior of the car, Ashley eased into the seat and smoothed the skirt of her gown as straight as possible to reduce the inevitable wrinkles that would form at her hips. Then, as Toni's parents watched, she helped her friend arranged the train and veil between them and tried to make Toni as comfortable as possible for the ride to the church. Taking a sideways glance at her friend's father and mother, Ashley made mental note of how handsome they looked that morning in their formal attire. Toni's mother's soft pink satin gown highlighted her pale complexion perfectly, and her father was particularly striking in his gray morning coat.

For the first time since returning from Egypt, Ashley took a deep breath and allowed the moment to wash over her. She had no worries that her friend was marrying the right man. Craig would give Toni security and the life behind the white picket fence they both had dreamed of having one day. Although Ashley was not in the least jealous of her friend's happiness, she wondered if she would ever wear that expression of nervous contentment that made Toni glow that morning. Even though she had occasional second thoughts about her decision regarding Kasim's proposal, Ashley still thought that their cultures were probably too different to allow her the freedom she needed in a relationship and in her life. Almost with sadness, Ashley mentally placed him on the shelf with her other abandoned passions and teenage memories . . . the dolls, the old love letters, and the records. Toni was not the only one standing on the threshold of a new beginning.

Sitting in the limousine, Ashley only half listened to Toni's father's last words of advice as they drove along old familiar roads on the way to the church. Her mind jumped from the beach to the pyramids to the reality of walking down the aisle ahead of her best friend on this special day. She felt both happy and sad at the same time. Ashley knew that Toni's life would be wonderful as she and Craig worked side by side to make a home for each other, but she longed for the past and the friendship that she knew would change forever. Ashley was a bundle of confusion. The only thing she knew with certainty was that the car had come to a stop and the driver was holding the door open. The time had come for her to leave the safety of the limousine and make the long walk down the aisle accompanied only by her dreams of what might have been.

As soon as Ashley heard the first strains of the carefully selected music and saw Craig's nervously smiling handsome face, she knew that she had to put all thoughts of herself from her mind and concentrate on making this the most memorable day of Toni's life. She felt her heart swell with pride at the sight of her friend waiting patiently on her father's arm. Blowing Toni a quick kiss, Ashley assumed her position at the head of the aisle and waited until the flower girl and the last bridesmaid took their places for their march down the aisle.

Gazing around her, Ashley saw that the old church glistened from top to bottom with careful cleaning. The sun

shone brightly on the stained glass windows casting a color-
ful glow over the assembled guests and the altar. The tall
wedding tapers flickered with the breeze from their position beside the cross. Pale pink and glistening white flowers
filled all of the vases and overflowed onto the sanctuary
steps. The baptismal font overflowed with pink and white
roses that scented the air in a delicate sweet perfume. The
florist had attached a cluster of matching roses to each
pew with a cascade of white satin ribbon. The altar guild
had unrolled a white cloth down the center aisle. Everything was ready for the grand processional.

Standing at the back of the church, Ashley watched as
the assembled guests devoured the sight of the adorable
little ring bearer in a junior tuxedo and the angelic little
flower girl in a pink gown so delicately colored that it
almost looked white. The children played their roles to
perfection as they carried the wedding bands on a sparkling
white satin pillow and scattered white and pink rose petals
along each side of the white aisle cloth.

The four bridesmaids in pale pink gowns glided down
the aisle with their heads high and their faces aglow. When
they reached the chancel steps, they inclined their heads
briefly in respect for the cross and then took their places
to the left of the aisle. They turned and waited for Ashley
and ultimately Toni to appear.

Walking down the flower-lined aisle, Ashley forced herself not to search each face for Kasim's. She hoped that
he was among the assembled guests who smiled and
exclaimed at her beauty as she led the way for Toni's
appearance. She wanted him to see how stunning she
looked with the desert sand and dirt washed off her face.
Yet, she could not bear the disappointment of not finding
him, and she did not trust her reactions if she did. She
preferred to think that she had conquered her emotions

and her passions by not looking for him rather than to admit that she had only pushed aside her weakness.

Arriving at the foot of the sanctuary steps, Ashley winked at Craig and stepped aside. Briefly the music stopped and the church drew still as everyone waited for the next chords that would signal Toni's arrival. Turning to face the rear of the church, Ashley watched as her friend emerged from the shadows on her father's arm. She could see Toni's radiant smile from behind her veil as her friend fastened her eyes on the man she loved. Tears of joy sprang to Ashley's eyes as she watched the happiness of her friend, hoping that one day she would experience such bliss, too.

Toni's feet seemed to never touch the carpet as she sailed to Craig's side. Her eyes never left his as she gently placed her hand on his outstretched arm. Ashley could see silvery tears of happiness on her lashes.

After Toni handed Ashley her bouquet and took her place beside Craig, everyone waited for her father's response to the age-old question of "Who gives this woman into the state of holy matrimony?" The guests all exclaimed with joy when Toni's father answered in a firm but too loud voice just as all fathers did on this special day. Then everyone settled down for what they knew would be a rather routine service. According to the service leaflet, nothing unusual would happen in this well-organized ceremony of prayers, hymns, and communion.

As the priest intoned the words of the liturgy in his usual monotone, only the very sentimental paid any attention to what he said or the manner in which Toni and Craig replied to the age-old questions. No one ever expected anyone to object to the marriage and they only half listened as the cleric momentarily paused after asking the required question. Mentally criticizing the flowers or the lighting or the bridesmaids' gowns was much more fun than listening to the recitation of vows they all knew by heart and could repeat in their sleep. Even Ashley was busy imagining the beauty of her own wedding and was paying little attention to the proceedings.

But something different happened this time as the minister whipped past the customary inquiry on his way to the blessing of the rings and the final vows. A male voice rang out from the back of the church startling everyone out of their daydreaming and into a shattering reality. Ashley could hardly believe that someone might object to Toni and Craig promising to love and cherish each other forever. There must be some mistake. Surely this was someone's idea of a pathetic joke. The unthinkable and the dreaded had happened.

"Stop! Please, you must stop! I apologize for interrupting the wedding, but I must," the figure in black called from the rear of the church as he slowly made his way forward past the open mouths and startled expressions of the guests.

Ashley felt her knees grow weak and her head begin to spin as she turned and stared at the approaching man. Other than the voice with its slight accent, there was nothing about him that would give away his identity. The body in the black business suit, white Oxford shirt, and black and silver striped tie stood lean and trim, the broad shoulders square and confident. The curly black hair had been combed into conservative submission. The beard that masked the lower half of his face had been neatly trimmed and contoured to the chiseled cheeks and lay perfectly under the high-bridged nose.

But the black eyes . . . the black eyes sparkled with determination . . . and love. He was the man at the pyramid—the man who haunted her dreams. He was Kasim.

"Come with me, Ashley. Leave here now. Take a chance. Forget about our differences. How can you go wrong? I love you, Ashley. We will have such a wonderful life together. You know you will never be happy when your nights are filled with dreams of me. I am in your soul. Try as hard as you might, you will always remember me," Kasim coaxed from midway up the aisle where he stood with his arms open waiting for Ashley to join him. When she did not move, he slowly lowered his arms to his sides. Lines of concern replaced his hopeful smile. He had gambled his life and his pride that their love would outweigh Ashley's innate need for security. Now he was afraid that he had lost everything—the woman he loved and his dreams of a life with her.

No one in the church spoke as they waited in one body for her to answer. All eyes turned from the man to Ashley knowing that with a single word she could send him on his way. Toni and Craig looked from one player on this stage of life to the other with a smile of amusement, while shock, excitement, and confusion danced across Ashley's face.

And Ashley looked deep within her heart and knew the answer.

Looking first at Toni and Craig who stood smiling at her side, Ashley watched as they nodded encouragement. As reality replaced wonderment, Toni nodded and whispered, "Go for it, girl! This is your chance for true happiness. You have to go. I'll keep a light on for you."

Craig echoed his future wife's sentiments by giving her shoulder a slight push as if to propel her toward the waiting figure and said, "Give the flowers to Sallie. I think we can handle the rest of this service without you. Go and be happy."

With her heart feeling lighter than it had since before she left Egypt, Ashley turned to gaze at the expressions of confusion that covered the faces of the astonished congregation. They had never heard of a man interrupting a wedding to beg the maid of honor to go away with him. This would be one ceremony that they would never forget.

Looking at her parents for guidance, Ashley saw that they looked almost as stunned as the rest of the congregation. They had heard all about her kidnapping and her fondness for Kasim, the man who had rescued her. Thinking that this passion would soon pass, they had encouraged her to proceed with her life now that she had returned from Egypt without him. She had told them that Kasim was a charming, intelligent member of a different culture. They did not think that she had known him long enough to make a life decision. However, seeing the smile of happiness and the look of determination that slowly spread over Ashley's lovely features, they knew that she was about to do something that would change the course of her life forever. Yet, they could not advise her. Ashley had to make her own life. She had to follow her heart. They would do nothing to stop Ashley from pursuing her dream.

Even the family priest who had married hundreds of couples could not utter a word in counsel. In all the years that he had been performing the same ceremony, never once had someone come forward at the last moment and objected to a union and definitely no one had ever called the maid of honor away from the altar. He was not sure what he should do next and hoped that the people involved would lift the responsibility from his shoulders. With simply one word from Ashley, this uncertainty would end and the proceedings could continue.

Turning again to Kasim, Ashley could almost feel the pressure of his lips on hers, the warmth of his body against hers, the strength of his arms around her. She felt strangely secure, needed, and loved. She was not afraid of the future and did not worry about the perils of the present. She knew that as long as Kasim stood at her side, she could weather the storm with the man of her dreams. She loved him and that was all that mattered.

Placing the bouquets in Sallie's outstretched arms and yanking off her gloves and the flowers that adorned her hair, Ashley took two tentative steps toward Kasim. As the confining bobby pins sprang loose, her hair tumbled free and curled around her face as it had when she was a young girl and every experience was new and exciting. Running toward the waiting future, she stopped only long enough to place the little pinkie ring carefully among the rose petals on the white cloth that lined the aisle. She wanted no old memories to get in the way of her new happiness.

The worried expression immediately left Kasim's face as he again held his hands out for her. As the congregation took in a collective gasp of air, Ashley threw herself into his waiting arms and buried her face in his neck. His arms wrapped around her body holding her to him as if their lives depended on each other's strength. For a moment, they stood frozen in time, unaware of the stares of disbelief that filled the faces of the guests. She only barely heard Toni shout, "Go girl! I'll miss you. Give me a call sometime," as she laughed happily.

Searching his smiling face, Ashley noticed the little scar over Kasim's right eyebrow. Touching it lightly she asked, "You've been hurt. What happened?"

"I joined a new dig after you left Egypt to try to take my mind off you. I thought that if I immersed myself in work, I would not feel so empty. I was not paying attention while walking through the pyramid. I stumbled over an irregular step and received a rather nasty gash on my forehead. I am afraid I will always have the scar as a reminder of my folly and my heartache. I hope you will not mind being married to a marked man," Kasim replied as everyone watched.

"It looks rather distinguished. Besides, I've seen it many

times in my dreams,'' Ashley commented as she beamed into the face of the man she loved.

For only an instant, Kasim wondered what Ashley meant about her dreams, but then he remembered what she had told him about her phantom. He threw back his head and laughed heartily. He took her hand, and running toward the doors at the back of the church, Kasim and Ashley fled into the sunlight that streamed through the multicolored stained-glass windows. Stopping for only a moment, Ashley pulled down the zipper and stepped out of the gown that slowed her progress. Leaving it a pile of crumpled rose satin on the red carpet, she ran into the summer sun in her shorts, eyelet shirt, and rose sandals. Ashley could have been any tourist out for a Saturday of sightseeing in the nation's capital with a strikingly handsome bearded man at her side except for the sprig of ''forget-me-nots'' that lingered in her hair.

As Sallie rushed to the church door with the rose satin dripping from her fingers, the nondescript black rental car disappeared into the traffic heading for the airport and Egypt. She smiled and waved, knowing that Ashley would find a lifetime of happiness mingled with the dust of the ages waiting for her beyond the pyramids.

Dear Readers:

This has been a very busy year for me. I took time off from teaching high school English to devote my attention to our son, who graduated from high school in June 1998, and to my writing. PARADISE, as well as the short story in the holiday anthology, SEASON'S GREETINGS, and my next romance, is the product of that effort. I hope that you will enjoy this novel as much as I relished having the time to spend in writing it.

I have thoroughly enjoyed receiving e-mail from you. I encourage those who wrote to me after reading BLUSH and IT HAD TO BE YOU to send me a note again with your response to PARADISE. Those who have not voiced their opinions, I ask that you take the time to drop me a line or two. It is through reading your thoughts that I grow as an author. If I do not produce characters that you would like to meet, settings that you would want to visit, and plots that keep you turning the pages, I have not accomplished my goal as a writer. I want you to take pleasure in my work and sit on the edge of your chair in anticipation of the next novel. Please send your comments to me either at my e-mail address, *courtni@erols.com,* or through my publisher.

Best wishes always!

Courtni Wright

ABOUT THE AUTHOR

Born in Washington, D.C. in 1950, Courtni Wright graduated from Trinity College (D.C.) in 1972 with an undergraduate degree in English and a minor in History. In 1980, she earned a Master of Education degree from John Hopkins University in Baltimore, Maryland. She was a Council for Basic Education National Endowment for the Humanities Fellow in 1990. She lives in Maryland with her husband, Stephen, and their son, Ashley.

Ms Wright's first romance novel entitled BLUSH was published by Kensington Publishing under its Arabesque imprint in September of 1997. IT HAD TO BE YOU followed in August 1998 and a novella entitled "New Year's Eve" in the SEASON'S GREETINGS anthology in December 1998. Her children's books JUMPING THE BROOM, selected for the Society of School Librarians International's list of "Best Books of 1994"; JOURNEY TO FREEDOM, named a "Teacher's Choice" book by the International Reading Association; and WAGON TRAIN were published by Holiday House. Her venture into Shakespearean analysis entitled THE WOMEN OF SHAKESPEARE'S PLAYS was published by University Press of America.

She has served as consultant on National Geographical Society educational films on the practice and history of Kwanzaa, the history of the black cowboys, the story of Harriet Tubman, and the African American heritage in the West.

Her next romance will follow in December of 1999.

COMING IN APRIL . . .

A TIME TO LOVE   (1-58314-008-5, $4.99/$6.50)
by Lynn Emery
To discover his roots, Chandler Macklin takes a job in Louisiana.
He's interested in Neva Ross's insight on the history of Louisiana
. . . and her charm. Neva's hesitant. Her past relationships
failed—why would this one be any different? When his ex-wife
wants to reconcile, Chandler's torn between giving his son a
stable family and true love with Neva.

ISLAND ROMANCE   (1-58314-009-3, $4.99/$6.50)
by Sonia Icilyn
Carla McIntyre, co-founder of a London advertising agency, is
in Jamaica for her agency's first major international account.
With business resolve, she meets with coffee plantation owner
Cole Richmond. But she loses her poise in his presence, and
Cole's set on proving he's the one for her . . . even when someone
from his past threatens their chance at love.

LOST TO LOVE   (1-58314-010-7, $4.99/$6.50)
by Bridget Anderson
To start over after a painful divorce, family counselor Deirdre
Stanley-Levine returns with her daughter to her hometown in
Georgia. But after an article by journalist Robert Carmichael is
featured in his newspaper, Deirdre becomes the target of a mad-
man. Now, while falling in love, Robert must help save the woman
who roused his burning passion.

SWEET HONESTY   (1-58314-011-5, $4.99/$6.50)
by Kayla Perrin
Samona Gray falls for the handsome writer who moved in next
door. He's the first man in a very long time she feels she can
trust. Then she learns that Derrick Lawson is really a Chicago
cop on a special assignment: to get close to her and learn the
whereabouts of a fortune in missing jewelry. Her faith in men is
tested once more, and ultimately, her faith in love.

*Available wherever paperbacks are sold, or order direct from the Pub-
lisher. Send cover price plus 50¢ per copy for mailing and handling
to BET Books, c/o Kensington Publishing Corp., Consumer Orders, or
call (toll free) 888-345-BOOK, to place your order using Mastercard
or Visa. Residents of New York, Washington D.C. and Tennessee must
include sales tax. DO NOT SEND CASH.*